Visions

of

Rage

Shifter Force: Book 1

By A.M. Burns

&

A.T. Weaver

See what A.M. Burns is up to.
Visit his website www.amburns.com
And sign up for his newsletter

Copyright 2019 © MysticHawker Press
http://www.mystichawker.com/

ISBN: 13- 978-1-945632-45-7

Edited by Robert Bronson
Cover design by Silver Circle Images

Shifter Force Books:

1: Visions of Rage

2: Visions of Shadows

3: Visions of Stars

Other Books by A.M. Burns and A.T. Weaver:

The Black Fin Case

Other Books by A.T. Weaver:

Catriona's Curse

Earthquakes

Touching Yesterday

Other Books by A.M. Burns:

Blood Moon Yellow Sky

Dark Stars of Dallas

Coyote's Pup

Familiar Path

Familiar Spirit

Chapter One

Connor McGriffin lay on a ledge of rock in the Jemez Mountains and basked in the rays of the bright New Mexico sun. The May heat warmed his fur, but couldn't reach the ice in his soul formed by the darkness he'd seen over the last eighteen months.

There was no end to the atrocities one human being could commit against another, but when those atrocities were committed by an adult preying on small children, their magnitude was multiplied one-hundred-fold. If he could only have seen the final piece of the puzzle sooner, he might have saved those last two kids the horror they experienced before they received relief in death. It's a shame Chief Kennedy called him off. He could've saved the state the cost of feeding and convicting the S.O.B. There was something to be said for tearing a monster apart. As a hunter at heart, Connor understood the urge to kill, but always limited himself to those deserving of his attentions. One of the problems he ran into when he worked with the police on special cases was he had to play by the rules. He couldn't just shred the evil doers and go on about his business, but the police often found out about the really evil ones before he did. That was why he put up with the humans in his life.

They helped him right the wrongs of evil people. He worked hard to make the world a better place and just didn't have the resources to do as much as he wanted to.

Connor opened his mouth in a teeth-baring yawn, laid his chin between his paws, and willed his body to relax. He closed his eyes and started purring. Purring always helped him relax. He thought it was one of the advantages of being a cougar shifter. If he was a lion or tiger, he wouldn't be able to purr. Those cats just didn't have the right vocal cords. He liked purring, even if it set some people off. They didn't think mountain lions should purr. It made them too much like house cats and that was wrong.

He ignored the sound of a mouse scurrying among the rocks. He wasn't hungry. There was no point in exerting himself for little more than a taste of meat and fur.

A fly landed on his ear, and he twitched it off. It was going to take more than an insect to bother him when he had a nice warm spot in the sun. It wouldn't last too long; as the day drew longer, the tall trees around him would cast shadows. He wanted to enjoy the sun while he could.

He purred louder. Loud purring was meditative. It helped block out the rest of the world and gave him the privacy in his thoughts he so often missed. After a hard case, he needed down time to escape the human world into places few people could follow. There were advantages to being able to get away and disappear into the wilderness, or in this case, find a spot where few people wandered.

The scent of a rabbit grew strong and then weakened as it came close before scurrying away in a soft cloud of dust. Like most prey animals, it probably thought it was in danger and made a smooth retreat while it could. It had no way of knowing Connor wasn't hungry. He just wanted to relax and get away. He wasn't a threat to anything that day.

Visions of Rage

The sun felt so good. Connor yawned again and then dozed with his eyes closed, but remained alert. There wasn't going to be much that bothered him, but, like other cats , he never completely let his guard down.

The all-too familiar sound of a distant gunshot echoed through his sub-conscious and brought him to full alert. He opened his eyes, raised his head, and sniffed the air. The breeze carried the scent of human blood. He closed his eyes and reached out with his thoughts until she became visible in his mind. He had the mental training to understand the vision that came to him. Precognition made him good at tracking down criminals the humans couldn't. His psychic gifts were also what made him seek out solace when the things he saw and experienced got to be too much to bear. Once he'd opened himself up to the energies around him, it was impossible to shut out the images and emotions he perceived. He would feel them until they no longer mattered, until the ghosts of the dead were finally laid to rest and he could again find his peace.

She was young, early twenties, dark eyed, and bleached blonde with about an eighth of an inch of dark roots. Vivid red lipstick smeared her mouth, and dark eye shadow covered her eyelids. Her red blouse was unbuttoned revealing ample cleavage. The blouse's tails were tied under her breasts, although one end appeared to be torn. She posed provocatively in front of a shadowy figure. Her smile became a look of surprise as the bullet entered her forehead. She fell backward, one knee bent upward.

Connor strained, but was unable to see more than a shadow of the killer, not even the gun nor the hand that held it. Too often the emotions encompassing a killing blocked out details that would make it easy to wrap things up. She had been surprised someone had taken an interest in her. The killer had told her how pretty she was and how he wanted to immortalize her beauty. He'd picked just the right words to make her block everything else out. Nothing else about him mattered. He said she was pretty.

No reason to hurry to the scene. He knew the odor of blood in his connection to the event meant it had already occurred, and she was dead. Scents never happened in visions of future events. In many ways, the future was a lot more sterile than the past or the present.

He stood, arched his back and lowered his shoulders in a leisurely stretch, gave another big yawn, leaped from the ledge, and then trotted toward the scent. It wasn't hard to follow. The odor of blood smothered everything else. There was no fragrance from either the Jemez River or the pines. The trail of a herd of elk was just a faint passing. In many ways, human blood distorted the peace and quiet of the forest, and Connor resented the killer who had disturbed his quiet time.

Connor had followed the road for a quarter of a mile when a vehicle roared toward him. He moved off the side of the road and slipped behind a tree. Humans were so easy to avoid; they didn't catch scent and rarely did they spot movement, but he stayed still, just in case. Even if he had been spotted, there were wild mountain lions in the area. As long as no body stopped to take pictures, he'd be able to continue in less than a minute. If they did stop, he'd have to slip away quickly, over the rocky, tree-covered hillside.

A white RV with green pinstriping and swirls sped past and careened around a curve, its speed a little too fast for the narrow paved road. It moved too fast for him to see the license other than the fact it was a New Mexico plate. If he hadn't been hiding, he might've gotten a better look, or scent. As it was, the scent seemed to cross itself when he stepped out into the road and walked back and forth for a moment. He tried to remember if he'd been down the road before. He hadn't spent much time venturing into the mountains west of Santa Fe. Most of the time he was in the city or nearby. His current trip was the farthest he'd come in this particular direction. Connor shook his head, and then gave up. If he was in his human form and had access to his phone, and there was a signal, he might be able to pull up a map, but it didn't really matter. He knew the direction the scent originated from. The fact that the RV's scent went both directions might only be a coincidence. Or he could've been driving from and to Santa Fe or Los Alamos. Either location was close enough for someone out on a day trip.

Another quarter of a mile at a slow jog brought him to a primitive campsite carved into the brush along the east side of the river. He approached cautiously. Next to a well-used log, nearly indiscernible wisps of steam rose from a crude stone fire pit. Someone had recently doused the few partially burned logs with water. He sniffed around the fire pit and picked up the vague sensation of a shadowy man.

He circled the campsite. The banks of the river extended, like an oxbow had filled in and created a beach that a lot of people used as a rest stop in their exploring of the mountains. Some trampled grass and the scent of two people led up the hill from the beach area, into the rocky outcropping that gave way to the thick forest beyond. One, the female, was definitely human. Connor sniffed, trying to get a good scent on the male, but it was elusive. He smelled human, but he smelled of something else too. It was too jumbled. Intermingled was the scent of a bear who'd recently wandered through the area.

A piece of red cloth fluttering from an old broken stump caught his attention. There was a freshly torn edge on it, and the color matched the woman's blouse in his vision. The scent of the woman clung to it, but it was a happy smell. The aroma from the pheromones released when the man had told her she was pretty. The torn cloth had been an accident. There was no fear on it.

Connor rose on his haunches and stretched his front paws upward. He envisioned his human form and his body changed until he stood six feet, three inches tall. He looked in the direction the path led up between two rocky outcroppings.

He was glad he could shift fully clothed. He'd been born with magic to make it possible. It was a habit he'd gotten into working with Kennedy, and often came in handy when he had to deal with humans. Something about a naked body made most of them uneasy. He'd hadn't planned on running into anyone when he shifted, but had opted to stay clothed, just in case he was in strange territory when he resumed his human form.

He continued up the path a little farther. Behind some large boulders, a slender leg stuck out at an awkward angle. Her hiking shoes were damp, like she'd waded in the river on her way up the trail. The soles of her shoes were worn almost smooth with just a bit of mud on them. They looked old, but well taken care of. Her shorts were also well worn, but fairly clean. The red blouse was newer than the rest of her clothes, and Connor wondered if it might've been her favorite top. She hadn't been happy for too long after she tore her shirt.

Taking care to not disturb the area too much, Connor circled around and approached the body from the other side. He'd worked enough crime scenes to know not to contaminate things too much. Even on the other side, he couldn't get a good scent on the man. There was only the faintest scent of fear from the woman; she'd been more surprised than scared. At least the spirits of the surprised ones didn't tend to stay around long. She would find her peace fairly easily.

Lifeless brown eyes stared unseeingly into the sky. The only mark on her was one bullet hole in the middle of her forehead. Although he hated touching the dead, there was too much of a chance a lost spirit might attach itself to him, Connor forced himself to put his fingers against her cheek for just a moment. The warmth of her body indicated she hadn't been dead long. It was about the same temperature as the mountain around them, but he'd long ago learned the difference between sun-warmed skin and the warmth of a living body. Her murder must have been happening when he saw it. Glancing back along the hiking path he'd trotted down, he wondered if the green and white RV back on the road was somehow involved. He'd headed cross country when he reached the point where the road curved away from the direction he needed to go. He wasn't sure if there were other vehicles driving along it or not.

Connor pulled his special cell phone case from his pocket. The case had spells cast on it to let him shift with it in his pocket and not have to worry about the magic of the shift disrupting the delicate electronics of the phone. He turned on the phone and glanced at the display. Two bars. He was glad to find a decent signal. He must not be as far from the highway as he thought he was. That would speed things up; he wasn't going to have to shift back and forth as he ran to try to find a signal. He dialed 911—since he wasn't exactly sure what district he was in, it would be the fastest way to get someone out there. If he'd been in Santa Fe, he'd just have called his contacts and got them to handle it.

"Sandoval County sheriff's office," an impersonal female voice said. She sounded rather bored. "Deputy Jeri White speaking. How can I help you?"

"I just found a body." His voice betrayed his southern roots. He kept it still and quiet, knowing how authorities, be they police, FBI, Border Patrol, or CIA, liked it when the civilians they dealt with knew how to keep things quiet and direct.

"Who are you, and where are you?" Excitement suddenly colored the voice.

"My name is Connor McGriffin, and I'm at a makeshift campsite about half a mile north of the Las Conchas Trailhead on the east side of the river. It's near some rocky outcroppings."

"Are you sure the person is dead?"

He rolled his eyes. "The bullet hole in her forehead would indicate it." There was no way the deputy could know how many dead bodies he'd seen. After the kids in the last case, he'd really hoped he'd be able to go a while without seeing anymore, but that wasn't his lot in life. Death seemed to find him, or maybe the spirits always put him where he was needed, he wasn't sure. But he really wanted some down time.

"Don't touch anything and wait right there. I'm sending the sheriff." There was a slight edge of excitement to her voice that made Connor wonder how many murders they had in the area.

Connor carefully followed his path back to the campsite and put his hand over the still-warm fire pit. The only thing he picked up was the fact that a man built the fire. For several minutes, he wandered around the campsite trying to open himself to more, but there wasn't anything. As with the scents, there weren't any images or feelings he could follow.

Visions of Rage

There were people in the world who didn't leave feelings when they did things, but they were few and far between. Anyone who had just killed a young woman should've left something he could follow. But there was nothing. Either the killer had a way of camouflaging himself, or he was a true sociopath who could kill without any feelings, either for himself or his victims.

Giving up trying to find any clues, Connor hoped the sheriff wouldn't take too long to get there. He sat on the log and waited. He considered shifting back to his mountain lion form, but decided it might not be a good idea if the authorities managed to get there before he could change back. Even though people knew about shifters, there weren't a lot of them 'out' to the humans, and people tended to freak out if they weren't prepared. Cops rushing to find a dead body were likely to be a bit on the jumpy side. It would be a good way to end up with holes in his hide.

Deputy Danny Lupan pulled into the Sandoval County Sheriff's Department's parking lot in Jemez Springs, New Mexico ready to get some downtime, but hoping something interesting would happen. He was so tired of sitting out by the truck stop waiting for speeders to go by. Sure, he caught a fair number of them, and for a minute or so on each one, he enjoyed the chase, but it wasn't the same as when he was running free in the desert chasing rabbits and deer. The speeders always gave up so easily and let him catch them, plus there was no feast after the chase. It just wasn't fulfilling. Sure, he'd been on the force for ten years, and it was a great outlet for his wolf, but it wasn't enough. He was ready for something interesting to happen. Even the drug dealers weren't coming through the way they had before so many states started legalizing pot. At least the drug runners would give him a good chase. It had been six weeks, at least, since he'd had a drug bust. If something didn't happen soon, he was going to dry up and blow away like the dust storms that kept ravaging the area due to the ongoing drought.

He turned off his squad car, grabbed his laptop and rifle, and then headed into the station. The smell of freshly brewed coffee hit him as he opened the door. It was midafternoon, but someone, probably Jeri White, the deputy who worked dispatch when there wasn't anything else for her to do, had filled the pot. From their daily talks, he knew Jeri was as bored as he was.

"Hey, Jeri, anything exciting going on that you didn't bother telling me about?" He put his shotgun in the weapons locker, then headed into the main squad room.

"Nope. The action around here is as dusty as the wind outside," Jeri replied. "The Sheriff wanted us to do our weekly weapons check. Might as well do it now so you can be out on the highway in time for rush hour."

Danny laughed. It was an ongoing joke in the department about making lots of ticket money during rush hour. They were lucky to get one or two speeders through town in a day. Rush hour tended to be when old man Begay drove his sheep through town twice a year, moving them from his winter field to his summer pasture and back again. They were still a couple of weeks away from the summer move, although Danny wondered how much fun it would be to make the flock of sheep stampede down Main Street.

The phone rang and Jeri took a moment to stop laughing and yawn before answering it.

Another of the department jokes was to always answer the phone sounding as bored as possible. It had been an office policy since before Danny joined the force. He'd asked Jeri about it when he noticed what they were doing. She explained that if they all sounded bored, that maybe the people on the other end of the call wouldn't expect too much out of them. It sounded lazy, but it kept calls down to a minimum, or that might just have been the lack of people in the county.

"Sandoval County sheriff's office." Jeri gave it her best bored voice. "Deputy Jeri White speaking. How can I help you?"

After a second, Jeri sat up straight. "Who are you, and where are you?" She pointed to her ears, indicating she wanted Danny to listen in on the call.

With his acute wolf shifter hearing, Danny didn't need to pick up the other line, he just sat on the side of her desk and eavesdropped.

"My name is Connor McGriffin, and I'm at a makeshift campsite about half a mile north of the Las Conchas Trailhead on the east side of the river. It's near some rocky outcroppings." There was a polite but urgent tone to the man's voice. It had a sultry Southern twang to it. Danny wondered what the man looked like. There was something about Southern men that got his attention. It might've just been the sexy way they talked, but he wasn't sure.

"Are you sure the person is dead?" Jeri sounded excited, but Danny understood her sudden change of tone. It had been a long time since they'd had a murder, or even a death that hadn't occurred either at home or in the small hospital a couple of blocks over.

"The bullet hole in her forehead would indicate it." The calm way the man said it didn't come across as snide, but Danny wouldn't be surprised if he wasn't shocked by the question. His voice remained sleek and sultry.

Jeri stood up, then sat back down. Every movement she made was fast and excited. "Don't touch anything and wait right there. I'm sending the sheriff."

Jeri hung up the phone and picked up the radio mike. "Sheriff, this is Jeri. We just got a call from a Connor McGriffin, just north of Las Conchas Trailhead. Says he's found a body."

The sheriff's voice crackled over the speaker. "A what?"

"A body," Jeri repeated. She acted like she was ready to jump out of her skin.

"As in human body, not another deer or coyote that someone hit with their truck?" The sheriff didn't sound like he believed her. Not that Danny could blame him. It had been several years since anything really exciting happened. He got off the desk and headed toward the weapons locker.

"Sounds like a human body. He said there was a bullet hole in her forehead." Jeri gestured for Danny to grab her a shotgun too.

"I'll be there in about thirty minutes," the sheriff said. "You and Danny meet me there."

She put down the mike and looked at Danny as he walked in carrying two shotguns. She glanced at the receptionist. "Mary, call the paramedics and have them meet us there. Cover dispatch for me until we get back. There shouldn't be much going on."

Mary looked up from her word-find book and flashed Jeri a thumbs up, never putting down her pencil.

"Come on," Danny urged as he headed for the back door. "We haven't had a dead body in a long time. Let's get out there before the vultures get to it."

Jeri stopped on the threshold. "Do you think we should get the coroner out there?"

Visions of Rage

Danny shook his head. "Not until we know for sure what we're dealing with. Rusty'll make that call." The urge to get to the scene and sniff around was nearly overwhelming. He'd been bored for so long, Danny wasn't sure how he was going to contain the wolf inside him long enough to make it out to Las Conchas Trailhead. He wouldn't be able to run faster than he could drive, but he desperately wanted to. There was a hunt starting and he wanted to make sure he was in on it.

A short, stocky man in his mid-fifties, wearing a brown sheriff's uniform, walked down the hiking trail toward Connor. After wiping his head with a handkerchief, he placed the wide brimmed hat he carried onto his balding head as he approached.

"You McGriffin?" His tone was questioning and cautious as he huffed out the question.

Connor couldn't blame him for that, he'd be suspicious of someone who'd called in about finding a dead body in the forest. There were a fair number of times when the person who reported a crime was the one who did it. "Yes, sir." He dealt with the authorities on a regular basis. He knew how to talk and move to keep the suspicion from swinging his way. He stayed on the log, doing his best to look innocent as he looked up at the sheriff.

"I'm Sheriff Callaway. Where's this body?"

Connor pointed toward the rocks above him. "I saw some disturbed rocks and thought it might be the path the killer took out there, so I went around it."

"Good move." Callaway moved his gaze about, glancing from Connor to the scene.

Connor grinned. "I watch TV." He figured it might be better if he didn't let on too much until he had an opportunity to get some of his contacts in Santa Fe to speak with the sheriff and open the way to him lending a hand. Cops always took strange news like mountain lion shifters who were experts on things like serial killers better when the news came from other cops, and not the mountain lion shifter in question. Or at least that had been his experience.

"How'd you happen to find her?" He looked back at Connor, his gaze intense.

"I was jogging and stopped for a breath. I saw something red waving in the breeze, and then saw her leg sticking out." Connor knew how to lie, and was pleased when the sheriff didn't even flinch at his. There were times he was very happy humans were easy to fool.

The sheriff walked away, moving up the hill toward the body. He kept his head down, obviously observing everything he could about the area. He moved with the slow deliberation of someone who'd investigated a fair number of crime scenes and didn't want to miss anything, no matter how minor.

Connor appreciated him trying to be thorough and wished he could explain there wasn't much to find. He'd thought about calling Santa Fe and getting introductions made, but figured he'd give Callaway a few minutes to get a feel for the situation, then drop the other shoe.

Two people dressed in brown uniforms, but hatless, jogged up the trail toward him. Based on their hurry, they were excited by the idea they had a dead body to investigate.

The smaller one was a petite redhead in her mid-thirties. She said something to the man, and her voice was the same as the woman who answered the phone when Conner called in the body. She sounded a bit out of breath.

Visions of Rage

The man caused the hair on the back of Connor's neck to stand up. A growl formed in his throat, and he swallowed it back down. It wouldn't do to antagonize the deputy, even if there was something about him that screamed not human. Being as sensitive as he was, Connor was better than most other shifters at spotting their own kind.

The man was just under six feet and lanky with the dark skin of a Native American. His hair was shoulder length and raven black.

The wind blowing along the river carried the reek of wolf. The man must be a werewolf. There weren't many wolf shifters around that he knew of. Most non-humans who smelled of wolf were werewolves.

Sheriff Callaway called from where he stood between the two outcroppings, "One of you two get McGriffin's information, and the other tape off the area and see if there are any footprints in that trampled grass."

"Sure thing, Rusty," the man said. "Jeri, you tape the area. I'll question this *gentleman*." He changed course from heading toward the sheriff and strolled toward Connor.

Once again, Connor forced back a growl. The way he came right at him, he hadn't noticed he was heading toward another shifter. The wind was still enough, he would probably have to either be closer or in his wolf form to pick anything up. It could also be he just had a bad nose. Although it was a fairly cute nose.

The deputy took a notebook out of his pocket and walked toward Connor. He seemed to be giving Connor more than a customary once over. If Connor wasn't mistaken, he liked what he saw.

Then the deputy sneezed. He cocked his head and sniffed. "Well, well, hello, kitty cat. I'm Deputy Sheriff

Danny Lupan. What are you doing out here?" he asked, sounding suspicious.

Connor stood and stepped away from the log. He wanted to have a little bit of maneuvering room if things got hostile. He doubted either the deputy or the sheriff would be carrying silver bullets, but he didn't want to find out. Even if they weren't, if the werewolf went after him, damage from a shifter would take a little while to heal. Standing also put him on equal ground with the deputy. He always liked being on equal standing with other shifters. Some, like werewolves, understood dominance positioning, and he didn't want the man staring down at him and having the high ground.

He turned his gaze from Deputy Lupan, but kept watch out of the corner of his eye. It would be too easy to glare, and he really didn't want to antagonize the locals.

"Name?" Deputy Lupan asked, then moved as if he were trying to circle around Connor.

"Connor McGriffin." He spun, keeping Deputy Lupan in front of him. He wasn't about to let a wolf get behind him.

Deputy Lupan made notes on his pad and didn't look at Connor. "ID?" Everything about him said he was also doing his best to be polite, as much as his natural animosity would allow.

"In my back pocket." Connor pointed to his right hip pocket.

"Okay."

Keeping his face toward Deputy Lupan, Connor turned sideways so the deputy could see his hands as he reached into his pocket with his thumb and forefinger. He removed his drivers' license from his wallet and handed it over. He knew how to move to keep a situation from getting out of control, but Deputy Lupan was the first cop he'd dealt with who was also a shifter. That made things a lot trickier than he was used to.

"Santa Fe? What are you doing in this area?" Deputy Lupan squinted at the license. He seemed to compare the picture on the license to him.

"Taking a break from the city. Doctor ordered me to take a rest. I leased a cabin about two miles from here for the next six months. Just moved in yesterday." He understood the need for the deputy to be asking questions, but he had to push back the urge to snarl. Deputy Lupan was hitting him wrong. His day was going from unsettling to bad.

"Doctor?" the deputy asked suspiciously. "Didn't know someone like us needed doctors. Most of us can heal ourselves just by shifting."

Connor shrugged and ignored the question. Not wanting the local cops to think there was something mentally wrong with him, he didn't reveal that the doctor mentioned was a psychiatrist.

"Brown or green?" the deputy continued, seeming to not be overly worried about what kind of doctor sent him out for a rest.

"Excuse me?" Connor raised his eyebrows in surprise.

"I said, is the cabin brown or green?" Deputy Lupan said with an impatient tone.

"It's brown, but what does that have to do with anything?" Connor snapped. He wanted to get away from the cop and his questions. With any luck, he could shake the entire encounter out of his system on his run back to the cabin.

"The only cabins for lease around here belong to Brian Epson," Deputy Lupan said as he made more notes. "He has two. One is brown, and the other's green."

Connor nodded. "I see." It all made sense, and he suddenly wondered why this werewolf was getting under his skin. He sighed. His agitation was part of the reason the department shrink in Santa Fe had suggested time off. Not that he was officially part of the police department there, but when the doctor said he wasn't going to get any more cases until he got some down time, he listened.

Two EMTs came up the hiking trail, dragging a gurney with them. They looked and sounded more winded than the sheriff had. Connor immediately wondered how they were going to sound after hauling the body down to the parking lot at the trailhead.

"Where's the body, Danny?" one asked between gasps for air.

Deputy Lupan pointed toward the sheriff. "Over there with Rusty. Go around where Jeri's working."

He turned back to Connor. "What do you do in Santa Fe?"

Connor had hoped that maybe with the EMTs arriving, the deputy would find something else to occupy his attention for a while, but that wasn't happening. "I'm a consultant."

"What kind of consulting?" The deputy swept his pen back and forth at an ever-increasing speed as if they were getting to the really interesting stuff. Connor knew if he were on the other side of the interrogation, he'd be more interested.

Connor raised an eyebrow in irritation and sighed. "It varies."

Deputy Lupan paused and looked up from his pad with a hard frown that worked its way up to become a glare in his deep brown eyes. "Anyone we can check with?"

With a shrug, Connor acknowledged that he wasn't going to get the opportunity to call Santa Fe and get proper introductions. He wondered if maybe he shouldn't have done it while he was waiting for the sheriff to show up. Maybe if he hadn't been so stressed by the last case he helped out with, he'd be making better decisions. "You could try Police Chief Kennedy, the police commissioner, or the mayor." He counted the men off on his fingers.

The deputy squinted at him again. "Are you trying to be a smart ass, kitty cat?"

Connor shook his head. "Wouldn't think of it, Dawg." He purposely exaggerated his southern drawl. He'd already irritated the werewolf, he didn't see any point in holding back.

"You know I'll have to tell the sheriff what you are?" Deputy Lupan handed him his driver's license back.

The existence of shifters was common knowledge, but not all were out to the public, some weres were not even to their families. Shifters were the new invisible minority, replacing gays in that respect. "He know what you are?"

"Most of the people around here know what I am." The way he said it, sounded like he was proud of it. Connor didn't have much contact with Native Americans, but the little he'd heard said they didn't hide their shifters. Some tribes didn't trust them when they'd come out during the First World War, but once they figured out they weren't evil witches, they accepted them with an almost religious reverence.

"I'll bet your special 'abilities' are a help in your job. You'd be *real* good at tracking." Connor made it a point to add a bit of a jibe in his tone, hoping the good deputy would decide to go do something more constructive than questioning someone who was trying to help them.

"You got a phone number?" Deputy Lupan asked with an agitated tone.

"Yeah." Connor knew he shouldn't be continuing to irritate the wolf shifter, but things were taking too long and he hoped that if he got him irritated enough, maybe they'd wrap things up. Or there was always the chance he'd piss off the deputy enough he'd end up in jail. If that happened, a couple of quick calls to Santa Fe would get him out. Kennedy was always warning him to watch his tone with the authorities, and would get a kick out of having to pull strings to get him out of jail.

Deputy Lupan glared.

"505-888-5132."

"I'll have to test your hands for gunpowder residue."

Connor shook his head; the continued questions were growing old and he wanted to be on his way. With each one, he wished more and more he'd already called his connections in Santa Fe. "You know you won't find anything. If I were going to kill her, I wouldn't use a gun any more than you would."

"I know," the deputy said. "But it's . . ."

Connor interrupted, "Standard Operating Procedure. Like I told your boss, I watch TV. And that's before I started working as a consultant. I know how these things work."

"How did you happen to find the body?" Deputy Lupan frowned and was obviously changing tactics to try and get him to give more information, or if he was the killer to slip up and give them something useful.

"You want what I told your boss or the truth?" He tilted his head. He knew a werewolf would be able to tell a lie if he repeated what the told the sheriff.

Deputy Lupan's frown deepened and he blew out a pained breath. "Let's try both."

Connor repeated what he told the sheriff. "I wasn't sure how the sheriff would take the truth, but if you insist, I was soaking up the sun about half a mile from here. I thought I heard a shot. The wind shifted, and I smelled human blood. I thought someone might be injured, so I followed my nose. When I arrived, the campfire was still barely steaming from being doused, and I was too late to help the woman." He left out the parts about what he felt from the area. Even shifters were more than a little bit suspicious of people who could reach beyond the psychical world and feel more than they should. He'd lost count of the people who thought he was a witch or something because of what he could sense that others couldn't.

He noticed the deputy's slim, elegant fingers as he made notes. There was something about those fingers, about the man they were attached to. He couldn't decide it he wanted to tear him apart for being a werewolf and thus more than a little bit of an inconvenience while he was supposed to be relaxing, or if he wanted to find out what it would take to get the deputy to relax. He hated people who yanked him around in any form, and Deputy Lupan was definitely pulling his chain on several levels.

"Another thing," Connor added. "As I was headed here, a green and white RV nearly ran over me. It was one of those that looks like a camper on a truck, but is all one piece. Not sure, but I think it was a Dodge."

"I don't suppose you got a license number?" Deputy Lupan flipped a page and made a few more notes.

"I was trying too hard to stay out of the road. I did see the Zia logo that identifies it as a New Mexico plate."

"That might help." He finally sounded a little bit less grumpy.

The sheriff walked up to the two men. "McGriffin, I'll need to get a DNA sample from you. Looks like she was raped. Danny, there's a kit in my car."

Deputy Lupan pulled off a backpack and dug around in it for a moment. He moved in the relaxed, easy way shifters did. It made Connor wonder if he might be a born shifter, or if he'd been a werewolf long enough he was comfortable with it and let it blend over into his human body.

Unbidden, a picture appeared in Connor's mind.

Two people engaged in sex in a camper bed. Again, the impression that the man had her well under his spell hit. He told her again that she was pretty.

Connor wondered what he'd promised her. With the other cases he worked where the prey went willingly, they'd always been promised something.

"Are you sure it was rape, Sheriff?" he asked.

The sheriff frowned and looked from Connor to another man who'd arrived while Connor and deputy Lupan talked. "I can't be sure, but she had intercourse not long before she was killed."

"You can have a DNA sample, but I can tell you it won't match even if you find anything. She isn't my type."

"And just what is your type?" Deputy Lupan asked as he returned with the collecting kit.

Connor just cocked an eyebrow and let his gaze travel down the deputy's lanky frame and back up to his lovely brown eyes.

Deputy Lupan glared and handed him a swab.

He rolled it around in his mouth and handed it back before he asked impatiently, "Am I free to go, Sheriff?"

"You have everything we need, Danny?" the sheriff asked, looking from Connor to his deputy and back.

The deputy's voice was almost a growl. "Yeah. For now anyway."

"Just don't go too far, McGriffin," the sheriff said. "We may have more questions."

"No problem. The Dawg knows where to find me." Connor turned and stalked up the highway toward his cabin.

Once out of sight, he stopped, leaned over with his hands on his knees, and took a few deep breaths. The atmosphere, both physical and psychic, was starting to hit him harder than he wanted to let on. He needed a chance to catch his breath. He needed the opportunity to shift, and he tried his best to not do that in front of people. Running on four legs would help him more than anything. After making sure there wasn't anyone within sight, he envisioned his cat form and his human form slipped away. As he always did, he gave a brief thanks for not having to strip down before shifting. It made things easier.

As his human form fell away and he dropped to all fours, he wondered if Deputy Danny Lupan would have to strip to shift, or if he also had a bit of magic that allowed him to keep his clothes. Either way, he was looking forward to seeing much more of the deputy. With any luck, they might even be able to work their way through their animosity, if they both wanted it badly enough.

Danny watched Connor McGriffin saunter away. His body again reacted as he admired the tightness of McGriffin's jeans across his ass. It was a shame he was a cat, although it might prove enjoyable. It had been a while since he'd met a shifter who caught his attention like McGriffin had. Gay shifters weren't all too common. There was something about him, more than just being a shifter. He was hot as hell, intelligent, and more. He wanted to find out what the more was. Danny wasn't a big fan of coincidence, and with it being a fairly slow few years, he wondered what it meant that a cat shifter found a dead body in his jurisdiction. His grandmother always told him to watch the signs and over the years he'd done just that. That meant he had to look deeper, there was still something McGriffin hadn't told him. Something important, if not to the case, then to McGriffin. He knew it in his gut.

"What was that about 'the Dog'," Rusty asked, drawing Danny's attention back to the present and the wind that was blowing the scent of drying human blood around.

"Just a jibe. He's a shifter, too," Danny replied. "Some kind of cat. I'd guess cougar. Don't think he's a bobcat. That's probably why he isn't heading toward the trailhead parking lot. He's got a cabin rented not far away and will probably shift and go through the woods." He was too self-assured to be a smaller cat. There was something powerful about him, and Danny wanted to find out more about that power dwelling deep inside him.

"This could prove interesting." Rusty frowned. "Was he indicating he's gay by that remark about the girl not being his type?" Even though he was a small county sheriff, Rusty Callaway didn't miss much. He also didn't have a lot of the hang ups people expected small rural people to have.

"Yes, if my gaydar is in working order," Danny said.

Rusty chuckled. "A gay cougar and a gay wolf. Sounds like a match made in Heaven to me."

Danny snarled. He didn't want Rusty to spend energy trying to fix him up with anyone. The last time that happened, it hadn't turned out well.

Chapter Two

Danny walked into the station the next morning. He hadn't slept as well as he would've liked. He'd kept dreaming about Connor McGriffin. That damned cat had stalked him all night, taunting him from every rock and tree along the Jemez River. At one point when they'd taken a run through the forest, McGriffin had stayed just far enough away from him that he'd been taunting, but seemed to not want to get intimate. They'd run in both human and animal forms. McGriffin was a sleek, powerful cougar. With everything his grandmother had told him about believing his dreams, he didn't doubt for an instant that when he found out what McGriffin was, it would be a cougar. His dreams never led him astray.

"Danny, my office, now!" Rusty yelled, bringing Danny back to the here and now.

Danny hurried into the room. He tried to think of what he might have done to make Rusty sound so pissed off.

"Shut the door and sit down." Rusty pointed at the door and frowned.

Danny sat on a chair facing Rusty's desk. He leaned back, stuck his legs out in front of him, and crossed his ankles. As much as he wanted to appear relaxed, between the lack of rest the night before and the general air of impatience in the room, he also wanted to get up and pace.

Rusty twirled a pen between his fingers. "I read your report from yesterday. Some of these questions and answers are a little confusing."

"Like what?" There were several things about Connor McGriffin that were confusing. He didn't even want to go into it with the Sheriff.

"He's a consultant?" Rusty tapped the pen on the stack of papers that Danny recognized as his report. "What kind of consultant?"

"He wouldn't say." Danny shrugged. "Just said to check with the Santa Fe chief of police or the commissioner.

Rusty picked up the phone and dialed. "Good morning. I'm Sheriff Rusty Callaway from Jemez Springs. May I speak to Chief Kennedy?" There was a moment of silence before the Rusty continued. "Hello, Kennedy. I have one of my deputies here in the office, and I'm going to put you on speaker. Deputy Lupan, this is Larry Kennedy, chief of police in Santa Fe."

"Hi, Rusty." Kennedy sounded fairly congenial. "What's up?"

"What can you tell me about a man named Connor McGriffin?"

Laughter erupted over the phone.

Rusty looked at Danny and frowned.

Danny spread his hands in a gesture of confusion. He wasn't sure if Kennedy's response was a good one or a bad one.

"Good luck to you. Didn't you tell me a couple of years ago one of your deputies is a wolf shifter?"

"Yeah." Rusty raised his busy gray eyebrows and his frown deepened.

"Well, McGriffin's a cougar." Kennedy continued. "Around here they call him the 'Big Cat'. I'd like to be around when he and your wolf meet."

"We met yesterday." Danny pushed back his growl. "I knew he was a cat of some kind." Then he smiled, remembering his dream and silently thanked his grandmother's spirit again for telling him to listen to his dreams. It was all laid out there for him. He wondered if the way McGriffin had taunted him had really been flirting.

"He said he's a freelance consultant for the police department." Rusty pulled out a fresh sheet of paper and started taking notes.

"You could call him that," Kennedy said. "Did he tell you anything about his other abilities?"

"There's more?" Rusty asked. He started twirling the pen again, telling Danny he was more than a little bit interested in what Kennedy was explaining. Danny had worked for Rusty Callaway long enough to know that he liked odd things coming along in their quiet town. He always said the unusual kept life interesting. That was one of the reasons he kept Danny around; with a wolf shifter on staff, the unusual got sniffed out before it became a problem.

"Tell me how you met him." Kennedy said.

"He found the body of a young woman in the hills yesterday." Rusty kept twirling the pen. He was making Danny more nervous. "She'd been shot."

"He probably *saw* the murder," Kennedy said.

"You mean he was there?" Danny straightened up in his chair. The urge to go to McGriffin's rented cabin and drag him out to face justice hit him hard. "He didn't say anything about that." He'd had more than one case where the person reporting the problem had been the one to cause it. He'd never had a murderer call in a body before.

"No. I mean he saw it in his head," Kennedy answered. "Do you believe in psychics?"

"You mean like fortune tellers?" Danny wondered if Kennedy was some kind of nut. Or maybe this McGriffin was a freak. Then Danny remembered tales his mother and grandmother told him about some of the other old women in the pack who could sense things the rest of them couldn't. It just didn't feel real. But if it wasn't real, what were his dreams that gave him warning of things to come?

"Yes and no. Connor *'sees'* things. Sometimes as they happen, sometimes he picks up visions after the fact, and sometimes he sees them ahead of time. I'm not sure if you'd call him psychic, seer, clairvoyant, or what. He's great at locating lost people or objects." He paused. "Did he say anything about why he's in your area?"

"Told me the doctor ordered a rest," Danny said. "I wondered about it, because if he's like me, we don't usually need doctors." He'd thought about pursuing that line of questions with McGriffin the previous day, but the way he'd been getting agitated, he'd decided to hold off and ask later, if they decided they needed the information.

"There're different kinds of doctors. Did you read anything about the case we've been chasing down here for the last eighteen months?"

"You mean the guy who was snatching, torturing, raping, and killing kids?" Rusty asked. He set the pen down and leaned back in his chair.

"That's the one." Kennedy's voice suddenly sounded tired and drawn.

"I heard you caught him last week," Rusty said.

"Have you ever seen a cougar attack someone?"

"You mean a human?" Rusty asked as he shook his head, not liking the only logical connection to a case and a cougar attack. Shifters weren't supposed to attack humans. It was part of the rules shifters followed and enforced on each other.

"Yeah. I thought we were going to have to tase Connor to keep him away from the guy. Not that tasing would have really done anything to him. He was in cat mode, had knocked the guy down, and was standing on top of him. I've never seen him so far from human. He's normally the calm, cool, collected one. He completely lost it. "

"Can't say as if I blame him." Danny rubbed the back of his neck. "I'd probably have trouble keeping my wolf in check if I cornered someone who was torturing kids." The very idea of it elicited a growl from deep inside him. He knew how protective a lot of shifters were of the weaker members of society. It was why a lot of them worked in law enforcement, or other civil servant jobs, to make sure the innocent had strong voices and protectors in the world.

"Getting back to your murder victim—" Kennedy said, "—you might want to ask Connor if he can describe the killer."

"We'll do that." Rusty picked up the pen and making a couple of notes. "Thanks for your information."

"You're welcome." Kennedy chuckled. "Good luck with your cat and dog."

"Thanks. I may need it. They've already sized each other up. One other question." Rusty glanced at Danny as if asking permission.

Danny was fairly sure he knew what Rusty was going to ask. He didn't mind one way or the other, although it would be nice if his boss would stay out of his love life.

"Shoot."

"Is your cat by any chance gay?"

Not being able to stand it anymore, Danny finally gave in to the urge to pace. He prowled from one side of the small office to the other. It wasn't much, and he knew Rusty would understand. He was ready for the phone call to be over so he could get out of the office and keep working on the case, even if it was getting stranger by the second. Maybe if he went out and caught a few speeders, it would give him some breathing space. He wasn't sure if he wanted to know if McGriffin was gay or not. Even if he was, he didn't know enough about him to decide if he was interested.

"Why do you ask?"

"Because my wolf is."

Kennedy laughed. "Have fun. I'm glad it's you and not me."

With a polite closing, Rusty ended the connection.

Danny growled deep in his throat. "Don't know what he meant about that. Just keep that cat away from me and nothing will happen." He stomped out of Rusty's office and sat at his desk. He didn't want to sit still. He opened his desk drawer, stared at it for a second, and then slammed it shut. There was a pile of papers he needed to go through, but he didn't want to touch them. He was tired after a long night of chasing McGriffin through the forest, and wasn't in the mood to deal with Rusty wanting to play matchmaker. He didn't see how he could ever be interested in a cougar. His family would laugh their asses off, and his alpha would have a fit.

"What's up, Danny?" Jeri asked, coming over to sit on his desk like she normally did when she was being friendly.

He curled his lip and growled. "Stay out of it." He stood and stormed out of the sheriff's office, not even caring as people rushed out of his way when he started down the sidewalk, not exactly knowing where he was going.

Visions of Rage

Danny stood at the window with a cup of coffee. His stomach growled, signaling it was lunchtime. An unfamiliar, topless, black Jeep Wrangler pulled in and parked across the street in front of the Star Café.

McGriffin slipped out of the doorless driver's side of the Jeep, brushed his windblown, tawny hair out of his eyes, stared at the window of the sheriff's office, saluted, turned, and sauntered into the café. He had a subtle arrogance that most cats, shifter or otherwise, had. It didn't help that he looked so good, and it had been a long time since Danny had felt a connection to another man, even a human one.

"The cat just drove into town, Boss." Danny again admired the tight jeans and t-shirt on Connor and attempted to stop the reaction of his body. After all, it wouldn't do. A cat and a dog? Never. But he couldn't deny he was attracted to McGriffin. But then he had always had a problem with the unobtainable men, or men who'd get him into trouble. That was one of the reasons he lived in Jemez Springs and not Albuquerque. There were fewer men there for him to get into trouble with. A cat shifter? That was just asking for trouble. "He just went into the Star."

Rusty hurried out of his office. "Come on. I have some more questions for him." He cut across the office and held the door open for Danny. "And behave yourself. I don't want any trouble."

"None from me, Boss." As he set his coffee cup on his desk, Danny opened his eyes innocently. He was far from innocent.

Connor sat facing the door of the café. He wondered how long it was going to take Deputy Lupan to get across the street. The way the man had been watching out the window when he pulled up made him wonder if that was how he normally patrolled the city, or if he was on his lunch break and people watching.

A perky black-haired woman in her mid-twenties approached. "Hi. My name's Angie. What can I get you?" Her voice carried a slight Spanish accent.

"I'm Connor." He smiled. He made it a point to try to be nice to waitstaff. They were the ones handling his food and he didn't like surprises. "What's good?"

"I can recommend our burgers," she said without any real thought to the question. That must've been the truth, or it was her standard answer to the question she received many times every day. "They're grilled over mesquite."

"Sounds good. Make it rare." He tapped a line on the menu. "I see you have grilled onions and mushrooms. Those would be great. Do fries come with it?"

"Sure do. What are you drinking?"

"Do you serve beer?"

She shook her head. "Sorry. We don't."

"Make it iced tea then." He winked. Charm also helped him make sure his food and service was good. "With lots of lemon."

"You got it." Angie turned toward the kitchen.

Sheriff Callaway and Deputy Lupan came in the door. They paused for a moment, glancing around the restaurant that was only minorly busy, since it was slightly before the official start of lunchtime. Deputy Lupan spotted him first, tapped the sheriff on the shoulder and pointed in Connor's direction.

"Hi, Sheriff, Danny," Angie called as she took Connor's order to the pass-through that went to the kitchen. "Be right with you."

The two officials walked over to Connor's table.

Deputy Lupan turned a chair around, and straddled it. "Hello again, *Big Cat.*"

"You must have talked to Kennedy," Connor said. The way the deputy had stressed the words, like a name, it was obvious to him that they had. Kennedy and the rest of the Santa Fe police department had stuck him with the nickname when he'd come out as a cougar shifter. It was different from the kitty cat Deputy Lupan had used the previous day.

Sheriff Callaway sat between his deputy and Connor as if putting himself between them would make them play better. "Danny, I warned you to play nice."

"I *am* playing nice." Deputy Lupan looked astonished. The way he did it made Connor wonder if he often had to pull exaggerated looks when he was with the sheriff, hell, with everyone. The wolf had an overly laid-back feeling. "I haven't bitten him *yet.*"

Sheriff Callaway turned to Connor. "Looks like you left out a little about yourself yesterday."

"I thought I answered all the questions." Connor stared at Deputy Lupan who glared back, also without blinking. He had some very lovely brown eyes. More like a cow's than a wolf's. But Connor could feel the deputy's furry side when looking at him so intently. He wondered if the feeling went both ways. He didn't know too many people who could hold his gaze for long. How long would it take before the wolf blinked?

"Well, there's answering questions, and then there's answering questions," the sheriff said. "You were right about talking to Kennedy. We had a nice conversation this morning. He had some interesting things to say about you."

"I can imagine." Since he was a civilian consultant, Kennedy would've been a little more open with his information than he would've been with a member of the force. It was the brotherhood of the badge, and Connor wasn't an actual part of it, even if he did work closely with them on a regular basis. He was an outsider, and he didn't mind that. Being outside of the official channels gave him freedom the cops he worked with didn't have. It also made him more vulnerable, in a lot of ways.

Angie came to the table carrying three glasses of iced tea and a small dish of lemon wedges. "What can I get you, Sheriff, Danny?" She set a glass in front of each of the men and the lemon wedges between them.

"I'll take my usual, Angie." Deputy Lupan finally broke eye contact with Connor and smiled at the waitress.

A small thrill of triumph went through Connor since the deputy blinked first. It gave Connor the first step up on him.

"Me, too," Sheriff Callaway said.

"What did Kennedy have to say?" Connor asked, still watching the deputy. He didn't want to let his guard down around the wolf. He might be sexy as all get-out, but he was still a dangerous predator. Connor picked up a lemon and squeezed it into his glass of tea.

"Something about how you *see* things," Deputy Lupan said. His eyes returned to Connor's. It seemed he was ready for round two.

"So, tell me, Deputy Lupan, can you hear me?" Connor asked mentally. Some shifters could hear him when he tried speaking to them telepathically but not many. Most were just as dense as humans were to his mental powers.

Lupan spewed tea across the table as his eyes widened. *"What's this? I knew I could communicate with pack members, but never tried it with another species."*

"Danny!" Sheriff Callaway grabbed some napkins from the small dispenser in the center of the table. "What's wrong with you?"

"Sorry," Lupan muttered as he dabbed tea off his smooth dimpled chin.

"Maybe that's one of the things I didn't tell you." Smirking into his glass, Connor took a drink of tea. Maybe playing with the wolf was going to be more fun than he thought. It had been a long time since he'd had someone he could just be playful with. There was no telling how long he could draw things out with the deputy, but he wanted to enjoy himself. After all, he *was* supposed to be relaxing.

Once the deputy had cleaned up his mess, Connor turned to the sheriff. "Did he say what kind of things?" He didn't doubt that Kennedy had explained everything to Callaway. The odds were he'd even told him he was gay, which Connor didn't care about one way or another. It wasn't illegal, and if Callaway had a problem with it, he could just get over it if he wanted Connor's help in finding their murderer.

The sheriff slowly stirred in the sugar he'd added to his tea. "He said you may have seen the murder."

"I did, and I didn't." He shuddered, as the details of what he'd seen flashed in his mind. "I saw the woman's face just before the bullet entered her forehead."

"Did you see the shooter?" Lupan asked, as he wadded up his damp napkins and put them next to the napkin dispenser and the bottle of catsup.

"Not really." Connor pursed his lips and tried to dig a little deeper into what he had seen. Sometimes, visions solidified a little over time. Things that might've been blurry at first, could become clear if he stood back from the scene and gave them the chance. Closing his eyes to make it easier to remember, he replayed the vision and noted the new details that came to him. "I saw a male form with a camera in front of his face. His skin was dark and his hair was black with a little gray. He may be Hispanic or Middle Eastern. He called her Connie and told her to smile. Not much of an accent. I'd guess he was born and educated in this country even if he does look foreign. I'm not sure where the gun was since he had the camera in both of his hands. There may have been another person, but I didn't sense one. From the shadow cast in front of him, I'd say the man was close to six feet tall. The woman wasn't afraid. I could feel she was relaxed and laughing. She was posing for the camera. She was happy up until the end. I bet he told her she was pretty."

"You know it was a man?" the sheriff asked.

"Yeah. When you said something about rape, I saw a man and woman having sex in a camper." On a personal level, he was thankful he wasn't getting more details on that vision. He did his best to keep other people's sexual lives from impacting him.

"You should be able to describe him then," Deputy Lupan grumbled. It wasn't exactly a growl, but something close.

Wondering if he was making the deputy start to relax enough to be more civil, Connor shook his head. "She was on top of him, and her body was blocking my view of his head. Again, I could see the dark hair. I don't really have any control over what direction I view scenes from." There had been times when he could get more control of what he saw, but that took a lot of effort, and he could rarely forget those details. He'd had to do that on the last case. He'd never,

ever, be able to not see that poor boy when he closed his eyes. Every night he had to go past that vision to get to sleep. In Santa Fe, it had been impacting him big time and that's why the doctor sent him for some down time. None of them had ever thought he'd get caught up in another case so quickly. He just hoped this one wouldn't drag him under like the last one had.

He picked up his tea glass and brought it to his lips. Suddenly a vision hit. Connor swallowed as the tea in his mouth went sour. As it hit, he relayed what he saw in vivid detail; sometimes when the vision came fast, in bits and pieces it was just easier to speak what he was seeing, and hope the people around him could remember the bits he wouldn't.

"It's happening again. She gets out of a white RV with green pinstriping like the one that passed me yesterday. She's wearing black slacks, a white blouse with lettering embroidered on the left front of it, and low-heeled black shoes. I can't make out the words on her blouse. Her hands are tied together in front of her. She has long red hair pulled back in a ponytail. He's wearing jeans, a white t-shirt, and boots. I can't see his face. His shirt is dirty, looks like food stains. She's crying. He pushes her over the low wall. She turns and starts running. She trips and falls. He walks over to her and turns her over on her back. A single shot to her forehead. She isn't happy like the one I found yesterday was."

Angie fumbled the plate of burger and fries she was carrying but managed to keep it upright. She set it on the table and stared at Connor. The look on her face was one that edged on fear. He'd seen it and worse on other faces over the years when his gifts showed themselves in public. With practice, he'd learned to ignore the looks, but sometimes, they still hit him hard. He didn't like being someone people feared.

He jumped up, yanked a $20 bill out of his wallet, threw it on the table, and grabbed the burger off of the plate. "Keep the change, Angie. Come on, Dawg. Let's roll." He ran for the door.

"You heard him, Danny," Sheriff Callaway said loud enough the whole dinner must've heard. "Go."

Deputy Lupan followed on Connor's heels.

Connor grabbed the roll bar with one hand and swung into the open side of his Jeep. If he hadn't had a shifter's reflexes and strength, he'd have dropped his burger as he slid into his seat. He held the burger in his mouth as he fastened his seatbelt. The juices from the burger made him drool, and he didn't care. He was hungry, but needed to get out to where the latest body was cooling in the New Mexico heat.

Deputy Lupan stood on the sidewalk, his brown eyes wide and questioning.

"You coming, Dawg?" Connor snarled as he pulled his keys out of his pocket, wishing he'd done that before he'd gotten in and fastened his seat belt, but then he might've dropped his burger.

Without a word, Deputy Lupan jumped into the passenger side.

Connor stuck the burger in Lupan's face as soon as he had the seatbelt fastened. "Hold this." He started the Jeep, backed out of the parking space, and took off.

"Will you slow down before I fall out?" The deputy grabbed the bar in front of him with his free hand. "Where're the doors to this thing anyway?"

"Back in Santa Fe along with the top." Connor figured he didn't need to obey speed limits since he had the county deputy in the car with him; he never did in similar situations in Santa Fe. He put his foot hard on the gas pedal.

"Where are we going?" Deputy Lupan snapped as Connor turned hard to the right, and he white-knuckled the bar in front of him.

"Following the scent." Connor reached over, grabbed the burger, took a large bite, and handed it back. "You're a wolf. You should be good at that."

Lupan lifted the burger to his mouth and also took a bite. "Mushrooms? Yuck!" He spit something out the side of the Jeep.

Connor glared. "I said hold it, not eat it," he hissed and snatched the burger back once he had the Jeep in fifth.

"You didn't give me time to get my lunch." Lupan growled.

Connor swung the Jeep into a roadside campsite, slammed on the brakes, and turned off the engine. Before the dust settled, he leaped through the missing door, shifting into cat form as he did. He landed on all four paws, and took off running. It was good he'd finished his burger on the way out. The shift took a bit of energy, and if he hadn't eaten, he'd have been ravenous enough to pause and hunt any small critter that happened to cross his path.

"You coming, Dawg?" He glanced over his shoulder as he ran in the direction the vision led him. The landscape was rough and uneven. He tried to remember where the woman had been shot, but there was a lot going on. The trees and rocks got confusing.

"Right behind you, Big Cat." Deputy Lupan also shifted shapes in mid-air and landed running.

The ease with which he did it, told Connor that he was a true wolf shifter and not a werewolf. He didn't leave clothes shredded on the ground behind him, so he also had at least a little magic to make his shifter life easier. Having things like that in common made Connor grin as they ran up the slope.

"I hope you know where you're going, Cat."

A siren blared in the distance.

Connor stopped. Everything was wrong. He was in the right place, but that was it. He tried to recall his vision. Where was the rock the man had thrown the woman over? He glanced around. It was a few feet in front of him. There was no body, no blood. The shadows were wrong. The sun was directly overhead, but in the vision it had been closer to evening. The shadows had been long and dark. *"Damn! It was a premonition. It hasn't happened yet."* He shifted out of cat form.

Lupan followed suit and stood there with an odd questioning look on his rugged face.

The sheriff screeched to a halt beside the Jeep, sending up another plume of dust. He rushed out of the Bronco before the engine completely died, and ran to Connor and Danny.

"What exactly did Kennedy tell you about things I see?" Connor asked. He felt like he'd just let them down. He should've known it was a premonition and not a vision of current events. There were subtle differences. There was something messing with his thoughts, and he wondered if it wasn't Deputy Lupan. Ever since he'd begun having visions, he hadn't found anyone he could be comfortable with, but there was something about the wolf that made him relax enough to tease. Maybe there was something more as well.

"He said sometimes you see it after it happens, sometimes when it happens, and sometimes before." The sheriff walked around the area, frowning.

"Right. This hasn't happened yet, but it will." Connor rubbed his forehead, feeling a little lightheaded after two shifts very close together. He was going to need another burger, or more, fairly soon. He also figured Lupan would too. "No telling when, but I think it'll be here."

"You think? You don't know?" asked Lupan. He sounded grumpy and Connor couldn't tell if it was irritation at their interrupted lunch, or feeling off from shifting twice within minutes. Things like that affected different shifters differently.

"Not for sure. It isn't like rocket science." Connor managed to block the snarl that tried to come out at the deputy questioning him. Even if the man did have a bit of magic about him to help make shifting easier, he obviously didn't know anything about visions and the forces that drove Connor.

They ambled back to the parked cars. There was a feeling of a missed opportunity, mingled with a bit of doubt.

"I can have the area patrolled, but I can't put a man here 24/7." The sheriff leaned up against his Bronco.

"It wouldn't do any good." Connor shook his head. "He'd just go somewhere else if he sensed a cop." That was one of the problems with premonitions. It had happened in the past. He'd have a vision and take steps to prevent it. The person would still die, but in a different location or at a different time. There were too many variables when dealing with future events.

"But if you saw it happen here..." Lupan sounded like he didn't believe what he was hearing.

"What I see is something that *may* happen." Connor cut him off in mid-complaint. "Circumstances can change things. What I see isn't carved in stone. Sometimes I see enough to prevent it and sometimes I don't. You know how weather forecasters often get it wrong? They say two inches of snow before morning, you wake up to a dusting, and by noon there's two feet?"

Lupan frowned. "Ye-ah."

"Well it's the same way with what I see." Connor continued. "It isn't an exact science like math. You know that every time you add two plus two, you're going to get four. This doesn't work that way." For years, Connor had wished his psychic skills were something as solid and logical as math, but they weren't. They were wild and barely controlled. He'd met a few psychics over the years who'd let the abilities get the better of them. Sometimes those people couldn't tell the difference between past, present, and future. He hoped if he ever reached that point he'd put a silver bullet in his brain and make sure he didn't go through the hell those people existed in.

When they reached the cars, the sheriff reached into the Bronco, pulled out a paper bag, and handed it to Lupan. "Here's your salad. Both of you guys' fries are in there. I hope I don't have to divide them up one by one."

Connor grabbed the bag, pulled out the salad, and took one of the chicken strips off the top. He handed the cardboard container to Lupan and grinned. "Now we're even, even if yours isn't as tasty as mine."

Lupan glared, then took his own bite. "At least mine doesn't have mushrooms on it."

As the stress of their fast trip out of town, and then being wrong faded, Connor laughed. It did feel good having someone around who he could tease and who would tease him back. Even his friends on the Santa Fe police force mostly kept him at arm's length, afraid to get too close to the strange shifter who had visions. Lupan didn't seem scared of him, and that mattered…a lot.

43

Chapter Three

Connor got up from his chair on the porch of the rental cabin and stretched. He glanced around and there wasn't anyone nearby. One of the reasons he'd chosen those particular cabins to rent from was their isolation, even from each other. Although he could see the other cabin through the trees, it wasn't in easy sight. That made shifting simpler. If it had been closer, he would've wandered into the woods before dropping his human form.

The need to run consumed him. For the past two weeks he'd been working closely with Deputy Lupan, Danny, and they weren't getting anywhere on the case. With a simple thought, he shifted and took off at full speed. The pine-needle-covered ground felt good under his paws as he raced through the trees. He hadn't had much time in fur since the case began. Sure, there'd been a couple of short times, but nothing real—he'd been too busy chasing his tail, or Danny's tail to get out and relax. They'd gone through the DMV records for any vehicles matching the RV he'd seen on the road, registered within two hundred miles of Jemez Springs. There had been a fair number of them, and they'd visited most of them. Not all of them had been home. But it was the middle of summer, the height of tourist season, and it would've been really stupid of them to think that everyone with an RV would be home. However, they hadn't found anything useful.

They also checked the spot in his vision every couple of days. Sheriff Callaway checked it on the days he and Danny hadn't. So far, there wasn't any evidence of a murder. He hoped their activity in the pulloff wasn't disrupting his vision. The future was pliable. Not every precognition he had became reality. Just knowing a bit about the future had a way of changing things.

A large rocky outcropping caught his attention and Connor ran up it. The sun had warmed the boulders to an almost unbearable level, but the heat was part of what he desperately needed. Stretching out to his full length, with his tail sticking straight out from his body, Connor yawned and let the heat from the rock soak in.

He closed his eyes and was thankful none of his visions came back to haunt him. Sometimes he got lucky and the sunlight and warmth helped keep away the dark scenes that ate at his soul.

With a heavy sigh, he surrendered and let sleep come over him. Unless some hunter was in the forest with silver bullets, he didn't have much to worry about. There weren't many things in the Rockies that would mess with a napping mountain lion.

As he had been doing the past two weeks, Danny ran in Connor's dream. They were nearly perfectly matched. Danny had a little more endurance than Connor, but Connor's initial burst of speed, when they ran, was faster. They covered great swatches of mountains and desert as they charged along, side by side. In the flat desert, Danny easily outran Connor, often laughing as he did.

As Danny went past him, Connor launched himself at the wolf. They rolled in the brown dirt until they came to rest with Connor on top of Danny. In the dream they shifted in the blink of an eye, faster than either one of them could shift in real life.

"Getting slow, Dawg," Connor said, leaning heavily against Danny's shoulders to keep him pinned.

"Maybe I'm ready to be caught, Big Cat." Danny smiled up and didn't try to throw Connor off like he often did in their dreams.

Connor stared at him, trying to find the right words, but they failed him. He was enthralled with Danny. He bent down to kiss him and something landed on his head.

Suddenly awake, Connor jerked and stared around. He growled low.

A brown kestrel landed on the rock a few feet from him and laughed at him in a high-pitched trill.

Connor shifted and pulled off his shirt. "How many times did you almost get eaten while you tried to find me?"

The kestrel shimmered and seconds later a delicate young woman stood there. Officer Lisa Collins of the Santa Fe police department held her arm outstretched for the shirt he offered her. "Only a couple." She pulled the shirt over her head. "As I figured things out, you kind of look a bit different from the regular lions in the area."

He sat on the rock and crossed his arms, giving her a hard stare. "How do you figure that?"

Lisa settled, cross-legged, across from him. "Well, as I just observed, most mountain lions don't sleep stretched out like they're road kill. The other two who were asleep were curled up in balls. You looked like you were trying to absorb every little bit of heat you could."

"I was." He was a little surprised Lisa had been able to find him, and wondered if she'd flown all the way from Santa Fe. For a kestrel that would've been a lot of flying. If her animal form was a large hawk or eagle, it would've been different since the flight would've been just an hour or so of hard flying.

"So how's your vacation going? One of the beat officers said he saw you in town a couple of days ago."

He nodded. "I was." He sighed. There wasn't a lot to be gained from lying to Lisa. She was his best friend on the force, and one of the better friends he'd made in years. "To be honest, I'm working a case up here."

Her face scrunched up in worry. "You're supposed to be relaxing. Working a case isn't relaxing."

"Well." He shrugged. "You know how my visions are. I can't control when I see something." She'd known him for a couple of years and had even been around during a few of his visions.

Lisa nodded and pulled her knees up so she could put her chin on them. "So how bad is this one?"

"Not bad yet. Well, one death. An adult female. I saw her die. But I had a precognitive vision about two weeks ago. We went racing over there and found nothing. We've been checking the site every day since and so far nothing."

"And by 'we' you mean?" She cocked an eyebrow at him.

"The local sheriff and his deputy," he replied.

She grinned. "Is this Sheriff Callaway, the one who called Chief Kennedy a couple of weeks ago?"

He nodded. "That's him."

"You know, Kennedy laughed so hard after that call that I had to go in and see what had struck his funny bone. He said you were up here and messed up in something that involved a gay wolf shifter."

"Is that why you're here?"

She raised her hands in an innocent gesture, then stood and paced a little away from him. As a kestrel she had a lot of surplus energy and had trouble sitting still for very long. "None of us had heard from you in a couple of weeks. Folks got a little worried the big bad wolf might've eaten you."

"I wish." Connor mumbled.

She stopped pacing and fixed him with her sharp falcon gaze. "Spill."

He leaned back on the rock and put his hands under his head. "Nothing really to spill right now. Deputy Lupan, Danny, is cute, obnoxious, flirty, and thoughtful. A real wolf shifter, not a werewolf."

"Danny?" She put her hands on her hips. "Are you calling him Danny already?"

"What do you mean?" Connor tried to think about that. He'd only just started thinking of him as Danny.

"Look. How long have you been working the Santa Fe Police department?"

"Three years?" He could've gotten more exact, but he didn't think that was what she was getting at.

Lisa nodded. "And how many of the officers do you call by their first name?"

Connor tried to think of how many of the officers he even knew their first names. Police officers normally went by their last names. He pursed his lips, sat up and stared at her. "You."

"Right." Lisa started pacing again. "And you've known Deputy Lupan…is that really his name? I mean come on, a wolf shifter named Lupan. How much more obvious can you get?"

"Yes. It's his name. That's what's on his badge. And okay, I've known him two weeks."

"Okay, are you sleeping with him yet?"

He jerked back at the question. "No!"

"Then you should be." She stopped pacing and stood directly in front of him with her hands on her hips looking like a large Tinkerbell. She even had her foot tapping. "Connor, you're one of the hardest people to get to know I've ever met. I think the only reason we're good friends is we're the only two shifters around the police department. It gave us a starting point. But you let your visions keep everyone at bay. Has Danny seen you have a vision yet?"

Connor nodded.

"And how did he react?" Lisa didn't move, well other than her tapping foot.

"He didn't freak out, if that's what you're asking. It was the precognition that hasn't come through yet. We were having lunch in the local dinner. It freaked the waitress out as I relayed what I was seeing as it happened. Danny and Sheriff Callaway were there. As soon as it finished, I ran for the Jeep and drove out to the site. I wanted to get there while I still had a fresh trail. Danny went with me."

"And he didn't freak out. Connor, until folks get used to your visions, they're more than a little disturbing."

He nodded. "I understand. I wonder if Danny hasn't been around someone else who has visions. He's Native American. I don't know what tribe."

"There's a lot of psychics among their population. I think the Romany are the only ones who have more." She nodded, then resumed pacing, thoughtfully pointing to nothing in particular as she spoke. "So, he's used to psychics."

"He doesn't freak out over them. Or maybe he just doesn't freak out easily." All this was stuff Connor had been over in his own mind.

"Yeah, whatever." Lisa continued pointing and pacing. "He's cute. He's a shifter."

"A *wolf* shifter," Connor objected. In all the times he'd been over this same train of thought on his own, that was really the only real problem he could find with Danny.

Lisa waved his comment away. "Whatever. One of my cousins married an owl shifter. I don't want to hear about mismatches. You guys can work it out."

"I'm supposed to be relaxing up here."

She again waved him off. "And how much more relaxed can you get than finding a sexy shifter to get involved with?"

"He's a cop."

She paused and stared at him. "And you're a psychic consultant who gets led around the country by your visions in an effort to be everyone's avenging lion. You know if this was a fantasy book you'd have a big mane and roar a lot."

"Whatever." He stood and was suddenly hungry. "Look, I've got some steaks in the cabin; would you like to stay for dinner. If you're not in the mood for steaks, I'm sure we'll cross paths with a mouse, a sparrow or something more your speed."

"Sure." She pulled off his shirt and threw it at him. "Race you there."

He yanked the shirt over his head, and was shifted before she finished hers. He yowled at her.

She screeched at him and they took off down the mountain toward the cabins. Running through the woods with Lisa flying above him was nice, and combined with the dreams he'd been having of Danny running with him, it made Connor wonder what it would be like to get Danny alone in the woods without a pressing investigation going on. As he got closer to the cabin, he had to admit he'd been alone for a long time, and if he'd found someone who wasn't going to be put off by his visions, maybe he should see if something could develop.

Lisa's car was parked next to the Jeep. That answered his question as to whether she flew all the way from Santa Fe.

She shifted and reached into it for her clothes. "You know, Cat, I wish I knew how to shift clothed the way you do. Think I could learn?"

"I doubt it. You either have the magic in you to tap into or you don't. Besides, if your clothes shrank to fit your bird form, they'd probably weigh you down too much to fly." He headed for the cabin door, happy to not be spending the evening alone. Chatting with Lisa was a great way to spent some down time.

Danny glared at the pile of reports on his desk. During his time searching for the killer with the RV, he'd let things like traffic reports pile up. There just hadn't been enough time to keep everything on an even keel, and even with Jeri helping out on things that didn't need his personal touch, he was still way behind. Although the two other deputies besides Jeri and him were working most of the traffic cases, he couldn't help himself from stopping speeders and drunk drivers in his jurisdiction. And the fight that erupted at the Broken Antler Bar and Grill two nights earlier only added to his paperwork. At one point, he'd even had McGriffin helping him with those guys. Nothing major, but he did know about processing people and suddenly having fifteen frat boys and a dozen sorority girls involved in a brawl with a biker gang, they'd needed all the hands they could get.

McGriffin had done his part without complaining and had been a great help, staying well past midnight and not even complaining about the cold pizza they'd all had for dinner.

Danny picked up the first report and started filling in the blanks so Jeri or Mary could get it filed the next day.

Halfway through the pile, he looked up and out the window onto Main Street. The setting sun painted the stucco buildings a vivid shade of red. Danny stood and walked out the front door. Out on the sidewalk, he leaned against the old wooden post that had been holding up the roof for so many years it was rubbed smooth from all the hands that had touched it and shoulders it had supported. The western sky was ablaze in light that danced off the high clouds that promised no rain and were useful only in making the sunset more vivid.

It had been a long time since Danny had spent any time looking at sunsets, and even longer since he'd had anyone to watch them with. He glanced away from the desert that began about the point where the southern edge of Jemez Springs ended and up toward the northeast, in the direction of Connor's cabin. He wondered what Connor was doing with the first quiet day he'd had since he found the body. He'd probably spent a good part of it lounging on a rock somewhere. In their long drives across the state checking out RVs that matched the description of the one that nearly ran over Connor, he'd confessed how much he liked finding a nice outcropping and lying in the sun. He found it calming.

"What are you thinking about so hard, Fuz Cuz?" a voice asked from behind him.

Danny spun around, alarmed that he hadn't sensed someone near him. "Hey Jime, what brings you to town?" His cousin hadn't been to town in several months, and he normally didn't come in without being sent by Cortez, the local alpha, Jime's father and Danny's uncle.

Jime shrugged. "Just in for a bit. Thought I would swing through and see what's happening with my favorite upstanding relative. What you been up to lately? Looks fairly serious from the lines on your head."

If there was one thing Danny didn't want to do was talk about Connor with Jime. It wouldn't take an hour and his whole family would know there was a mountain lion in their territory, and Jime would probably go off and tell everyone the two of them were already an item. Just what he didn't need.

"Trying to figure out a case," Danny sidestepped. It wasn't exactly a lie, but it wasn't the whole truth either. He did his best to never lie to family.

Jime leaned on the bricks on the corner of the wall. "Is this a real case? Not trying to figure out who's stealing old lady Johnson's chickens?"

Danny hadn't heard anything about missing chickens. "Someone's stealing old lady Johnson's chickens?"

"No." Jime laughed. "Gods, you're so easy sometimes."

Danny frowned. He wasn't in the mood for his cousin's weird sense of humor. If he hadn't been so wrapped up in thinking about the case and Connor, he wouldn't have fallen for it. He knew old lady Johnson, one of the few humans who lived near the pack territory out on the desert flats to the west of the mountains, hadn't had chickens in a number of years. She was barely able to take care of herself, let alone the huge flock of chickens she'd had for most of her life. "Look, I need to get back inside and back to my paperwork."

Jime grinned like a fool. "Okay. You do that, Fuz Cuz. But your mother wanted me to remind you that you need to come out some time. She hasn't seen you in a while. Cortez wants to talk to you too."

Danny cringed. If Cortez wanted to talk with him, that could mean trouble. Although he was officially an active member of the pack, Danny was all but a lone wolf. Working for the sheriff had put him on that path. He knew of other wolves who were police officers or in other forms of law enforcement. The responsibility to their jobs made it hard for them to handle the duties that came with pack membership. The Jemez Pack was one of the older packs in the Southwestern U.S. Cortez had been named after the Spanish explorer. He had been around when the first missions popped up in New Mexico. He was a fair alpha; he let his wolves mostly live their own lives as long as they didn't go around turning people. When the shifters had come out to the humans during World War I, Cortez had been the spokesman for the wolves, and even worked closely with the Army. Danny worried that he'd been too lax in his minimal pack duties of late and Cortez was about to demand more of his time. With Connor and the killer taking up a lot of his time, he wasn't sure when he'd be able to get out to the pack, but also didn't want to piss Cortez off by putting it off too long.

"Tell Mom and Cortez, I'll do my best to get out there soon." Danny walked past his cousin, toward the sheriff's office front door.

"Will do." Jime continued to grin. "And, by the way, let that puma of yours know that Cortez knows about him. Since he's working with you, everything's cool, but if he stays too long he needs to check in, so Cortez can decide if he's long-time cool or not."

Danny felt like Jime had just punched him. "Okay." He couldn't think of anything else to say. He was going to have to go out to the pack and take Connor or the pack would come looking for both of them and that wouldn't go well.

"Later, Fuz Cuz." Jime waved and jogged down the sidewalk to the public parking lot and disappeared.

It felt like hours that Danny stood there as the last of the sunlight faded from the sky, leaving things in darkness even as the streetlights came on. He didn't want to deal with the pack while they were trying to find a killer, but he wasn't going to have much choice. After he talked to Connor about it, he'd come back to town and talk to Rusty and get a day off, maybe two. It wouldn't take that long to drive out there, but it would depend on how fussy Cortez was being as to how long they would have to stay. He'd never had to involve the sheriff in pack business before. He made a point in handling things on his days off or during vacation time. He kept the various parts of his life separate. When he'd lived in Albuquerque, it had been easier to do things for Cortez. He hadn't had a career, a profession that made it hard for him to drop and go. But since he had that, he'd put more distance between himself and the pack.

He walked in and stared at the stack of reports for a little while before he forced himself to get them done. If he was going to have to ask for a day or two off, he'd need to have them done. Sometimes, not even family emergencies trumped paperwork. The world thrived on paperwork.

Chapter Four

Connor walked into the sheriff's office carrying two coffees. Although the brew in the office wasn't bad, he'd discovered a small coffee house a few doors down from the diner across the street and had starting going there with Danny before they set out on their drives across the state trying to locate the RV they were looking for. Having the previous day to himself and getting a visit from Lisa had been nice, even if she had brought his thoughts of Danny up to the forefront of his mind. The dreams he'd had that night had reinforced things, and he'd decided to stop and get some coffee for both of them on the way in.

"Hey, Dawg." He set the coffee he'd brought for Danny down in front of him.

Danny looked up with bleary eyes. "Thanks, Cat." He took the cup, opened it, and then sipped at it. He closed his eyes and hummed. "Just like I like it. I guess you've been paying attention." He sounded tired.

Conner settled in the worn wooden chair on the opposite side of the desk. In the past weeks it had become his customary spot to sit when he was in the office. "You look and sound tired. I thought we had a day off yesterday."

Shaking his head first, Danny took another sip of coffee. "Hope you had a good day. I had a bunch of paperwork to do."

"And from what I can tell, he stayed here all night working on it." Deputy White walked over from her desk near the front of the office. "He's got nearly everything filled out and ready to be filed. But his car hasn't moved all night."

Danny frowned at her. "Jeri, how do you know my car hasn't been moved?

She grinned. "There's still a huge splatter of bird shit on your windshield that was there when I left yesterday. Unless I'm mistaken, it's right where you'd need to look to see out. I know you well enough to know that if you'd left last night, you'd have cleaned it off. That and the drop of grease on your shirt from your lunch yesterday means you've been here all night and haven't changed clothes."

Connor grinned. "Good detective work, Officer White." He studied Danny as he sat there drinking his coffee and glaring at his coworker. There were dark circles under his hooded eyes. His face drooped a bit and was pale. He also had a barely discernable shake as he held the coffee. They'd been going non-stop for two weeks. He'd lost track of how many miles they'd traveled trying to find the RV and the killer driving it. Connor didn't need to be psychic to tell Danny needed rest.

"Okay, so are you finished with all the reports?" Connor set his drink down on the desk and picked up one of the stacks of paper.

"Hey," Danny snatched it back, nearly upsetting his own coffee. "That's official police business. You're just a consultant."

Connor leaned back in his chair and looked at Deputy White. "So, Deputy White, do you think he's finished all his reports?"

She took the papers out of Danny's hand and scanned over it. "Hand writing's atrocious, worse than normal. We'd better hope nobody actually needs to read this, but it looks like the last one, and it looks finished."

"Good." Connor downed the last half of his coffee in a single gulp, feeling like he was wasting perfectly good brew by drinking it so fast. He threw the cup in the trash can someone had moved in front of the desk a couple of days earlier, presumably for his use. He glanced at the glass-enclosed office where Callaway normally sat; the sheriff wasn't there. "Since the sheriff isn't in, who needs to know Deputy Lupan is taking a sick day?"

"I can let Rusty know," Deputy White said with a sly smile.

Danny glared at both of them. "Look. I don't need a rest day."

To Deputy White's advantage, she locked gazes with him. "I'm with McGriffin, you're wiped out. Now get out of here before I put you in a cell to sleep for a few hours."

"We need to keep looking for this guy." He crossed his arms, and yawned.

"And if you keep yawning, you're going to put all of us to sleep," Connor said as he stood. He walked over to Danny's chair. "Now, I'm going to take you to your place so you can get some sleep."

"You don't even know where it is," Danny objected.

"He lives about six blocks to the south, Edgar Street, number 54, in the rear," Deputy White supplied with a sly look.

"Jeri, you're a traitor," Danny mumbled.

Connor grabbed his arm and pulled him to his feet. "I'll drive you home; that way I'll know you get there."

"You don't have to. I'm perfectly fine to stay here and get some work done, then drive myself home later."

Deputy White put her hands on her hips and glared. "Tired driving is nearly as dangerous as drunk driving. McGriffin, take him home and put him to bed. When you get back here, you and I will follow up on those last couple of addresses in Albuquerque this afternoon."

Connor gave her his best grin and guided Danny toward the front door. He was a little surprised when Danny stopped objecting. "I'll be back as soon as I have him settled."

"Take your time," She walked back to her own desk. "Rusty's in court this morning, and we can't go anywhere until he gets back."

"Will do." Connor kicked open the front door and kept hold of Danny's arm as they started down the sidewalk to where his jeep was parked halfway between the sheriff's station and the coffee house. It wasn't how he'd planned on spending his morning, but it was obvious Danny wasn't getting enough sleep and was about to make himself sick, if a wolf shifter could get sick from exhaustion.

"I can walk on my own." Danny tried to jerk his arm out of Connor's grip.

"I'm sure you can't. Just relax, Dawg and let…me take care of you." Inwardly, Connor cringed. He'd almost referred to himself as your cat. He wasn't quite ready to do that, as much as he wanted to take care of Danny and make everything okay.

Warm, early-evening sunlight woke Danny. He stretched and yawned. Glancing out his curtainless window, he wondered exactly how long he'd slept. He'd been pushing himself for two weeks. It was hard not to. He felt the need to prove something to Connor, but what he couldn't say.

Although he balked at openly admitting it, he liked working with the cougar. In many ways it was refreshing to work with another shifter. He didn't have to explain things like scent or catching the sound of a mouse scurrying across a field as they walked across it. Even though Rusty and Jeri knew what he was and accepted it, he often worried they were being just a bit standoffish, particularly when he displayed his differences openly. The first time he'd shifted around either one of them, he'd thought he was going to get shot. Rusty had the knee-jerk reaction a lot of humans did and had drawn on him without thinking about it. They'd laughed about it afterwards, and it hadn't happened again in the ten years he'd been on the force, but he always worried about it. When they'd talked to Kennedy, from Santa Fe, about Connor and he'd mentioned almost tasing him, it reminded him that they were different, and always would be.

But with Connor, the only difference was a species thing. They were both shifters. They were both trying to fit into the human world by showing the best their kind had to offer. He didn't have to worry about Connor getting afraid of him and shooting him. Scratching him, maybe. Biting him was a possibility, but he wouldn't shoot him.

As Danny got out of bed and headed for the bathroom, he wondered if Connor felt the same way. If Kennedy had been prepared to tase him, that said they weren't completely comfortable around Connor. He made a mental note to question Connor about it later.

Although they'd spent a lot of time together, they hadn't gotten around to talking about things like feelings. Other than knowing Connor was single and had been that way for years, he didn't know much about his personal life. They'd mostly talked about various cases they'd both worked. He wasn't shy about admitting that Connor had a lot more interesting stories to tell, but then he'd been led around the country by his visions. Danny had just spent lots of time trying to stay out of trouble.

As he shuffled out of the bathroom, he spotted his phone laying under the antique lamp on the small wooden table next to the bed. He didn't remember putting it there. He picked it up. It was turned off. He frowned as he turned it on.

He sat back on the bed and debated crawling back into it. The afternoon of sleep seemed to have done a lot for him, but tiredness still gnawed at him.

The phone beeped and he glanced at the screen. Four messages. Danny groaned. He never turned off his phone. He lifted it to his nose. Connor's pleasant scent was all over it. Like it had done before, Connor's scent made him smile. His sneezes were long past at the odor of cat. He'd check with Connor and see if he'd been the one to turn off the phone. If their murderer struck while he'd been asleep and he'd missed all the action, he'd be royally pissed.

Two messages were from Rusty, one checking on him, wanting to make sure he wasn't getting sick, and the other telling him if he needed the next day off too, he could take it. If there was one thing Danny wasn't going to do was take another day off until they caught the killer, or he fell over again.

The third message was Jime, just calling, which was his way of giving a brief reminder that Cortez wanted to talk to him. Danny didn't think he was going to forget about that, as much as he wanted to.

The last message was from Connor, left a couple of minutes before Danny woke up. He said he and Jeri were back from Albuquerque and hadn't found anything, and if Danny wanted to join them for dinner, they'd be heading to the diner across from the Sheriff's station about seven.

Danny pulled the phone away from his ear and looked at the time. Six forty-five. He'd have just enough time to grab a quick shower and get over there. At the thought of food, his stomach rumbled.

Since scaring her the first time he'd met Angie, Connor'd been doing his best to be mellow and normal when he went to the Star. He hated scaring people, even if he had no control over his visions.

Beside him, Jeri yawned. "You know, this is one of the things I hate about police work."

"All the hours of nothing?" Connor relaxed a little when he saw Angie wasn't on duty, or at least not presently visible.

"Right." Jeri steered them to a table in the corner where they could watch the door. It was the one where the members of the sheriff's department tended to sit when they were there, unless the table was occupied at the time they showed up. "I just wish things could be simple. We get a lead. We run down and bust the perps. Wham, bam, thank you ma'am."

"The regulars tonight?" Stephanie, the regular night waitress asked as she approached the table with some napkins and silverware.

"Sure." Jeri eased herself down onto the booth's red leather cushions.

"Yeah." It was odd to have a place that knew his regular food order, but Jemez Springs was a small town, and the Star was one of the few restaurants. Being across from the sheriff's station it was where they normally ate. Connor slid to the far side of the booth. Since he'd left Danny a message, he was going to make sure there was room for him if he decided to show up, that was if he woke up in time. He knew from personal experience how little sleep some shifters needed, but like humans, it would eventually catch up to them. When he'd seen Danny so tired that morning he couldn't help himself at being pushy and over-protective. It was strange being protective of someone, but somehow with Danny it felt right.

"I think those two were the last two on the list, weren't they?" Jeri asked as they waited.

Connor pursed his lips and nodded. "So we're at the point of no leads." He also hadn't had any more visions since the last one in the diner. They were at a dead end until the next body showed up, or they managed to get a lead on the killer and stop him before his next kill.

"What do you normally do when that happens?" Jeri moved her hands as Stephanie set their teas in front of them.

"Food will be up in a few." Stephanie started to turn away.

"Can you bring me a burger too?" Danny asked, rushing up to the table.

Connor's heart started pounding like crazy, and he rubbed his suddenly sweaty palms on his jeans. Just seeing Danny sometimes hit him like a freight train.

"Sure thing, Danny," Stephanie smiled and went over to the kitchen.

Danny slid in next to Connor. He'd started doing that when they were at the diner with other people. They hadn't really discussed it, it was just something that started about a week earlier and had continued. "So, what did you guys find today?"

Jeri shook her head. "Absolutely bupkis. Not even an RV of the wrong color. Two dead ends."

"Damn." Danny sighed. "Now I guess we have to wait around for something to happen."

"We were just starting to talk about that," Connor said, then picked up his tea. He started to take a drink, then realized he hadn't put any lemon in it and grabbed three wedges and squeezed them in. He could never have enough lemon in his tea. Lisa often accused him of liking a little tea in his lemon. "I think at this point we just have to wait. In a week or so we can probably run back through the list where no one was home. It might be our guy took a vacation or something."

"Should we be looking for other killings in other states?" Jeri asked, then took a sip of her tea, frowned and reached for several packets of sugar.

That was something Connor didn't have a concrete answer for. Sure, there had been a couple of times his visions had pulled him across state lines, but he wasn't sure how far his visions were good for. If someone did something all the way across the country he wasn't sure if he'd get a vision for it or not. "Maybe. It might be a way to get a feel for the guy we're looking for. See if we can find a pattern."

"Are you a profiler too?" Danny asked as Stephanie set a soda down in front of him.

"No, but sometimes I think it might make life a little easier for me if I could use more than just my visions to home in on criminals," Connor swirled his tea around, trying to not be too violent with it so it wouldn't slosh out. A lot of times the limits of his gifts made them feel more like curses. If he couldn't be right on top of something when it happened, it was difficult to make much headway unless he happened to get lucky. Even working with a team like he had in Santa Fe, it hadn't been easy to make progress. Some criminals were determined to not get caught. There were times he wondered if some of the bad guys had gifts like his and were able to stay a step ahead of him, at least until they misstepped.

"Have you ever worked with a profiler?" Jeri asked as she put her fork in her tea and stirred.

"A couple of times." Connor sipped his tea. It was perfection. "Most recently in Santa Fe."

Danny nodded. "I think I heard something about the FBI being called in on that one. Too many kids dead."

Connor hated remembering the boys who'd died, some of them because he hadn't been fast enough at figuring out where his visions were telling him to go. "Yeah. The FBI folks weren't too thrilled with my help, but they had to admit I helped them out a lot. If I hadn't been there, that priest would still be roaming the missions killing altar boys and homeless kids."

Jeri's eyes got big. "I hadn't heard it was a priest."

"That should come out as it goes to trial." Connor unrolled the napkin containing his silverware and set it in his lap. "I think they're trying to keep that part really quiet right now. You know, the Catholic Church and its sexual issues."

"Right." Danny nodded. "A lot of my friends growing up were altar boys."

"Dawg, you had friends growing up? I figured you just ran wild in the desert." Connor welcomed the opportunity to change the subject. He wasn't in the mood to relive the case that had sent him up into the mountains for some much-needed mental recovery time.

Danny turned and glared. "Yeah. And I spent most of that time chasing jack rabbits and quail." He chuckled softly. It was a sexy sound. "Cortez, our pack leader, thought it was a good idea if we all had a fair amount of contact with humans, so everyone was sent to public school. I had a lot of friends there. You might say I'm a people person."

Connor didn't like thinking about his own school years. Once his gifts emerged, school had been hard. He never knew when he might bump into someone and have a vision. Even with his Scottish grandmother helping him learn control, it was difficult. It was also why he rarely took a lover, or tried to make real connections with people. He never knew when his gift was going to flare up and show him something he didn't want to see. Being a shifter just gave him another reason to avoid getting close.

"Yeah, I've seen the way you handle people," Jeri said with a sly laugh. "Remember that one guy you pulled over for speeding. You had him so mad he was ready to punch you, all because of your charming people personality."

"Hey, if we're thinking about the same guy, he was stoned out of his mind, and I ended up arresting him for impeded driving and obstructing an officer." Danny rolled his eyes. "There's a lot of these fools no amount of charm will help."

Stephanie showed up with their food and, for a few minutes, silence fell over the table. Connor hadn't realized how hungry he was until he bit into the rare burger. It was warm and delicious. The fries had just the right amount of crunch. Dinner was great, and then it was gone.

Jeri's phone beeped as she pushed her plate toward the center of the table. She glanced at it. "I need to take this."

"So, Cat, what are we going to do for the rest of the night?" Danny asked as he cleaned up the last little bit of catsup with his final fry.

Connor took a sip of his tea, wishing Stephanie would come by and refill it for him. He was a little surprised by Danny's question. They normally went their separate ways after a day of following leads that went nowhere and having dinner. "Unlike some of us, I didn't sleep all day."

"Right, but you had a good night's sleep last night," Danny countered. "So you should be up for a bit of late night speed traps or something."

Jeri tapped her phone off. "As fun as that sounds, I need to get home. I clocked out before we came over here, and that was my sister. Mom wants to talk to us about something." She looked at Connor. "Well, McGriffin, that was a lot more fun than Danny here normally thinks it is. Thanks for riding along, even if we did get nothing done." She swung her gaze to Danny. "See you tomorrow. Don't spend too much time tonight chasing cars." She grinned, then slipped out of the booth.

Danny glared at Connor. "You know, I won't be too happy if everyone starts calling me Dawg."

Connor laughed and held up his hands in mock surrender. "Not my fault. But you know, I think she likes you."

"No." Danny shook his head. "She's like a little sister to me. Plus she knows I'm gay."

"I know she does. She's also fairly protective of you." Connor didn't want to tell him how much of their afternoon had been spent talking about him.

"Right. She's a cop. She's protective of everyone." Danny pushed his plate away and shook his head.

"That's a good quality."

"I know it is." Danny sighed. "Okay. Can we change the subject?" He looked a bit sheepish.

"Sounds serious. What's up?" Connor wiped his mouth with his napkin and put it on his empty plate.

"One of my cousins stopped by last night." Danny started, then turned and looked at Connor.

"While you were doing all your paperwork?"

Danny shrugged. "I was actually taking a small break from the paperwork to watch the sunset."

"Dawg, that's a side of you I didn't know about. A bit of a romantic?"

Color darkened Danny's checks. It was a cute look. "Sometimes. But anyway, Jime stopped in with a message from my mother and Cortez, our alpha. I need to go out to the pack and check in. I've been busy lately and haven't gotten out there."

Connor nodded. If there was one thing he understood, it was being busy. He was thankful mountain lions didn't have the same social structure wolves did. Having to answer to a pack alpha would be a pain in the butt. "And that's why you were up so late doing paperwork? You were trying to get caught up so you could take a couple of days?"

"Right. I hate having to run off in the middle of a case, but this is pack business. My alpha calls. I have to answer." There was a pained look on Danny's handsome face, like he didn't want to go, but he had to.

"I think Officer White, Sheriff Callaway, and I can handle it without you." Connor knew from Danny's devotion to his work that missing out on the chase would get to him, but there wasn't really any way around it if he had pack business to attend to.

"See, there's a hiccup." Danny frowned. "Cortez wants you to come too. You're officially in his territory. Even if you're on police business, he wants to meet you and decide if he wants you to stay or not."

It wasn't the first time Connor had stumbled into a pack territory, but he wasn't used to knowing the wolf who delivered the message for him to meet the alpha. That little bit of information also explained why Danny wasn't real happy about delivering the message. Various shifters had different ways of declaring their territory, and wolves tended to be the ones most often getting pissy about strangers in theirs, although he'd heard lions in Africa could be the same way. There were rumors of a jaguar who controlled most of Central and South America. If he was lucky, he wouldn't find out if that was true or not.

"Okay. So you get to haul me home to meet the folks." Connor decided to try and make the situation a little lighter. That was normally Danny's forte, but he gave it his best shot. "So Dawg, does that mean we need to at least go out on a date first?"

Danny's face hardened. "Dude, you don't get it. This is serious. If Cortez decides he doesn't like you, we might not be able to finish up the case, you might have to get out of northern New Mexico or be killed. Just because the world knows about us, doesn't mean that some packs aren't still more than a little backwoods."

Connor nodded. "Right. Sorry, just trying to lighten the mood." He wished he'd known how Danny was going to react first, before he tried to ease things up a little bit.

"It's okay." Danny shook his head, then picked up the napkin he'd quietly been shredding in his lap. "So, I'm going to go talk to Rusty and see if I can get a couple more days off, with the understanding that if we get a solid lead on the killer, he calls, and we get back here ASAP. Then, in the morning, you and I take my car and drive out into the desert so we can meet with Cortez and get permission for you to stay here, at least until the case is closed."

"Okay." Connor wasn't real sure how he felt about driving out into the desert to meet the local pack, but he didn't really have a choice. The one time he'd refused to meet an alpha it hadn't ended well. He'd been rather banged up and then had to leave town as fast as possible. Luckily in that case, he'd already given the police enough to catch the bad guy.

"Fine." Danny stood and dropped his napkin on his plate. "I'll pick you up in the morning. Now I get to go talk to Rusty and hope he understands."

Connor almost stood and followed, but settled into the squeaky leather seat and tried not to stare too hard at Danny's ass as he paid his ticket and headed out the door.

As Danny pushed the door open, he looked back at Connor and waved.

Again, Connor's heart raced as he returned the gesture.

Chapter Five

Danny gripped the wheel of his old Chevy truck. The short trip from his house to the cabin Connor was renting wasn't enough time for him to mentally prepare for their journey out to the pack lands, especially after calling Jime to let him know they'd be out before noon. He wished he didn't have Cortez breathing down his neck. It felt like he was pushing Connor into something, but he really wasn't. He was just doing what most shifters would, seeing that he checked in with the local alpha before staying in a territory too long, but somehow it felt like it was something more. He pulled onto Brian Epson's land and took the right drive, going deeper into the property. Connor's cabin was the more isolated of the two. He wondered if Connor had chosen that one due to the heavy trees around it that would keep too many people from seeing what was going on. Although people knew about shifters, most shifters kept to themselves so as not to not remind the humans of their differences. People dealt with things better when things weren't thrown into their faces.

The narrow drive opened up to a well-maintained cabin. Connor's Jeep was parked in front of the porch, and Connor was lying on the porch in his cat form, basking in a pool of early morning sunshine.

Danny parked next to the Jeep and grinned. There was just something very natural about the big mountain lion lying there soaking up heat. He leaned out the open window. "So, kitty cat, are you going to come with me, or just lie there looking like a rug?"

Connor stood in a slow languid motion, stretching gracefully as if trying to show off his body to its best benefit. Then he turned toward Danny and stuck out his tongue. His shift was swift. As he started descending the steps, he didn't pause, and by the time he was halfway down, he was a man. His jeans seemed impossibly tight, and his light blue T-shirt exposed every contour of his muscular chest. He stopped and picked up a long-sleeved, button-down shirt that was draped over the hood of his Jeep.

"Dawg, you know, I think I like your sheriff's-department Bronco better than this." He slapped the top of the truck with a heavy thud.

Danny sighed. He wasn't about to admit that he did too. But he'd had the truck for years, and police work wasn't known for its huge salary. "Kitty cat, just get in, unless you'd rather ride in the back, but the roads can get fairly rough."

Connor flashed a playful grin as he stalked around the front of the truck. "As long as I'm not going to get fleas from this thing." He opened the passenger door and slid in. "We could take my Jeep if you'd prefer."

"Nope." Danny put the truck into reverse even as Connor snapped his seatbelt closed. "Too dusty on the roads we're going to be going. I want to be able to roll up the windows and have some AC when we hit the desert."

"Desert? I figured the local pack would be in the mountains."

Danny started back down the drive. "Nope. Cortez comes from a Navajo people. Desert dwellers. But it's not far from the mountains, and he claims this whole area." Talking made things easier. In their two weeks of driving around, he and Connor had settled into a fairly easy relaxed manner with each other. It was good. If nothing else they were friends, but he kept wondering what it would be like to be more.

"It's interesting how some species of shifters claim different amounts of territory in various parts of the country." Connor settled into his seat with a look of comfort.

Danny knew his old truck wasn't in that bad of shape, but he'd just redone a good portion of the interior the previous year, and planned on working on the engine next with the hopes of getting the exterior fixed after that. One thing at a time, that's how he liked it.

"Other than a couple of wolf packs, a condor flock, and a herd of javelinas, we really don't have any organized shifter groups in the area," Danny said as they pulled out onto the highway. "I think Cortez and the other alphas have tried to keep the others out."

"Doesn't make him sound real friendly," Connor tapped on the dashboard as if expecting there to be a bar there like he had in the Jeep.

"He's okay." Danny glanced at his speed. Even if he wasn't worried about a ticket, he kept his speed down when he was driving his own truck. Expecting to get away with speeding was a little too much privilege, and he did his best not to abuse his position. "I haven't heard any complaints when I run into other shifters."

"Are there many out here? I know a couple in Santa Fe."

"Not really. Most of the smaller ones tend to keep to the cities, while the larger ones find their own spots where they can live without problems." As they drove through town, Danny thought about stopping at the coffee house. "Want a coffee?"

Connor shook his head. "I'm good. But if you want something, feel free."

After half considering it, Danny decided that maybe he shouldn't. He was already keyed up about what they were doing, and if he got caffeine in his system it would be worse, at least for a few minutes until his metabolism burned it out. "Nah." He kept driving past.

A comfortable silence settled over the truck. It was nice they'd reached the point they didn't have to be constantly chattering at one another. That was one of the many things he found himself liking about Connor.

Danny gripped the steering wheel tighter. "Cat, there's something I've been wondering about."

"What's that?"

"When Rusty first talked to Kennedy, he said something about nearly tasing you. What happened? I thought you had a good relationship with the police."

Connor took a deep breath and looked out the window. "It was the night we finally caught the priest in that last case. He'd just disemboweled a young boy. I jumped on him and knocked him down." He took another breath and ran his fingers through his hair. "I swear, I've never felt like killing a human the way I did then. Kennedy finally talked me away from him."

Danny turned away from the road, looked at Connor, and nodded. "I understand. I would have had a hard time letting him go myself." He reached over and placed his hand on Connor's knee.

Connor covered it with his own hand.

When they reached the turnoff from the highway onto the dirt road that led to the center of pack territory, Danny did his best to not be nervous. He didn't really care if Connor noticed or not, but he always did his best to not let Cortez or any of the other wolves see him in any way that might make him look weak in their eyes. If he was nervous they'd smell it and exploit it.

After a couple of minutes on the rough road, Connor squirmed in his seat. "How much farther?"

Danny chuckled. "Don't tell me the kitty cat is going to get all 'are we there yet?' on me."

"You should know better than that," Connor said, shifting slightly. "But the coffee I had with breakfast wasn't expecting to ride down a rough dirt road."

That made Danny laugh loudly. He couldn't point out exactly what it was, but Connor made him laugh more than any man he'd been around in a very long time. Laughing was good. "Cat, there's plenty of dirt out here if you want me to pull over so you can go."

Connor rolled his eyes. "Like there's anywhere to go so I wouldn't get arrested for indecent exposure, not to mention how is your alpha going to react to me pissing in his front yard? Is he going to take it as a challenge and spend the next couple of months following me around to pee every place I do?"

It wasn't something Danny could see Cortez doing, but he could see him assigning someone else to do it. With Danny's luck it would be his job. But he opted to play with Connor a bit. "Maybe. You know how some of these alphas can get. Very insecure about some things."

"Right." Connor nodded slowly. "And from what I've seen, you're fairly secure in things, Dawg. This truck makes me realize I'm right. With this thing you aren't compensating for anything."

A slow grin spread across his face. He liked it that Connor didn't think he was compensating for anything. "Kitty, knock it off on my truck. We've been through a lot and I like her."

Connor held up his hands in surrender. "Not saying anything negative about your truck…this time."

"And don't." Danny bit back the laugh he wanted to spit out. He tried to think of anything he could say about Connor's Jeep, but other than it lacking doors, that he claimed were in Santa Fe, there wasn't anything. He wondered how Connor would react if they had a rainstorm while he didn't have a top or doors on.

A few more miles down the drive, which was more of a road than an actual drive, they reached the first of several forks. It was a protective thing. Only people who knew the right combination of forks to take would make it to Cortez's house. Most of the forks ended up at dead ends, dry washes, edges of canyons, and on rare occasions the houses of pack members. The land was just rolling enough to hide things from casual eyes.

"This area does have a simple, rugged beauty to it," Connor said, staring out the window. "Not exactly my kind of place, but not horrible."

Danny shook his head. "I grew up around here. Gets old after a while. I think that's why I like it up around Jemez Springs. Just different enough to hold my interest. That and there's trees. Didn't used to think that was important, but now I do."

Connor nodded. "Yeah. I like trees, although probably not in the same way a dog does. I think if my visions ever let me completely settle down somewhere, I'd like there to be trees around."

"So you've mentioned little things before, but haven't said much about how your visions force you to where you need to be," Danny said as they went down a fairly steep drop that put them almost on top of Cortez's place, but the drive was still going to circle around a bit before they came to the entrance to the underground house.

Connor shrugged. "That can be a rather complicated thing, and I haven't actually figured out how it works. My ancestors came over to the States back in the seventeen hundreds from Scotland."

"So that's where the McGriffin comes from," Danny said. He figured it was either Scottish or Irish.

"Right. They brought the gift of Sight. From what my grandmother said, my fourth great-grandmother was fairly scary with her visions. Incredibly accurate. She thought the way the English settlers treated the Native Americans was just awful; even worse than the English had treated the Scots. She made it her life's work to do what she could to make things easier on them. Even married a Sioux chief, Running Cat. But he was killed in a fight between the Sioux and the Crow, and she went back East to do what she could there."

"Ah, so you have a bit of Sioux in you."

Connor nodded. "It's why I'm a mountain lion. That grandma was a lynx so it all worked out fine. Her gifts passed on and Grandfather's shape passed through the family."

"Funny how that works out, isn't it? Many humans in your family?" Danny knew some shifters had humans scattered throughout their family trees. They tended to breed with humans easier than other shifters who weren't as compatible a species. One day he figured someone was going to sit down and work out the complicated stew that was shifter genetics.

"A few, here and there, my mother was the most recent. Mostly we keep with big cats. Grandmother always said it's better to keep the bloodlines pure as possible. I guess being gay, I don't need to worry about that."

"As long as you've got siblings to pass the genes along," Danny said. "That's our rule in the packs. Since I've got a sister who's already had a couple of kids, it's not a big deal for me to have kids. Plus I've got cousins. If I was an only child, the pack would demand I at least father one child." He shuddered at the thought. Although he could be very protective of children, he hadn't ever thought about having any of his own.

He made the final turn, taking a right fork that ended a couple hundred feet beyond in a large parking area. Several other trucks and SUVs were parked near the steps that went down to the front door. Most of the pack houses were, like the main house, underground. It made them cooler, but also more defensible.

He parked next to Jime's truck that was a lot more beat up than his. Like a lot of the pack, Jime didn't have an official job, and didn't have the money to keep his truck more than serviceable.

Two men stood at the top of the stairs. One of them was Jime, the other one of the new pack members, a previously lone wolf named Phillip, who Danny had only met a few times. Phillip always seemed happy to have his lower place in the pack. Some wolves were like that. They didn't like being in charge of anything, so they stayed on the lower end of the pack hierarchy. Danny could understand. He didn't want to have more responsibility in the pack. He was happy being almost a lone wolf.

"Hey, Fuz Cuz," Jime called as Danny stepped out of the truck.

Connor snickered. "Fuz Cuz?"

His voice was soft enough and they were far enough away, Danny was fairly sure Jime wouldn't have heard it. "That's what Jime calls me. Kind of like you calling me Dawg."

"Is this the cat?" Jime asked, stalking toward them.

Phillip stayed where he was at the top of the stairs, but his gaze stayed on them as they strolled toward the house entrance.

"Conner McGriffin,"—Danny gestured between him and Jime—"Jime Mendoza. Jime, Connor."

Jime wrinkled his nose and sneezed. "Smells like a cat."

Danny punched Jime in the shoulder. "That's 'cause he is a cat, Cuz. Now act a little smarter before he starts thinking all wolves are imbeciles."

Connor patted Danny on the shoulder. The brief touch sent a little thrill of anticipation through him. "I know not *all* wolves are idiots."

His wording gave Danny a chill, and he hoped Cortez wasn't lingering nearby, listening. Although he liked the way he and Connor could keep things light and playfully antagonistic, he wasn't sure how that would go over with his alpha. Cortez was a bit sterner than Danny and his immediate family tended to be.

Jime looked from Connor to Danny as if trying to figure out what to say.

Danny pushed past him. "So where's Cortez? I'd like to get this done so I can swing by, see Mom, and then head back to town. We're in the middle of a major case right now and the sheriff wasn't real happy about me taking time off." The last bit wasn't exactly the truth, but if it helped him get done with Cortez faster, that would be good.

"I told him you were coming." Jime turned and started down the steps. "He said he'd be waiting for you." He paused halfway down the stairs to the front door. "I also called your mother. She'll have lunch ready for us."

"Thanks." Danny had been hoping to surprise his mother so that maybe she wouldn't try to feed them, but Jime had blown that idea. He and Connor would be lucky to get back to Jemez Springs by nightfall.

"No problem, Fuz Cuz." Jime continued down the stairs and Danny just wanted get back into the truck and go home.

Connor did his best to not be surprised by the house Danny and his cousin led him into. When he stopped to think about it, an underground house made a lot of sense on several levels. Out in the desert, it was probably easier to cool. As wolves, having it be den-like probably made them more comfortable. A lot of shifters liked finding a good balance between the two sides of their nature and this house was definitely that. As a cougar, he could see having a house built into, or from rocks.

There wasn't anything grandiose about the dwelling. Of the few alpha's homes he'd been in, this was probably the most down to earth. It was decorated with lots of exposed beams and adobe walls. Here and there ceramic tile added little accents. The floor was all tile, and Connor wondered how much trouble wolves would have running on it. Would their claws slide a lot, or had the local pack learned to navigate it without a problem? Being underground, there were no windows. Recessed lighting in the ceiling gave the feel of sunlight.

They went down a short entry hall and into a large room that looked like a cross between a dining room and a living room. A large fireplace dominated the center of the room with couches in a comfortable semi-circle and several casual chairs.

A short, powerfully-built man stood from one of the chairs and turned toward them. "Ah, Daniel, you've come, and brought the puma with you." He nodded slowly as he walked the short distance to Connor. "Cortez Mendoza." He extended a hand.

Connor took it. "Connor McGriffin."

Cortez's grip was firm, but not challenging. There was a soft smile on his lips that didn't reach his hard eyes. "It's been a while since I've had one of your kind in my territory."

That was a surprise to Connor. The population of mountain lion shifters in the states was fairly decent; not as large as the wolves or bears, but still there were enough of them to make a fair number. He couldn't name any who were living in New Mexico, but he felt sure there had to be at least a couple. He did his best to not let the surprise show on his face.

"Thank you for welcoming me. If Deputy Lupan had told me I needed to come see you, I would've been here sooner." He didn't want to reveal to Cortez just how close Danny and he had become by calling him by his first name.

Cortez waved for them both to have a seat on the couches nearest the chair he'd stood from. "Until you came to Jemez Springs, you weren't in my territory. Santa Fe is just east of my lands. There isn't an alpha who claims that city. I think the next time one of mine has a bit of wanderlust, I should send them that way to hold the city, in my name."

"Of course." Connor knew how territory expansions worked. They were always easier if there wasn't an existing pack holding a city. He wondered if there were other shifters who held Santa Fe. If there were, he hadn't encountered them during his time there. Lisa was the only other resident shifter he'd met, although there had been a few who'd come through on travels that he'd smelled from time to time, normally down in the square.

"We came as soon as I got word," Danny said hastily. "Since he is on police business, I wasn't sure if you'd be bothered with him not checking in with you. Particularly since I'm on the police force."

"Of course, Daniel." Cortez settled back into his chair. "But since he's been here for more than a week, you should've known to bring him to me."

His words were soft, but there was a level of discipline in them. Like a father who needed to let a child know they'd misbehaved, but didn't believe in spanking in front of company. If he was keeping Danny from being punished, he was glad he was there.

"I'm sorry for that," Connor said, hoping to come to Danny's defense. "I'm sure if we hadn't been so busy looking for a killer, he'd have brought me out before now."

"Yes, I know how important it is to keep the humans happy." Again, his tone was light, but his words a bit sarcastic.

"We've all got to do what we can to fit in," Danny said. "That's what you've told us for years."

"It is." Cortez tapped the arm of his chair. "I'm glad you've been listening." He turned his dark gaze on Connor.

"So, Connor McGriffin, how long do you plan on being in my territory?"

Connor shrugged, wishing he had a firm answer. "The sheriff's department has asked for my help in finding a killer. It will depend on how long that takes."

Cortez shook his head. "But some cases are never solved. Does that mean you'll be here forever? I'm not sure I like that."

"I'm sure it won't be forever." Connor hated being asked for definites in life. He wasn't about to take the time to explain to Cortez how he was driven by visions. He doubted the alpha would care what drove him in life.

"It shouldn't be." Cortez paused for a moment before he continued. "While you are in my territory, please make sure that Daniel knows where to find you. I'm sorry, but I can't have a predator like yourself just roaming freely without supervision."

Danny looked uncomfortable on the couch next to Connor.

"And what does that-" Connor started, then stopped as Danny's hand landed on his thigh.

"Of course, Cortez," Danny said, bowing his head in a slight submissive movement. "How often would you like me to report back on our movements?"

Cortez pursed his lips. "On this issue, once a week should be fine. But I also have another issue that requires your particular skill set."

Danny straightened. "My skill set?"

"Yes." Cortez pulled out a manila envelope and handed it to Danny. "This is something that has come to my attention and I feel you should deal with it."

Danny opened the envelope, and Connor peered over his shoulder. It was pictures of a decomposing human body.

It looked like it had been exposed to the desert for a month or more. The scavengers had been at it, scattering bones and clothing. "Where is this?" Danny slipped the pictures back into the envelope.

"Near the highway. Phillip found it two days ago while he was patrolling. As you know, there are parts of the territory we don't patrol on a regular basis due to fears that humans will become nervous." Cortez looked over his shoulder toward the entryway where Jime stood like a good guard. "Please relieve Phillip on the outside door and have him come in here."

"Yes, Cortez." Jime gave a short bow then retreated down the hallway.

Connor was thankful that from their seats, he hadn't had to turn far to see Jime and watch him retreat. However relaxed things appeared in the house, the pack still acted like any other pack he'd encountered; their setting was just a bit less structured.

Seconds later, Phillip came hurrying down the hall. "Yes, Cortez?"

Cortez waved him forward. "Phillip, please tell Daniel about the body you found."

Phillip nodded and turned slightly so he was facing Danny and Connor. "It was up by the highway. You know, near that rest stop that's on the way to Albuquerque."

Danny nodded, but didn't say anything.

"It was far enough away from the buildings that I doubt any humans would find it, unless they were walking their dogs or taking a long walk from their vehicles. I didn't bother it."

"Was it a man or a woman?" Danny asked, tapping the manila envelope. "The pictures make it hard to tell."

"It smelled like a woman. Human, I think. But a lot of animals had been all over her. Coyotes, bears, vultures, maybe even wild dogs. None of the bones looked anything but human."

Connor knew that didn't mean a whole lot. Most shifters stayed in the form they died in. That was part of what had kept the humans from getting firm evidence about their existence until they decided to come out to the world at a time it was mutually beneficial for both sides.

"Can you take us there?" Danny asked.

Phillip glanced at Cortez who nodded. "Of course."

Danny stood and looked at Cortez. "If there is nothing else you need, I'll go check this out."

"Please. It is one of the reasons I agreed to letting you join the sheriff's office. You can do what you can to earn your keep." Cortez waved them toward the door. "Please let me know when you have something on this death. I don't like bodies showing up on my land."

"Of course." Danny turned and started toward the door.

Connor stood facing the alpha for a moment. "It was a pleasure to meet you." Although he refrained from actually bowing, he gave a nod.

Cortez nodded. "Please let me know when you will be leaving my territory."

It wasn't hard to tell how difficult it was for Cortez to maintain a level of civility. He was upset about something and Connor was fairly sure it was more than a dead body on his property, or a lone mountain lion who hadn't checked in. There was something more gnawing at the wolf, and at that point Connor didn't care about it, as long as it didn't impact Danny.

Chapter Six

The smell of rot hit Danny as soon as he got out of his truck. They'd followed Phillip down almost to the highway, then taken one of the first tracks leading south. He wondered why anyone who wasn't pack would've taken the trail, since it didn't really go anywhere and wasn't well maintained. It only went a couple of miles before it ended. There were signs of other vehicles, but none of them overly recently. He figured Phillip had been on foot or paws when he discovered the body. Well, since there were pictures, probably foot. Connor was the only other shifter he knew who had a special magical pouch to put his cell phone in. So either Phillip had been human when he found the body, or he'd come back with a phone or camera to get pictures.

"Over here." Phillip pointed a little farther to the south as he got off his motorcycle. "It's not far."

Danny shook his head. "Not if we can already smell it."

Connor waved to their right. "And there's the rest stop he mentioned."

"Right." Danny glanced that direction and the tops of the buildings were barely visible over the rolling desert landscape. He turned away from the buildings and followed Phillip to the body.

Scattered and torn clothes were the first thing they spotted. Bits of fabric were caught on yucca fronds and cactus spines. Some of them were bright enough to stand out in the stark desert, while others had been bleached nearly white by the sun. The bones were tossed about, some of them missing, at least at first glance. Most of the flesh was gone, gnawed off by the various animals feeding on the corpse.

"Wow," Connor shook his head. "It's not horrible smelling right now, was probably worse a couple of weeks ago."

"Yeah, the animals haven't left a lot of evidence," Phillip said, staying a little back from the scene as Danny walked up to the remains.

Danny paused and looked toward the rest stop and the highway. They might be within his jurisdiction, if they weren't it would only be by a few yards. The county ended at the south edge of the pull-off's parking lot. He decided it was going to be his scene, and if the folks in Bernalillo County got picky he'd get Rusty to deal with them. Pulling out his phone, he called the office.

"Hey, Danny, aren't you supposed to be having a day off?" Jeri asked as she answered her phone.

"Supposed to, if we weren't looking at a skeleton." Danny bent down low and pulled out a pen to turn the skull. There was a perfect small hole in the center of her forehead.

"Skeleton! Danny, are you sure it's human?" Jeri's excitement level went up.

Danny understood her excitement. They'd gone years without anything more than a drug bust every so often, and then they get two bodies in as many weeks. "Yeah, I'm sure it's human. Connor's with me, I bet he'd back me on this. Plus, she's been shot in the forehead just like the first one and the one Connor saw in his vision."

"Wait a minute!" Jeri's tone went up a little higher. "Two bodies with the same MO? Does Jemez Springs have its first serial killer?" Then things got muffled. "No Rusty, he hasn't told me where yet. Danny, where are you?"

"A few hundred yards west of the rest stop on the south end of the county. The one on the way to Albuquerque. Not sure if it's in our county or Bernalillo."

"About forty-five minutes out. He says it may be Bernalillo County." There was the sound of Jeri's chair falling back against the floor. "See you soon. Rusty says he'll check the county line when we get there."

"Right." Danny tapped the end button on his phone. He glanced at Phillip. "You probably need to stay around and fill out an official statement. But we'll say you found it this morning. No need to make it look like you've kept this quiet for a few days."

Phillip nodded. "If you think that's a good idea."

"I do." Danny glanced at Connor. "Cat, you've been rather quiet. I know bodies don't bother you."

Connor shook his head. "They don't, but this one has me thinking. The one I found was near a trail head. There was a restroom there, so it's kinda a rest stop. This one is right behind a rest stop. I wonder if that plays any role in our killer's pattern."

"And the place you led us to two weeks ago, where the murder hasn't happened yet was just a pull-off, so it might be the pull-off part of things is the important piece of the puzzle, not necessarily the pit stop part." Danny thought again of the RVs they'd been trying to find. RVs weren't easy to maneuver down dirt roads. And they could be traffic hazards if stopped along the side of the roads, but if the killer was using the pull-offs and rest areas as his killing grounds, that might explain things. He was also doing his killing a short distance from the highway. There was still the chance for someone to catch them in the act, but highway noise could cover things up, or the killer might be using a silencer. There was still a lot they didn't know.

He glanced back at the rest stop and sighed.

"What's on your mind, Dawg?" Connor asked softly.

"I really wish this one wasn't so old. We could shift and sniff around, see if we could get any scents." Danny sat cross-legged on the ground a few feet from the body and stared at it.

"Don't killers always return to the scene of the crime?" Phillip asked.

"Only in crime novels or bad TV shows," Danny rolled his eyes as he put his elbows on his knees and rested his chin on his hands. "If they're smart they never look back."

Connor huffed. "If they're smart they keep driving and don't commit several murders in the same area, but most criminals aren't extremely smart and/or have limited funds. Which makes me wonder, if we aren't just chasing a false lead with the RV, he'd need to have a way to get plenty of money to fuel that beast."

"And something like that might stand out to the local gas stations." A minor hope sprang up in Danny. They were spending a lot of man-hours on the case already. He wondered how long before Rusty was going to have to either stop the active investigation, or at least put it to part time, but there wasn't anything else pressing that he was aware of.

"Right." Connor beamed. "We could check the most logical ones. It's not like there's a ton of them between here and Santa Fe. But if he's getting gas in Santa Fe, or Albuquerque, we might be out of luck."

"Yeah. You know, I wonder if we should check with your contacts there and see if there's been anything like these murders that's been unsolved. Might help if we had more info." He knew he was grasping at straws, but even after two weeks, Danny was getting ready for some kind of resolution to the case. Patience wasn't one of his better virtues.

"I'll give Kennedy a call this evening and see what he can drum up." Connor sat down next to Danny. "I think I might've been having visions if he'd been killing women in Santa Fe before this."

"But you were working that big case with the kids," Danny countered. "How do your visions handle two things at the same time? Do they prioritize one thing over the other?"

Connor pursed his lips, looking really sexy. Then he closed his eyes as if he was thinking about something. After a moment, he opened them again. "I don't know. I can't recall my visions ever working on more than one thing at a time. They do seem to be focused on a particular thing and helping me work through that to the end." He sighed. "So yeah, this guy could've been doing this for a while and just now came on my radar. We need to check."

"Hey," Phillip pulled Danny's attention toward the road. "You think that's the sheriff?"

A rooster-tail of dust rose off the road. Danny glanced at his watch. The timing was right. "Probably." He stood, dusted off his jeans, and then offered Connor a hand up.

Connor frowned at the phone as he explained the two dead women to Kennedy in Santa Fe. The more he talked, the more he knew he was missing something really important, but he just couldn't put his finger on it.

"Sounds like we need to do some checking and see if there are any other unsolved murders in the area that match that description," Kennedy said. "Tell you what, since this is originating in Jemez Springs, talk to Sheriff Callaway there and get him to poke around in the western counties, the local jurisdictions, and highway patrol. I'll send out some inquiries for points north and east."

"I can do that." He glanced across the desk where Danny was making notes on their skeleton. He hoped some DNA or something would help them identify her. The patchy black hair they'd found scattered around the scene could be either Native American or Hispanic. They'd gathered up some and sent it along with some of the smaller bones to the New Mexico State Crime Lab, but the odds were it would take a few weeks before they could get any response back. Crime labs weren't nearly as fast as most television shows portrayed them. He'd tried to get some kind of psychic impression off the bones, but there hadn't been any kind of residue he could reach. The bones were just too old. However, he did pick up the essence of coyotes and vultures that'd probably feasted on the body.

"Okay," Kennedy said. "I think Lisa's open after she gets her traffic reports filled out. Unless something major happens, I can put her on this and see what she can find."

"That would be great." Connor knew Lisa would hate spending days going through old records looking for unsolved cases that matched the little bit they had to go on. Just the number of women with shoulder-length black hair would be enough to drive her nuts since that would describe half to three-quarters of the women in New Mexico.

"I'll tell her to either call your cell phone or the Jemez Springs station with the information. Is your wolf handling the case, or should she ask for Callaway?"

Connor cringed at him referring to Danny as his wolf. He knew Lisa had gone back to Santa Fe and spilled the beans. "Either will be fine. Deputy Lupan is the one handling the case for Sheriff Callaway."

"Okay. Good luck with this. If it *is* a serial killer, the odds are he'll move on soon. Even with your psychic abilities, we might not be able to catch him."

"I have to have some luck sometimes." Connor wasn't going to give up easily. His visions were good at leading him to the people he needed to find, even when it wasn't very fast a lot of the time.

"Call me or Lisa if you get anything and need more help from us on this end."

"Will do."

Kennedy hung up without further ceremony. He wasn't prone to polite maneuvering on the phone if he could help it. Connor understood, but at times it hit him as rude. He was raised to always say goodbye or something. He stared at his phone for a moment before slipping it into his pocket.

"So, is Santa Fe going to lend a hand?" Danny asked as he laid his pen on the stack of reports. He sighed. "You know, sometimes I really wish this office would come into the twenty-first century so we could have computers to do all this."

Officer White laughed from her desk behind Connor. "Yeah, like the taxpayers are going to fund that. We were lucky to get that temporary tax hike last fall so we could get bullet-resistant vests and body cameras. I think if it hadn't been for the Black Lives Matter protest everywhere, including here, we wouldn't have gotten those."

"Really?" Connor asked, turning toward her. He knew from the talk around the Santa Fe office how hard funding could be for police, but figured they weren't completely primitive. He knew there were computers in the Broncos the deputies drove, then he realized the Broncos themselves were nearly twenty years old, they were just being kept in good condition.

"You have no idea how hard it is to get the county residents to fund things around here. I think most of them think we don't do a whole lot, so they don't need to worry about making sure we've got the modern tools to work with unless they get inconvenienced." Officer White sounded a bit bitter about things, but Connor knew from observing how hard it could be to do a good job without the right tools. Since college, he hadn't actually had a regular job. His visions kept him on the move too much for that, but luckily most of the police departments had it in their budgets to pay for consultants under special circumstances.

Danny chuckled. "You know, sometimes I think folks around here would be happy if we still had horses and six shooters."

Officer White frowned thoughtfully. "Say, can you even ride a horse?"

Glancing at Connor, Danny pursed his lips. "I've never actually tried. I always figured if I needed the speed of four legs, I've got my own. How about you?"

"Yeah." Connor nodded slowly. "Back when I was a kid, my mom used to take me riding. But once I hit puberty and I had my first shift, the horses didn't want anything to do with me."

Danny pointed at Connor. "That's right, you said you were a half-breed. I didn't have to wait until I hit my teens for my first shift. Both my parents are wolf shifters so I was doing it about the same time I learned to walk. Actually, according to Mom, they had to put a collar and leash on me to keep me under control." His face paled. "Shit. Mom." He jerked his cellphone out of his pocket and frantically pushed buttons.

Officer White raised her eyebrows. "What's wrong with him?"

"We were supposed to have lunch with his mother, and with the skeleton we forgot." Connor wondered how much trouble Danny was going to be in. If they'd missed lunch with his mother, it wouldn't be a huge deal. She was really understanding about things like that, particularly if they explained it was due to police work. She understood that things like that came up, and even how the visions pushed him around from place to place.

Danny stood and walked toward the front door. "Hey, Mom. Look, I'm really sorry. Cortez wanted me to take a look at the skeleton Phillip found and I kinda forgot about lunch." He went out the front door, still talking.

"I've met Danny's mom a couple of times," Officer White said softly. "She's fairly intense."

"A lot of wolves are. I think it comes with being a canine." Conner smiled.

"You know, you two are really cute the way you tease each other," Officer White said.

Connor shrugged. He wasn't sure he knew Danny's coworker well enough to discuss him with her. It had felt odd enough talking to Lisa about him. He hadn't had a man in his life in Santa Fe, so it had been new territory for them.

"You guys might be opposites in some ways, but you're good for Danny," Officer White continued. "He can get a bit broody from time to time and since you've been around, I haven't seen that."

Even though he normally saw the more light-hearted Danny, Connor had seen glimpses of a brooder, like when they'd spent all day checking for RVs and hadn't found anyone home. The idea that he might be helping bring out a lighter side in Danny made a warm spot in his chest. He wasn't sure exactly what to say, but he smiled. "Thanks."

"No. Thank you." Then she stared at him hard. "But let me tell you something, if you hurt him in any way he can't heal, you're not going to be just dealing with wolves, you're going to have to deal with an irate human woman with silver bullets in her pistol. Got that, Cat Man?"

Connor always thought it was a good sign when someone would illicit such overprotective responses in their friends. Good people did that, bad people didn't. He raised his hands and backed away from her. "Got it."

"Good."

Sheriff Callaway came out of his office. "Jeri, where's Danny? Does he have those reports ready yet?"

Officer White stood and walked over to Danny's desk and looked at the papers he'd been working on. "Report's here." She held it up. "He had to call his mother." She pointed toward the front window where Danny was visible walking up and down the sidewalk as he talked.

The sheriff came over and took the papers. "Got it. Tell him to come into my office when he gets off the phone. McGriffin, come in with him, if you wouldn't mind."

Connor wondered what the sheriff was going to want. He seemed a bit more agitated than normal.

Seconds later, Danny came back in, slipping the phone back in his pocket. "Man, she's pissed. We're going to have to go out sometime soon. Luckily, Cortez had alerted her to the fact we were going to miss lunch."

Connor frowned and raised his eyebrow. "We? Puppy Dawg have mouse in pocket?"

Danny met his gaze. "No, and white kitty better be on his best behavior when *we* go out there, cause Mom wants to meet *you.*"

"Why?" Connor was starting to feel like they had multiple people trying to force them together and he wasn't sure if he liked that idea or not.

"Don't worry about that right now," Officer White interrupted. She pointed toward the Sheriff's office. "Rusty wanted to see you when you got off the phone. Go in there."

Danny closed his eyes for a second and sighed. "Yes, ma'am. Seems like all I'm saying today." He turned and headed that direction.

"I'm supposed to come too," Connor stood and hurried after Danny.

"Alright you two. It looks like we do have a pattern." Sheriff Callaway said as they entered the office. "I have an idea. Might help us save some man-hours. McGriffin, what's the possibility you might have another of your visions before our next girl is supposed to die?"

Connor shook his head. The sheriff's words were a bit too harsh. "The future isn't always certain."

Callaway frowned. "How often are you wrong?"

Sitting in the chair in front of the sheriff's desk, Connor closed his eyes and thought back over the years. There had been times when things hadn't gone exactly as he'd seen them, but there wasn't a time a vision hadn't played out at least in some semblance to the way his vision portrayed. "Only about small details. The meat of the vision nearly always happens, unless I can find a way to stop it."

"Right." Callaway nodded. "Looks like we've got a situation we need to get more information on, and right now, that's being slow in coming. Danny, what else are you doing today?"

Danny shrugged as he settled in the wooden chair next to Connor. "Nothing, except hitting the streets looking for speeders."

"Leave that for me and Jeri." The sheriff slid a credit card across the desk to him. "I want you to go into Albuquerque and buy a couple of trail cameras. I'm sure any of the outdoor shops there should have them. Hell, you might find them at Walmart."

"Trail cameras?" Connor asked before the idea registered in his brain.

"Yes. If you're sure your vision is going to come to pass, then if we put cameras in the place you saw it, we might not be able to stop this one from happening, but we might be able to get some information about our killer."

The idea sounded like a good one. Connor nodded and grinned. "Sounds like a plan. We can't stake out the place because it might frighten the perp off, but hopefully he won't spot the cameras."

"I bet we can get some that will blend in with the surroundings," Danny said as he picked up the credit card. "How much can I spend?"

Sheriff Callaway frowned slightly. "Look at the card, Lupan. It's my personal one. I'm a civil servant. Don't bankrupt me."

"Oh. Okay." Danny put the card in his pocket. "I'll grab two with good battery life and large data cards. Be back tonight."

"Thank you." Sheriff Callaway waved them out of the office.

Once he got back to his desk, Danny paused and looked at Connor. "Do you want to ride with me? Remember, Cortez said I'm supposed to keep an eye on you."

Connor shrugged. They'd spent a lot of time the past couple of weeks riding around the state. What was one more trip to the biggest city around? "Why not. I was just thinking I could go lie on a rock somewhere and soak up some rays."

Danny rolled his eyes. "Cat, you've got to find more interesting hobbies."

"Maybe you can teach me to chase cars." Connor said with a wide grin.

"It's not that hard and kinda fun when you get right down to it." Danny waved toward the front door. "Since this is a professional trip, we'll take the Bronco."

"Okay." Connor fell into step with Danny as they headed toward the official parking lot. He hoped the sheriff's idea was a good one. He'd never thought about bugging a place he'd seen the future happening. If it worked, it might turn out to be a handy tool for future investigations.

Chapter Seven

Connor, in his cat form, stood next to Sherriff Callaway in the same field from his last vision. Danny, in wolf form, was just a few feet away, sniffing around. The sun was just starting to peak over the mountains to the east. The scent of decomposition Connor could pick up from her was very faint. She'd been lying there less than a day, more like about twelve hours or so. It had taken a month, but the vision had come to pass.

The woman's body lay on its back. Blood soaked the ground under her. Dark marks on her wrists showed where she had been restrained with a rope of some kind. She wasn't as peaceful and happy as the other one had been right before she'd died. Connor didn't want to have to touch her, afraid of what he might pick up. There were things he didn't want to see.

Danny sniffed the body. *"She had sex just before he killed her, but I don't smell him. It's just like the other one. Probably no DNA."*

Connor headed back toward the campsite and stopped near a bush. *"Do you have an evidence bag?"*

Danny also stopped, while Sherriff Callaway continued toward the cars.

"Should be one in the squad car. What'd you find?"

"Looks and smells like he peed on this bush. We might get some DNA from it."

"Is it human?"

"It's strange. Almost human with a wild scent."

Danny sniffed at the bush. *"I'm picking up a bear scent."*

The two shifted back to their human forms. It was strange how they were beginning to think alike and act in unison. Even with the few friends he'd had over the years, Connor had never really had that kind of synergy with another person. He was starting to like it.

"Hey, Boss," Danny called, "The cat needs an evidence bag."

Sheriff Callaway opened the back of the Bronco, removed a bag, and walked back to them. He held the bag out to Connor. "What is it?"

"Possible DNA," Connor said. "Somebody peed on this bush recently."

Connor pulled a pocket knife from his jeans, cut a sprig off of the bush, and placed it in the bag. It was good finally having a bit to go off of. The skeleton from pack land hadn't yielded much in the way of evidence. The crime lab came back with inconclusive results, claiming there was a lot of degradation due to it being exposed to the elements and scavengers for so long. The search for other victims was also being a little less than extremely helpful. There were a good number of missing women in the area, and there had been a few bodies found. Some of them matched the killer's MO, but most didn't.

More than a few times, Danny had asked if Connor could try and force a vision. He'd explained his gifts didn't work that way, even as much as he wished they would. He handed the bag with the leaf on it to Danny. "Guess you can send that off to the crime lab."

"Maybe we can get them to give us a rush job," Sheriff Callaway said from behind Danny. "I think this is the most we've ever sent them, let alone in a short time."

Connor chuckled. "I doubt it." In the time he'd been working with Santa Fe, he'd never known the crime lab to be fast on anything.

"Me too." Danny sighed. "But if they come back with something, and we're still without any real leads, that will be good."

"Yeah, it will." Connor paced a little, trying to figure out what they could do to find the killer. He hated how they had bodies piling up and no real lead.

"Well, these were a waste of time," Officer White said as she put the trail camera back where Danny had mounted it two weeks earlier. "Something bumped this one." She frowned as she turned her tablet toward them. A picture of a large furry paw hitting the camera housing was the last one from the direction they'd aimed it at. "It was a good idea. But this one's not been on target for a couple of days, and the one in the parking area over there." She pointed back to where the trucks were parked. "You guys put it too low. All it got were shots of dust and tires."

"Damn." Sheriff Callaway stomped over and glared down at the small camo-colored box on the side of a boulder.

"Yeah." Danny agreed. "That was one of the few spots over on that side of the area that had any kind of cover. Sticking it on one of the highway signs might've alerted the guy it was there. I was hoping we could at least get a license plate or something useful."

Callaway bent down and picked up the box. "A good idea that was just a waste of money. But I guess I can take them home and put them on the corners of my deck. I paid for the damned things, I may be able to get some use out of them by tracking the deer that wander through the yard."

Connor retrieved the other box, the one that had taken Danny and him nearly an hour to get just right based on his vision. He'd so hoped they'd be able to digitally capture their killer. Overall his vision hadn't helped much. Even if they had found a bush that had been peed on, it might not be enough. He still couldn't understand how their killer was managing to mask his scent. It was soon enough after a full moon, he and Danny were both still feeling the effects of the monthly strengthening of their animal sides. Their senses were sharp, but all he could pick up was the smell of a bear who'd come through recently. Since it hadn't done anything to the body, it had probably prowled the area right before the victim and killer had stopped. It was possible their arrival had scared it off.

Once they returned to the sheriff's office, Connor stalked around the office. The case was beginning to gnaw at him. There should be at least something coming to him. There was nothing. Nothing bothered him. He needed to think.

The sun streaming in the front window formed a warm puddle of light on the floor. It was too much to pass up. He stopped, shifted into cat form, turned around a couple of times, and lay in the sunlight. The warm sunbeam helped him relax. That was what he needed, to relax and hope something came to him.

"What do you think you're doing?" Danny asked. "Rusty doesn't like us to shift in the office. He even frowns on it in town."

Connor turned his head toward Danny, blinked, laid his chin on his paws, and closed his eyes. A loud purr sounded from his chest.

Officer White laughed. "He's acting just like a cat. Ignore everyone, lie in the sun, and purr."

Danny snorted, and pulled out his chair with a loud scrape. "Next thing you know, he'll be licking himself."

"I think he has more human in him than to do that." She chuckled. "At least in public."

Connor didn't bother opening his eyes to respond. *"Never when ladies are present."*

Walking to him and leaning over, Officer White scratched behind his ear. "Don't you, Big Cat? If I weren't married, I might try to take you home with me. But I'm afraid my husband might get jealous."

Connor lifted his head, rubbed it against her hand, and laid it back down. He purred louder. She had a light touch, but he really wished Danny was the one who came over and gave him a little affection. They were hesitant to touch, and Connor understood that was as much on his part as Danny's, but he caught himself wishing for a soft touch or a light kiss.

Danny chuckled. "More likely, you'd get jealous. The Cat would be more interested in Bill than he would in you."

"What's the matter, Dawg? You wouldn't be jealous, would you?" He took the opening to tease. Teasing Danny made him feel good, and he didn't totally understand why. *"Maybe you'd like to take me home with you and lick me."*

"Dream on, Big Cat." The playful edge to Danny's mental voice made Connor smile, and he was thankful he was facing toward the window and away from Danny's desk so Danny couldn't see his look.

Chapter Eight

Danny pulled up next to Connor's Jeep and stepped out of the Bronco in front of the east-facing cabin. His body reacted at the sight before him. Again he had to force his body to relax. He had no desire to get mixed up with a cat. He was beginning to treat Connor like a member of the pack, but there was something more. He knew the people around him wouldn't care if they found a connection, but their differences still bothered him. He was still having the dreams that had progressed to full-on wet dreams where Connor starred. The dreams were good, but he didn't know how far he wanted it to go. He'd only recently acknowledged that if Connor had been a wolf, they'd already be sleeping together, probably for a week or more. He never considered himself a speciest, but that was the biggest hurdle he was having. Maybe if he'd had good luck in the love department in the past it would be different, but he hadn't, and that made him wary, even when Connor was as incredibly sexy as he was in that moment.

Connor sat on the step naked with a cup in his hand. His hair and the tawny pelt on his chest glowed almost golden in the early morning sun. He grinned. "Mawnin' there, Dawg," he drawled stressing his southern accent. His grin broadened as his gaze landed on the bulge in Danny's pants. "You'd better be careful. Someone might think you see something you like."

"Sometimes the body does things the mind doesn't want it to." Danny snapped back. Connor attracted him even more when naked. It made him realize how long it had been since he'd been with another man and how much he really wanted Connor.

"To what do I owe the pleasure of such an early visit?" Connor asked.

Danny sat on the step next to Connor, took the cup from his hand, took a sip, and spit it out. "First mushrooms on your burger, and now cream in your coffee."

"I think the key point is it's *my* burger and *my* coffee." Connor took the cup back and gulped down the last of the coffee. "And everyone knows cats like cream."

"We've identified the victims," Danny said, thankful for a change of subject. He hoped if they were talking about dead women, maybe his body would stop reacting to Connor's naked presence next to him. "The first one's name is Consuela, Connie, Sanchez. She has a record in Santa Fe. She's been picked up several times for soliciting.

"The other one is also from Santa Fe. Lacey Simmons is a divorced mother of a four-year-old son. Her mother reported her missing two days ago when she didn't come home from the café where she worked as a waitress. Still nothing on our skeleton."

Connor tilted his head and knitted his eyebrows. "You couldn't tell me this over the phone?"

"Rusty wants me to drive down to Santa Fe and interview their friends and families. He thought you might be able to pick something up with that thing you do." He suddenly wondered if calling first might've been better. He could've spared his libido the glorious sight of Connor's almost perfect body on display in the early morning light.

"Okay." Connor stood and stretched. He seemed to take a little longer at completing the motion than a human would. It left his body on perfect display and certain things at eye level from where Danny continued to sit on the step. "Let me get dressed."

Danny looked sideways and let his eyes go from Connor's face to his feet and back up again. "Don't need to bother on my account." Then he smirked. "But you know, if this cabin wasn't so secluded, I might have to haul you in for indecent exposure."

Connor made a slow wave down his supple body. "Do you call this indecent?"

"Not exactly, but if someone complained." Danny suddenly wished he'd kept his mouth shut, but they fell into teasing so easily it was hard.

"I don't hear anyone complaining." Connor chuckled, then sauntered into the cabin, moving his furry ass much like a cat would.

Danny swallowed and paced over to the Bronco. Thinking about dead women, he hoped he'd relax enough Connor wouldn't smell his arousal and think he was turning him on, even though he was.

By the time Connor came out of the cabin, Danny thought he had himself back under control. Unfortunately, everything flared right back up when he caught sight of him.

Connor's neatly-pressed jeans fit like a second skin. The light green polo shirt brought out green highlights in his eyes. Even though he didn't appear to be trying to be seductive, he was. The realization that it was more than just Connor's naked form that turned him on really bad, hit Danny hard. He was lusting after a cat.

There was a small sports bag slung over Connor's shoulder. Danny let his attention go to it. "What's in the bag?"

"I figured it might take us longer than one day to question everyone."

"Didn't think about that." Danny mentally hit himself for not thinking ahead. Interviewing people always took a lot more time than just chasing down RVs all over the state. Going back to his place for some clean clothes would delay them a good half an hour and they'd have to drive past the Sheriff's office and he didn't want to have to explain a lack of forethought to either Rusty or Jeri.

"No problem. I have enough clean underwear for both of us. We're about the same size…I think." Connor walked to the passenger side of the Bronco and opened the door. "Besides, I have a place in Santa Fe. Just not sure what I have clean there. I left in kind of a hurry when Kennedy told me to get out of town for a while. Sometimes, jumping at opportunities makes me leave things behind."

Danny said. "We always keep a clean uniform in the car just in case someone bleeds or throws up on us. But tell me, don't those tight jeans get uncomfortable sometimes?" Danny couldn't stand tight clothes. He always made sure things were just tight enough to not fall off, but loose enough that he could move easily.

Connor grinned lazily as he leaned across the hood of the Bronco, looking for a moment like he was about to pose for a beefcake photoshoot. "If they do, I take them off or shift."

Danny opened the driver's side door. "Do you always shift fully clothed? I noticed you did it very easily the other day." He knew from the pack, not everyone could pull off the stunt. Normally the wolves who could pull it off were either older, or had a bit of magic in them. If Connor's visions come from his own personal magic, that made sense.

"Mostly." Connor straightened and shrugged. "Humans tend to get a little uneasy when I'm naked. What about you? You've been completely dressed the times I've seen you shift."

"Yeah." Danny slipped into his seat, suddenly wondering if Connor was trying to arrange a way they could get naked together. "If I'm out in the wild and alone, I'll strip first. It's less binding." He didn't take the time to strip when he shifted if it was an emergency, but if it was just a casual run in the desert, and he knew he'd be coming back to where he left his clothes, it was a lot more natural to shift naked.

Connor settled into his seat and clipped the seat belt securely in place. "Yeah. I hear you."

Connor studied the dashboard of the Bronco. It was as old as the rest of the vehicle, but had some upgrades, probably to make it more usable as a police truck. In the past couple of weeks, he hadn't really cared much since he and Danny normally had something to talk about, but there had been a weighty silence hanging over them since they left the cabin. "This thing got a radio besides the two-way?"

"No radio, but there's a CD player." Danny reached over and pushed a button that was slightly recessed in the dash. A couple of faint lights flashed, then the haunting sound of a flute filled the car. Behind the flute, a soft drum beat gave the music an earthy feel.

"Now that's a surprise," Connor said. It had been a while since he'd heard native flute music for longer than just walking past some of the shops in Santa Fe. It was nice, but often put him to sleep unless there was singing along with it.

"What?" Danny sounded a bit offended.

Connor tried to find just the right words, and stumbled. "I wouldn't take you for a flute man."

"It's a Navajo flute. My grandfather played one and taught me. I learned to love their sound as a kid." There was a note of pride in his voice.

"So where's this grandfather?" Connor asked. He'd heard about Danny's mother, sisters, and met his cousin and uncle.

"Dead." Danny's voice was little more than a whisper. "He died about ten years ago."

"What happened?" Connor pushed his seat back as far as it would go, put his feet on the dashboard, and tapped his fingers against his leg in time to the music. He knew some wolves died of old age, but that wasn't normally what happened.

"Get your shoes off the dash; this vehicle is county property." Danny turned and glared.

Connor reluctantly lowered his feet, kicked off his sneakers, and put his feet back up. "Happy now?" They'd had the shoes on the dash discussion before and he knew better. It was just a reflex.

"It's better. Just hope I don't stop suddenly."

Danny's mood was a lot darker than it had been before Connor asked about his grandfather. Connor decided to change the topic. "You know, you never did tell me how you ended up in Jemez as a deputy sheriff?"

Danny shrugged. "I met Rusty's son at college. We were roommates."

"Roommates?" Connor quirked an eyebrow.

"Yes," Danny snapped. "Just roommates. Sam was straight."

"Was? What happened to him?" Connor hoped he hadn't just wandered onto another subject that was going to upset Danny. For all the time they'd spent together, he was still learning to navigate Danny's moods to avoid things that would upset him.

"If you'll quit interrupting, I'll tell you." Danny shook his head and sighed. "Are you always so impatient? Anyway, Sam wasn't doing too well in school. He dropped out before senior year, and enlisted. He was killed in Afghanistan."

"Sorry to hear that." Connor frowned. "It must have hit Sheriff Callaway pretty hard."

"It did. There was a while I didn't know if he'd get over it. Sam was his only kid. He and his wife divorced soon after Sam died."

"That happens a lot." Connor mumbled, more to throw something in to keep Danny talking. He knew from experience how talking could help things a lot. "Each parent blames the other, and suddenly things escalate to the point there's no going back."

"When I graduated, Rusty asked if I wanted to work for him. He thought my 'special' talent might be an advantage in police work." Danny paused. "How about you? Where are you from? That accent isn't from New Mexico. You've said your visions tend to lead you around a lot."

"I was born in Tennessee." He hoped doing his share of the talking would help Danny lighten up.

"Is your whole family shifters?"

"No. My dad's family is as far back as I know, but my mother's human. How about yours?"

"One-hundred percent shifters back before the white man came to this country. How'd you get into helping the police?"

"A fluke really." Connor shrugged. "I was always using my Sight to locate lost objects. One day a friend's kid disappeared, and I used it to locate him. The friend told the press, and the cops called me the next time they lost a kid."

"Santa Fe's a long way from Tennessee."

"I just slowly moved along. Mostly going where the visions take me. Sometimes I'm in a place longer than at other times depending on what's going on. I think Santa Fe has been the longest. There was a case in Las Vegas, New Mexico, not Nevada, a couple of years ago where a guy was killing hikers who he thought were trespassing on a prospecting claim he never filed. He even tried dressing up in a Bigfoot costume to chase them off. Even though I knew where he was killing people it took me a while to get it all figured out. The costume had me fooled and threw off my Sight. Then there was a shooter on the highway just south of Santa Fe. By the time I had that one sorted out, I was working with Kennedy." He pointed to the exit sign on Highway 285. "There's your exit."

Their conversation dropped off for a little while as Connor directed Danny to the police station and into a reserved spot.

Danny whistled. "Wow! You must be some big shot," he said sarcastically. "Your own reserved parking spot."

Connor got out of the Bronco. "When they call me in, it's usually an emergency. They want to make sure I don't have to mess around looking for a spot."

Danny followed him, making sure to lock the Bronco. He didn't trust big towns like Santa Fe. Then he hurried to catch up to Connor who was almost to a side door. He'd been to the Santa Fe police department a few times, but normally went in the front door.

Connor took him through the door and down a long hall that was the back way into the squad room. He strolled into the squad room, grabbed a small woman with short auburn hair standing by the water cooler, swung her off her feet, and nuzzled her neck. "Hey, Lisa, have you missed me?"

"Put me down, you big ox." She batted him playfully on his shoulder. "What are you doing here? You're supposed to be on vacation. I haven't gotten any new info for you since the batch I sent over two days ago."

He set her on the floor. "I'm a cat, not a cow. Is Kennedy in?"

"In his office." She pointed to the office with glass walls on the far side of the squad room. "Wait a minute, is this your wolf I've heard so much about?"

Danny stayed a foot or so behind Connor. He'd heard people calling Connor his cat, but it was the first time he'd been called Connor's wolf and he wasn't sure how he felt about that. On the one hand, he liked the sound of it, but on the other, he didn't like the idea of belonging to anyone.

"Lisa, this is Deputy Danny Lupan." Connor waved Danny forward. "Danny, this is Officer Lisa Collins. One of the best officers in Santa Fe."

"I've heard good things about you, Lupan." Collins offered him her hand. "Both from Connor and Callaway. It seems you make a good impression."

"Thanks," Danny wasn't sure what else to say as he shook her hand. Other than Connor mentioning Officer Collins was working on finding similar cases to the one they were working on, he hadn't heard anything about her. But then there was still a lot about Connor he didn't know. What was interesting was the way he moved through the squad room, waving to various officers there, and flashing the occasional smile. These police people were ones he treated like family, like pack.

Connor opened the door to Kennedy's office.

Kennedy had his back to the door. "I said I didn't want to be disturbed." He turned around. "McGriffin, what are you doing here? You're supposed to be in the mountains. Has there been a break in that case you're working on up there?"

"Thought you might be able to help us with it," Connor said. "This is Deputy Danny Lupan."

"Is this Callaway's wolf?"

"Yeah. The old Dawg." Connor winked and grinned at Danny.

Danny glared. He stopped himself from snarling. He had only met Chief Kennedy once before and wanted to stay on good relations. He never knew when he'd be called to come back to Santa Fe, and he didn't want to be seen as a drama wolf.

Kennedy chuckled. "I can see I was right in wishing Callaway good luck with you two. Good to meet you, Deputy. Have a seat. How can I help?"

Danny sat facing Chief Kennedy. He liked being able to watch the people he was talking to, plus he'd grown to trust Connor to watch his back.

Connor leaned against a credenza. "We've identified our two victims. They're both from Santa Fe. Sheriff Callaway sent us over to talk to their families and friends."

Kennedy frowned. "Two victims. I only heard about one and the skeleton."

"The first one is a Consuela, Connie, Sanchez," Connor said. "She apparently has a rap sheet for soliciting. The second is a missing person named Lacey Simmons."

Kennedy picked up the phone. "Lisa, get me the file on a hooker named Consuela Sanchez and call missing persons about a Lacey Simmons."

"I'll be right back," Connor said and left the room.

Danny stared after him, wondering what had caused him to just up and hurry out like that. There was so much about Connor he was still figuring out.

"So what's your take on these murders, Deputy Lupan?" Chief Kennedy studied Danny with sharp gray eyes.

Danny shrugged trying not to take offense at being stared at. He knew it wasn't a challenge. "Most excitement we've had in Jemez Springs in years. So far we've been lucky and kept the local paper from getting wind of it. The local pack isn't happy that the skeleton was found on their land."

"I bet." Kennedy nodded. "I guess we're lucky we don't have a pack here in Santa Fe. From what I've heard from other departments where there are packs, it can be hit or miss as far as how they get along with the local law."

"That's true." Danny had heard the same thing. Some of the packs still held to age-old shifter laws and didn't feel that human law really impacted them. "I know Cortez tries his best to stay on Sheriff Callaway's good side. It's one of the reasons he agreed to me being a deputy." He didn't want to say anything about Cortez wanting to send someone into Santa Fe to establish the pack there.

"So you're sort of an unofficial ambassador." Captain Kennedy pursed his lips and nodded. "I like that. It's sort of like Officer Collins and the local shifter community."

Danny straightened a bit and tried to remember if Connor had said anything about Officer Collins being a shifter. If he had, he hadn't said anything about what kind of shifter she was. There hadn't been any overall scent that caught his attention when he'd met her. It wasn't uncommon for female shifters to mask their scents with perfumes.

"She works with them any time we have questions that might impact them," Kennedy continued. "I think it really helps to have cops who can connect with all segments of our populations, human and otherwise."

"Definitely," Danny agreed, then before he could say anything more, the office door opened and Officer Collins came in.

Connor followed her and handed Danny a can of soda. "Here, Dawg, thought you might be thirsty after our drive. I know I am."

Danny nodded his thanks and popped the top on the can. He was pleased Connor remembered his preference for root beer over cola.

"Thanks, Cat," he smiled as he sipped the soda.

"No problem," Connor said with a grin. "Is that the Sanchez file, Lisa?"

"Yes." She handed the folder to Connor. "By the way, there's an unfamiliar vehicle parked in your spot. Should I tow it?"

"Better not. The Dawg here wouldn't like it." He sat on the couch, opened the file, and read through it.

Danny bristled slightly. The truck was marked and obviously his. It was like Officer Collins was trying to get in on the teasing he and Connor enjoyed. That was something special between them. He didn't want other people getting in on that.

"Do you see anything, Connor?" Captain Kennedy asked, coming around his desk.

Connor shook his head. "Just what's on the paper."

The door opened and a patrolman hurried in and handed Kennedy a file. "Missing persons sent this over."

Without looking at it, Kennedy handed the folder to Connor.

Connor opened the file and closed his eyes. After a couple of seconds, a tear slowly trickled down Connor's cheek.

"You okay, Cat," Danny asked. Something had touched Connor, made him sad and that triggered a protective instinct in Danny he hadn't felt before where Connor was concerned. He stood and walked over to the couch.

"Yeah." Connor's voice was sharp and full of pain. "Let's get this done." He rose and headed for the door. "If you hear anything, Kennedy, call me."

"Will do. Keep me in the loop also."

Connor stopped at the copy machine and made copies of both files.

Danny followed behind him quietly, taking in this new aspect of Connor. He'd seen something in the pictures or the file. Whatever it was, it hit him hard enough to put a crack in the Connor he was used to dealing with.

Nothing was said as the copying finished up, and Connor dropped the files on Officer Collins' desk before heading for the door. Even the people he'd waved to previously seemed to sense his mood and stayed out of his way as he sulked down the hall toward the door. It was like he'd suddenly become a very dangerous big cat and they were just deer trying to stay out of his way.

In the car, Danny sat there with the keys in the ignition, but not starting the engine. "What did you see back there? Whatever it was broke you up a bit."

Connor hit his fist against the dashboard. "A mother telling her son she'd be there when he woke up. But she didn't get to keep that promise." He rubbed his forehead. "It's times like this I hate my *gift*." He closed his eyes and laid his head against the back of the seat.

Danny put his hand on Connor's leg. Connor flinched slightly, then let out a long breath, like Danny's touch was comforting.

"For what it's worth," Danny said. "I'm sorry you had to see that. Does your gift do cruel things to you like this on a regular basis? How does seeing something like that help you find the killer?"

Connor closed his hand over Danny's and shrugged. For several minutes they sat there like that. Neither of them moving, but slowly Connor's dark mood seemed to ebb slightly.

Then Connor sighed and lifted his hand from Danny's. "I don't know about you, Dawg, but I'm hungry. There's a good Mexican place a couple of blocks away. We can eat some tacos and plan our strategy."

"Tacos always sound good." Danny started up the Bronco, then backed out of the parking lot.

Beside him, Connor still looked pale and sullen.

He wanted to do what he could to help completely break the bleakness seeping from him. Something about seeing Connor sad hit Danny in a way nothing ever had. Connor's cool cat exterior had peeled away and he looked vulnerable. Danny wanted to protect that vulnerable side.

Chapter Nine

They sat at a table close to the door and ordered soft drinks and taco platters. Connor had always liked the restaurant. It was one of his favorite places to eat, and one of the cheapest. It was also more 'real' Mexican than 'Tex-Mex'. All of the wait staff and cooks were Hispanic, as well as most of the customers.

The waitress brought the drinks and left without any non-service questions. The place was close enough to the police station that Connor and most of the others came often enough she had long since stopped asking questions about the files that inevitably showed up with them.

Connor opened the file on Consuela Sanchez. "Not much here." He thumbed through the file, half hoping he'd get a flash on something beyond what he'd seen previously. There was nothing out of the ordinary in the folder. "She was last seen getting into a black Ford Escort on the evening before we found her body."

He closed the folder and took a drink from his soda. Even though carbonation bubbles were visible, it tasted flat. He hated going through the files of the dead and knew they were affecting his taste buds. There was either too much there, or not enough. Only on rare occasions would he find exactly what he needed.

He opened the file on Lacey Simmons. "Divorced."

"We knew that," Danny said, then took a sip of his soda.

Connor glared and continued, "Friendly terms with ex-husband who's currently overseas."

"So the husband's in the clear," Danny said.

"Sounds like it. Of course, he could've had someone do it, but it's highly unlikely. They've been divorced for nearly three years. Her car was found out of gas two blocks from where she worked. A receipt in her purse shows she filled up that afternoon on the way to work." Connor looked up from the file, thinking out loud. He found that talking about what he was thinking was a good way to work things out. And even as he wished Danny wouldn't interrupt, he hoped something Danny said would make things click in his brain.

Danny said, "So someone either put a lot of miles on the car that afternoon, or they tampered with the tank."

The waitress brought their food and silently left.

Danny took a bite of taco and washed it down with soda. "Tell me about Officer Collins. What is she?"

Connor laid his taco on his plate and tilted his head. "What do you mean?" The question wasn't helping them sort out the case. He wondered why Danny was asking.

"I mean she's a shifter. Kennedy said she's the local liaison between the force and the community. What is she?" He took another bite of his taco.

"If she wants you to know, she'll tell you. It's her secret; not mine." Connor felt bad about saying it, but there was an unspoken agreement in the shifter community that if someone wanted someone else to know what they were, they'd tell them, unless their scent was obvious. He knew Lisa's musky raptor scent was light, and she normally covered it up with a bit of perfume, so he doubted Danny's nose would be able to pick up what she was without having it spelled out for him.

"Okay. I'll do that." Danny looked a little hurt, but didn't press on the subject. "So nothing else hitting you in the files?"

Connor shook his head. "I'd like to find out who our skeleton is. With three people, it's easier to form a pattern. Two, unless there are some major similarities, it's just hard. So far the only similarities are that they were all women and were shot in the forehead with the same gun."

"I hear you." Danny finished off his tacos. "Maybe we can make some headway once we talk to family members. Sanchez and Simmons…you don't think he might be going for women whose last name starts with S do you?"

Connor glared across the top of his soda glass. He wasn't in the mood for Danny's cavalier attitude, then he realized that maybe he was trying to lighten his mood. That meant he cared. Connor had never really had anyone who cared about his feelings beyond family. He sighed and ate a chip with a bit of salsa before he picked up his second taco.

"It might be a place to start. I guess we'll know once we get more information."

Danny reached across the table and patted his hand. "Here's to more information."

A warm pleasant feeling went through him, like it had when Danny had touched his leg in the truck. No matter how much they tried to avoid it, something was building between them. He just wanted to get the case solved and *then* maybe he could have time to figure out where his heart and emotions were leading him. The food had a bit more taste as they finished up their meal.

They pulled up in front of an older, single-wide mobile home with a covered deck off Monterey Drive. The place had a lived-in look to it. It hadn't reached the run-down state yet, but it was quickly approaching it. Connor had seen his share of similar places on the last case, and they always made him sad for the people who worked so hard to live there.

"What's wrong, Cat?" Danny asked.

The sound of his voice made Connor realize he was sitting there silently. He hadn't even unbuckled his seatbelt or made any move to get out of the Bronco. "Sorry, just getting a feel for the place."

"Okay, but if we sit here too long the folks inside are going to get nervous." Danny pulled the key out of the ignition and put his hands in his lap.

"Good point." Connor unbuckled his seatbelt. "Let's get this over with." He was fairly sure no one had been out to tell Lacey Simmons' family that she was dead. There had only been a few times he'd had to be the bearer of such news, and he didn't like it.

They got out of the Bronco and headed for the front door.

A small red-haired boy played with some toy trucks on the floor of the porch. Connor recognized him from the vision he'd had at the police station when going through the missing person file. A chill went through him. This little boy was never going to be held by his mother again. He would only remember her good-night kisses as yet another thing that would be in his past.

"Hi. I'll bet your name is Martin," Connor said, stooping so he was at eyelevel.

The boy stared at him, then glanced over Connor's shoulder.

"Is it?" Connor prodded.

"I don't know you." Martin looked more intently at Connor. "I'm not supposed to talk to people I don't know."

"That's a good rule to follow," Connor said and gave Martin the biggest smile he could force. "Is your grandma home?"

Leaving his trucks where he'd been playing with them, the boy opened the door. "Grandma. A man wants you. There's a man who looks like policeman here too, but his uniform's weird."

Connor glanced back at Danny. He'd never stopped to realize the brown uniforms from the Jemez Springs Sheriff's Department were a lot different from the gray uniforms of the Santa Fe Police Department. The big thing was the color and the simplicity of it, even if Danny's badge was in plain sight on his broad chest.

"It's not weird," Danny mumbled.

"No, it's rather handsome," Connor replied with a chuckle.

A short, heavy-set woman came to the door wiping her hands on her apron. Wisps of red hair sprinkled with gray straggled from her tight bun. "Can I help you?" A look of fear entered her eyes, and she covered her mouth with her hand as she glanced behind Connor and must've spotted Danny in his uniform. "Lacey?"

"I'm very sorry, Mrs. Davis," Connor said, hoping he remembered her name correctly from the file and that there hadn't been an error there. "I'm afraid we have bad news. I'm Connor McGriffin, and this is Deputy Danny Lupan of Jemez Springs. May we come in?" His gut tightened and he suddenly wanted Danny in front of him to be the one to deliver the news. He was just a consultant. Danny was the official. He should be doing it. But, Connor's vision had led them to Lacey. He had to be there, had to hope something from the visit would help lead them to her killer.

Mrs. Davis opened the door and stood back for them to enter. "Martin, you stay on the porch for a few minutes." Tears seeped down her cheeks as she closed the door behind him. Her lips were tight as she turned to Connor and Danny who were standing patiently in her living room. "She's dead, isn't she? I knew something had to have happened." She sniffed and pulled a tissue from a box on the cluttered coffee table. "She wouldn't just leave Martin. Please have a seat." She indicated two mismatched chairs and sat on the overstuffed couch.

Connor walked over to some pictures on an end table and picked up one. The vision hit him quickly, like he was tuning into the uniformed man in the photo as he sat on a cot in a tent. He held a photograph in his hand. Martin's red hair was visible. His thoughts came through clearly. *I wonder if I'll ever see Marty again.*

Danny sat beside Mrs. Davis on the couch. "We found a body near Jemez Springs we believe to be your daughter." He handed her a picture of victim number two.

Officer White had photoshopped the bullet hole out of Lacey's forehead.

The woman covered her face with both hands, and sobs wracked her body as she rocked back and forth. "What am I to do? What will become of Martin and me without Lacey?"

Danny took her in his arms, rocked with her, and let her cry. He reached over to the box of tissues on the coffee table and handed it to her.

Connor turned the picture so Danny could see it.

Danny nodded as he raised his eyebrows in question.

"Martin's father is still alive, just deployed." Connor said quietly. "He'll need to be told so he can come home to his son."

When the woman finally stopped crying, Danny handed her another tissue and asked, "Did Lacey have any close girl friends?"

"Not really," Mrs. Davis answered. "When she wasn't working, she just spent her time with Martin." She blew her nose. "Wait. There is one woman at the café. Her name's Mavis. She and Lacey sometimes stop and have a beer to unwind after they get off work."

"I understand she usually worked the dinner shift," Danny said.

Connor silently applauded him for remembering what they'd read in the file. Dawg really was a good guy.

"That's right." Mrs. Davis nodded slightly and dabbed her eyes. "She liked that shift because she got to spend her days with Martin when he was awake and work while he slept. Also, the tips were better at dinner when diners had wine or cocktails with their meals."

"Mrs. Davis, could I see Lacey's room?" Connor asked from the chair he'd settled into while she grieved.

She frowned. "Whatever for?"

"Sometimes a stranger will see something you might not that'll give us a lead as to what happened to Lacey," Connor replied. It was true and easier than trying to explain that he might get a flash on something that would lead them to Lacey's killer.

"I guess," she said. "She shared the back bedroom with Martin, and I have the smaller front bedroom and bath. I wish we had more room, but even with my retirement check and her working, this is all we can afford. I don't know if I'll be able to keep it without her."Without saying anything else, and trusting Danny to keep the woman occupied, Connor walked through the kitchen, down a hall past a bathroom and a laundry area, and into the master bedroom at the back of the mobile home. It was a cluttered mix of little boy and hard-working woman. The number of toys outweighed the female clothes scattered about. He stalked around the room trying to let his extra senses lead him to something, but everything was too vague. He touched several items, both Lacey's and Martin's. None of them triggered any reaction. It was like she hadn't really lived in the room; it had just been a place to sleep.

Disappointed, Connor strolled back into the living room. Danny still sat on the couch offering Mrs. Davis tissues. He looked up with questions in his eyes.

Shaking his head, Connor asked, "Where's Martin's dad?"

"He's deployed overseas," Mrs. Davis said, then blew her nose again. "I guess I should notify the Army to get in touch with him. He's real good about sending money and stuff for Martin."

"Why did they divorce?" It was a logical question, but Connor wasn't sure it would help them find the killer.

"They got married because Lacey was pregnant. It just didn't work out," she replied. "But Doug's a good father."

"I'm sure he is." Connor wished he could explain the vision he'd had when holding the picture of Doug Simmons, but that would be awkward, particularly when Mrs. Davis was already grieving. It would probably be more than her human mind could handle.

"I'll contact the base in Albuquerque and have them get a message to him. Lacey knew how to reach him directly, but I don't." She dried her eyes. "It's going to be hard to tell him."

"I know." Connor wished there was more he could say. He made a mental note to keep tabs on the family and make sure they were able to stay in their home.

"We should go, McGriffin," Danny said, standing and nodding toward the door.

Mrs. Davis walked to the door with them. "Good luck finding her killer. I hope he rots in hell."

"We'll do our best, Mrs. Davis." Connor said, then looked down at Martin. He glanced at Danny. "Just a minute." He went over to Martin, and knelt down to his level. "Martin, you're going to have to be a brave boy for your grandma. She's going to need your help." He held out a hand for Martin to shake.

The boy looked at him through eyes swimming with tears. "My mom isn't coming home, is she?"

"I'm sorry, Martin."

"I'll be a big boy. I won't cry."

Connor reached for the boy, gently took him in his arms and laid his head against his chest. "Don't you ever let anyone tell you not to cry. There's nothing wrong with tears. Remember how much your mom loved you when she was here? She still loves you, and she's still here. You just can't see her."

Martin's tears flowed dampening the front of Connor's shirt. His grief hit Connor hard. He never liked to see children in pain, whether it was physical or emotional. It was all he could do to keep tears from running down his own cheeks.

Connor closed his eyes. A vision hit him hard. *A tall young man in a graduation gown stood next to an older Mrs. Davis. Strands of red hair curled around the miter board cap on his head. Cords representing honor societies hung around his neck. The man from the photograph, a woman, and two younger children stood with them. A building in the background pictured scales of justice.*

When Martin's sobs finally stopped, Connor stood and wiped the boy's checks with his fingers and straightened his rumpled red hair. It was only half an attempt to put the boy to rights. "Mrs. Davis," Connor said, glancing at the old woman standing in the doorway, looking out through the screen door, "don't you worry too much about Martin. He's a good boy and I have a feeling he's going to do you proud."

Once they were in the Bronco and Danny had the engine going, he asked, "What'd you see back there?" There had been an odd look on Connor's face, a look Danny was beginning to realize meant he'd had a vision.

Connor stared straight ahead. "Martin's going to live with his dad and stepmom, go to law school, and graduate with honors."

"You didn't tell her that. Why?" Danny would've told her. Anything to help the woman get through her grief.

"Don't like to be too specific in predicting the future. Things can change." Connor ran his fingers through his hair. "What I see is just a suggestion of what might happen. Take the vision where Lacey was killed. If Sheriff Callaway had staked out the place, he'd have gone somewhere else. Like I said then, it isn't an exact science."

Danny backed the Bronco out into the dirt road that served the trailer park, then started toward the pavement. "So, what now?"

"I need to make some phone calls. Go down here to the stop sign and turn right." Connor pointed the direction he'd suggested they go.

"Where are we going?" Danny followed Connor's directions like he was a living GPS. He didn't doubt Connor knew where he wanted to go, but he wanted some clue for himself.

"I thought cats were supposed to be the curious ones. You ask a lot of questions for a dog. Just drive."

After following Connor's directions for nearly fifteen minutes, Danny pulled into the driveway of a small adobe house.

From the files they'd read over lunch, it wasn't anywhere associated with either of the two women. "Who lives here?"

"I do." Connor got out of the car, picked up his bag, and walked to the front door. "Are you coming in or not, Dawg?" He opened the wood-plank door.

Danny scrambled to follow. He'd been to the rental cabin, but that wasn't Connor's real home. It hadn't really sunk in when they'd been driving to town that Connor had said he had a house there, and they'd be staying there. He stopped inside the door and looked around.

The room reflected the atmosphere of the area. An Aztec sun was inlaid in the tiled floor right inside the door. An open floorplan made the area seem larger than it was. The color scheme was in the shades of a desert sunset: turquoise, mauve, yellow, and orange. An island under a rack of hanging copper bottom pots and pans separated the living room from the kitchen area. The pans, although clean, appeared to be well used. A skylight in the living room ceiling threw a large pool sunlight on the floor. The whole area was spotless.

Connor walked into the kitchen, opened the fridge, and took out two cold soft drinks. "I'd throw this, but you wouldn't want to open it."

"Probably not."

"Sorry it isn't root beer. I'll remember next grocery trip."

"No problem." Still trying to absorb everything, Danny hurried over to take the drink. He'd known enough shifters to know their homes often reflected their animals more than their human selves. He'd heard how meticulous cats liked to have things. The condition of the place reflected that. It didn't look like anything was out of place. He smiled slightly. At least nothing was pushed onto the floor and left to crash the way some cats and kittens do.

"Nice place you have here." Danny said as Connor carried his bag down the short hall off the kitchen. "A lot different from the cabin in Jemez Springs."

"The cabin is temporary. It works for what it needs to." Connor came back and plopped into a chair next to a table with a landline phone. "This is home."

The new soda hit Danny hard and he realized he hadn't stopped for a bathroom break since lunch. "I'm assuming you have a bathroom."

"Most houses do."

Danny cocked his head to the side and frowned. Sometimes having someone who he could tease came with the difficulty of getting a straight answer.

"Down that hall, middle door on the right," Connor said with a slight grin.

Danny followed the directions. The bathroom was as clean as the rest of the house. He paused for a moment and straightened his hair. He'd been doing that a lot more than normal. Having Connor around made him want to look his best.

Connor needed to get more information. Luckily he'd been around Santa Fe long enough he had a few sources and during the last case those sources had grown immensely. He picked up the phone and hit a speed dial. "Hello, Alma, it's Connor."

"What's up, BC?" Her voice was soft and sultry with a soft purr to it, even though she was human. She always told him that her clients loved it.

He cut right to the chase; there were already enough dead women around; he didn't want to have another one if he could help it. "What can you tell me about a hooker named Consuela Sanchez?"

"Connie?" Her voice lost the purr and she sounded genuinely surprised. "Nobody's seen her for a few weeks. Juan is about ready to kill her."

"Someone already beat him to it." He didn't sugarcoat anything. Alma was a big girl and streetwise, she'd be able to handle it.

"She's dead?" Alma asked. "Oh, God. That's not good news."

"Do you know anything at all about a possible John who has a camper?"

Danny came back into the room, and Connor motioned him to keep quiet. He sat on the sofa and looked sharp, a sure sign he was going to listen to everything that was said. If it had been a call Connor hadn't wanted him to overhear, he wouldn't have made it on the landline, or placed it on speaker.

Alma hummed thoughtfully. Her nails clicking on wood carried through their connection. "There was one guy hanging around for about a month. He drove a black Ford Escort. He'd pick a girl up and take her to a camper for a trick. I didn't care for his looks."

"That could be our guy." A spark of hope shot through Connor, but he knew from experience not to put too much faith on getting lucky so quickly. There would be some kind of hiccup, even if it was the right guy. "Think you could describe him to the police artist?"

"I might be able to. You want me to see Kennedy?"

"Yeah. I'll tell him to expect you so no one will hassle you."

Alma and some of the other girls who occasionally helped out with various cases were a little reluctant to go into the police station as some of the officers didn't view their opinions as valuable, and if Kennedy or one of the detectives wasn't around, they were prone to be a little less than cordial. Connor knew he had to pave the way for her to get in and out without a problem.

"Okay."

"Another thing," Connor decided to press his luck and see if he could get more information, "if you know any of the girls who had sex with him, see if they can tell you anything about him."

"I'll do what I can."

"Also, see if they'll talk to me. Thanks, Alma."

"Sure thing, BC." She disconnected the call.

He set the phone on his knee.

"BC?" Danny asked with a chuckle. "I guess she knows you're a shifter, but that sounds like she's a friend rather than just a hooker."

Connor shrugged. "She lost someone to the predator priest. She helped me a fair amount on the case. I wouldn't exactly call her a friend, but she knows what's going on out on the street." He held up a finger for Danny to be quiet for a moment and dialed the station's number. "Lisa, there's a hooker named Alma coming in to talk to the artist, you remember her. Tell Kennedy to give her a twenty out of my desk drawer."

"Sure thing, Connor," Lisa said. "Are you at home?"

"Yeah, for a while. We just talked to Lacey Simmons' mother and are going to the place she worked later."

"Okay. Only wanting to keep track of where I should call if something comes up."

"Cell phone is always good. If you need anything, give me a call."

"Trust me, I will."

Connor chuckled. "I know. I'll call if I find out anything." He hung up. After a tension-relieving stretch, he stood, and walked over to sit beside Danny.

"I hate to keep asking, 'so, what now?'."

"We wait until dinner time and go see Mavis at Ruby's Café." Connor reached over and wound a strand of Danny's hair around his finger. His heart pounded loud enough he was fairly sure Danny could probably hear it. He wasn't normally so forward with men, but the case had him on edge and he needed a little something to put his head back in order. With all the tension building up between the two of them, he hoped he wasn't missing the mark.

Danny eyed him suspiciously, but didn't move. "Won't she be busy then?"

The tension in the room went up several notches.

"We'll wait until late so we can talk to her when she finishes." He tucked the hair behind Danny's ear, running his finger lightly down Danny's neck.

"What are you doing?" Danny jerked away.

"Hopefully living out one of my visions." He hadn't said anything about the vision he'd had about making love to Danny. But it was fresh on his mind.

"What vision is that?"

"The one I had when you touched my leg in the parking lot at the police station." He took a chance and leaned in and kissed Danny.

As soon as their lips touched, Danny pulled back. "Cat . . ."

Connor's heart pounded even harder. He was suddenly terrified he'd rushed things, even though his vision and his heart were telling him otherwise. He'd hate it if he'd just ruined the friendship he was developing with Danny. He didn't think he had. "Tell me you don't want me."

"I can't." Danny returned the kiss.

Connor felt like he could melt into Danny. There had never been another man who'd felt so perfect as he wrapped his arms around Danny's broad shoulders.

Chapter Ten

Connor dried his hair with a towel as he walked out of the bathroom. He sat on the bed behind Danny, who was sleeping peacefully on his side, leaned over, and flicked his tongue in Danny's ear.

Danny raised his arm and brushed a hand along his ear.

"Time to wakey, wakey, Dawg. We need to get to work." Connor licked the ear again. After the evening they'd had, he wanted to do so much more, but they had things to do. He didn't want to lose the killer's trail because he had found a good thing with Danny. More than ever, he wanted to get it all wrapped up so he could spend time exploring everything he could about the handsome wolf in his bed.

Danny rolled over onto his back and opened his eyes. He blinked a couple of times, then ran his finger along Connor's jaw, leaving tingles where he touched. "What time is it?"

"Ten after seven. We had a good nap." Connor kissed him, savoring the taste of his lips. "But right now, we need to get a move on. The shower's empty."

Danny stretched and studied Connor through half-open eyes. "Did what I think happened happen, or was I dreaming?"

Connor grinned, a feeling of happy completeness filled him in a way he'd never known. "If you were dreaming, so was I. It happened. And unless I'm mistaken, it's going to happen again."

Danny yawned and stretched more like a cat than a dog. "What're Rusty and Chief Kennedy going to think of this development?"

"Who says they have to know?" Connor kissed him again. It felt right kissing him. Even his cat side thought kissing Danny felt good. "You know we're going to keep teasing. It's the nature of the beasts inside of us. That doesn't mean we can't have a little fun on the side."

Danny got off the bed and headed for the bathroom.

Connor couldn't help himself; he flicked Danny's smooth butt with the damp towel. It hit with a resounding crack.

"Ow! That stung." Danny jumped, then rubbed the spot. He glared over his shoulder before entering the bathroom and closing the door softly enough Connor knew he hadn't pissed him off.

Connor dressed in black slacks and a green button up shirt. He wanted to have a professional look when he went to talk to Mavis.

Danny came out of the bathroom rubbing a fluffy white towel across his muscular shoulders, and giving his groin a few extra shakes as he sauntered over to the bed. "That's some tub you have in there."

"If you're lucky, I may let you try it out later." Connor cocked an eyebrow and flashed his most wicked grin. He liked playing with Danny. It felt natural, and had from the first day they met. Some people might see it as fighting, but they were just playing. He knew it, and he was pretty sure Danny knew it. "If you get my drift."

"I understand." Danny picked up his uniform pants and frowned. "I hate to put on my wrinkled uniform when you look so nice."

"It'd be better if you weren't in uniform." Connor looked at him. "We're close to the same height, although you're a little thinner." He rummaged in the closet. "Here try these." He handed Danny a pair of khaki slacks. "I've gained a few pounds since I wore them."

Danny put them on and moved them from side to side with ease. "A little on the loose side, but I guess that's better than too tight."

Connor grinned and winked. "Oh, I don't know. I wouldn't mind if they were a little tighter." He threw a brown polo shirt at Danny. It was something that would look good with his eyes. He suddenly wanted to play dress-up with Danny and find just the right look for him, but they didn't have time. He wondered when they were going to have time to go shopping so he could make some adjustments in the way Danny dressed. Some tighter jeans would be nice, even though Danny said he didn't like tight clothing, Connor felt sure he'd be able to talk him into it, given enough time.

They strolled into Ruby's Café just about an hour before the posted closing time of ten o'clock. The place was an old-fashioned greasy spoon, and Connor felt a little overdressed, but he didn't think it really mattered. They were just off the square and the place probably saw a lot of tourist traffic. He'd never eaten there, but he'd checked with Lisa, who said a lot of the force frequented there, so he felt confident enough they'd have good food that he hadn't bothered stopping for something else on the way over.

Connor told the hostess, "A friend of mine was in here about a month ago. He told me if I wanted exceptionally good service to ask for Mavis. Is she here tonight?"

"Yes, she is." The hostess consulted a chart on the table. "I can seat you in her section. Right this way." She seated them at a four-top table next to a window.

Connor slipped a twenty dollar bill into the girl's hand as she handed him a menu.

She gawked at the bill. "That isn't necessary, Sir." She quickly slipped the cash into her pocket.

"I know." He winked at her. He knew how a little extra cash could help grease the wheels of information, and if nothing else would ensure they got top-notch service while they were in the restaurant.

A couple of minutes later, a slender, blonde woman came to the table. "Peggy said you asked for me." She cocked her head slightly as if studying them. "Do I know you?"

"No, but a friend said you were a good waitress, and I trust his word," Connor answered. He kept his voice soft and conversational, nothing to make her possibly jumpy about them being there. It wasn't hard to keep people he needed to talk to comfortable, and a comfortable person was more likely to give him the information he needed.

She pulled out a small pad and a pen. "What can I get you to drink?"

"I'll have a glass of Chardonnay," Connor said, then glanced across the table. "How about you, Danny?"

Danny nodded slightly. "That sounds good to me."

"I'll be right back." Mavis made a quick note on the pad, then tucked it in her apron.

"You know, that's the first time you've called me by name," Danny said with a cute sexy smile. "It sounded nice." He took a drink from his glass of water.

"I thought it might be a little more discrete than Dawg," Connor said. It had felt nice too. Maybe he'd try and remember that, and when he wanted Danny to smile at him with that soft sexy look, he'd use his given name. "Just don't get too used to it. It probably won't happen often."

Mavis came back with the wine. "Are you ready to order?"

"I'll have a T-bone, medium rare, baked potato with lots of sour cream and butter, and a Caesar salad," Connor said, then folded up the menu and handed it to Mavis.

"I'll have the same, except make my steak rare," Danny said as he handed his menu to her.

"Got it," Mavis said and left, once again tucking her pad in her front apron pocket.

Connor took a sip of wine. It was good, but not great. "So the wolf likes blood in his steak."

Danny shrugged. "I'm surprised you don't."

"I like it a little red, but not bleeding." Connor just realized that most of their meals before that had just been burgers and salads. Thinking of all the salads Danny ate, he was even more surprised with Danny eating rare steaks. "I guess we still have a lot to learn about each other."

"Yeah," Danny sipped his own wine. "That's the point of relationships, isn't it? Learning about each other."

"I guess so," Connor agreed. He'd never really gotten close to anyone before. Sure there were friends like Lisa, with whom he wasn't intimately close. There was something great about knowing Danny was as interested in him as he was in Danny. It was also scary. The idea of letting someone close enough to him that his visions wouldn't be enough to protect his heart, was terrifying. But he was tired of being alone. The recent times with Danny was opening something inside him, and he wanted to feel more of that.

"So what's your favorite color?" Danny asked after taking another sip of his wine.

"Color?" Connor blinked at him. He hadn't expected a question like that.

"Sure." Danny chuckled and touched Connor's hand. "If we're going to get to know each other, we might as well start at more than just how we eat our steak."

"Oh, yeah." He felt really stupid, but grinned. "Blue."

"Red's mine." Danny said.

"I'll remember that when we go clothes shopping." Connor laughed.

Danny's eyes grew wide. "Clothes shopping?"

His look made Connor laugh louder. "Have you seen how you dress when not in uniform? We've got to work on that."

"Yeah, right." Danny drank half of his wine. "There's things we're going to work on, but my wardrobe is not part of it. Maybe we can work on your taste in wines, or should I say get you to drink more beer."

Connor shook his head. "Nope. Cats have more class than beer."

"Really?" Danny finished off the rest of his wine. "We'll see about that."

Mavis came over with their steaks. "Is there anything else I can get you right now?"

"Not right now." Connor picked up his fork and knife as he took a long breath to drink in the aroma of the steak.

"Looks good," Danny added. He glanced at Connor. "You don't do that with burgers."

As he cut into the steak, Connor laughed. "Burgers don't normally smell as good as steaks. I thought wolves had a better sense of smell than that."

Danny wrinkled his nose. "Of course we do, but you're acting like some kind of wine connoisseur or something. I mean, it's just a steak."

Connor chewed his meat slowly, savoring the warm juices that filled his mouth. Then he sighed. "Yeah, this one is just a steak. One of these days I'll have to take you to a really good steakhouse so you can have the experience of eating as close to perfect steak as you can get. There's a place down in Albuquerque that fits that bill." He closed his eyes, remembering the last meal he'd had there. "Great as far as human food goes."

Danny frowned as he started in on his salad. "Don't tell me you really enjoy the food we bring down in our animal forms."

"Sure." Connor cut another piece of steak. "It helps my cat feel better about things. Doesn't your inner wolf sometimes get pushy for fresh deer?" He'd met a few shifters over the years who had major problems between what their animal side ate and how their human side wanted to.

"That's as a wolf," Danny said. "That's different. I don't have to enjoy my human food the same way I do as a wolf." He gestured at his salad with his fork. "My wolf would hate this. Sometimes I think if it wasn't for being a wolf, I wouldn't eat much meat at all."

"But it soothes the soul." Connor gave him a knowing smile, although he was in a much better synchronicity with his mountain lion than it sounded like Danny was with his wolf. He wondered if that might be why Danny was able to be separated from his pack like he was. If he and his wolf didn't see things eye to eye, it would explain a lot.

"Sometimes." Danny agreed.

They made small talk as they finished off their dinner. Connor suddenly felt like Danny was trying to shut down, at least a little bit, on the information he was letting out on himself. He worried that maybe he was getting a bit pushy on things, and wondered if Danny was going to need time to think about the turn their relationship had taken.

The restaurant slowly emptied until there was only one other table occupied.

Mavis approached. "Did you boys save room for dessert?" She looked tired and ready to go home.

"Not tonight, Mavis," Connor said. "But we would like to talk to you when you get off."

She shook her head. "Hey, this isn't that kind of place." She put their check down on the table with a little bit of force, enough to try and get her point across.

"Nothing like that," Connor assured her. He'd been ready for her reaction. People often jumped to the wrong conclusion when approached causally like they'd just done. "It's about Lacey Simmons."

Mavis quickly sat in an empty chair between them. "Have they found her? Is she okay?" Her tone was suddenly inquisitive and at the same time apprehensive.

"I'm afraid not," Danny said. "Someone murdered her."

Mavis broke down in tears. She pulled her apron up and hid her face as sobs wracked her body.

A big man hurried over. "What's going on here? What happened?" He put his hand on Mavis' shaking shoulders and glared protectively at Connor and Danny.

"You the manager?" Connor asked. He was dressed too nice to be the dishwasher or the cook, but he didn't want to assume anything before he let out too much information.

"Actually, I'm the owner." His bulldog-like expression didn't change. "My name's Jeff. What did you do?"

"I'm afraid we have some bad news about one of your employees." Connor kept his voice low and even. "Lacey Simmons was murdered. My friend and I are investigating."

The manager collapsed in the other empty chair, placed his elbows on the table, and dropped his head into his hands. He didn't break down on the level Mavis had, but it was obvious the news had come as a major shock, and he had cared about his employee.

The couple at the other occupied table cast several wary glances their direction, then rose and left in a controlled hurry.

As her sobs lessened, Connor handed Mavis a napkin from a nearby table so she didn't have to keep using her apron. "Can you tell us anything about Lacey? Her mother said the two of you often stopped after work for a beer."

"We stop by O'Malley's sometimes. We'll have a couple of beers and play a game or two of pool." She paused as if she realized she was still speaking of Lacey in the present tense. Wiping her eyes smeared her eyeshadow and mascara. "It helped us relax and get to sleep easier when we got home. In fact, that was the last place I saw her. We came out of O'Malley's the night she disappeared and got in our cars to go home. She didn't show for work the next night. Her mother called and said she was missing. I never dreamed…" Her face wrinkled in grief, and tears gleamed in her eyes again.

"Was there anyone she was interested in?" Connor pressed. "Any man in her life?"

Mavis blew her nose on the napkin. "There was Robert. At least he seemed interested in her. I don't think she returned his interest. In fact, she laughed about it with me."

"Who's Robert?" Danny asked before Connor could.

"Robert Weeks, he was a cook here for a couple of months," Jeff said. "He just quit yesterday."

"So he still came to work after Lacey disappeared?" Connor asked.

"Yes, but only for a couple of days," Jeff said.

"Could we see his employee files?" Connor hoped they might have a lead. He didn't believe in coincidence, particularly with something like murder. "I'd also like to talk to anyone who worked with him, especially those in the kitchen."

"The files are at my house," Jeff replied. "I keep all that stuff off site."

"Why don't you keep it here?" Danny asked. "Looks like you'd want it handy."

"I keep phone numbers and addresses here, but the main files are at home in a locked safe. I don't have that much locked storage space in the office here. Wouldn't want nosy eyes seeing stuff they shouldn't. Plus it keeps all the grease off everything important."

The way he threw in the last part, Connor wondered exactly how clean the back of the restaurant was.

"Do you know what kind of car he drove?" Danny asked as he pulled out a small notebook and started taking notes.

Mavis spoke up, "It was a black Ford Escort."

"Do the two of you think you could describe Robert to a police artist," Connor asked.

They both nodded.

"Can you go down to the police station tonight?" Connor pushed, then by the tired looks they gave him, realized he was asking a lot. But he didn't want any other kids to have to go through what Martin was going through. Children shouldn't lose their parents to serial killers.

"It's rather late," Mavis objected, with a heavy sigh. She looked a lot more tired than when she sat down with them. "I've been on my feet for the last four hours. Can it wait until tomorrow?"

"I guess," Connor said. "The artist is probably not on duty at this time of the night anyway. Since one quit last month, we only have one artist. She usually works the day shift. I hate to call her in at night. I'll tell Officer Lisa Collins to expect you in the morning."

"And please bring the files with you," Danny added. "And if you happen to have a staff photo or even a selfie someone took of Robert that would be great."

"Anything we can do to help catch Lacey's killer," Jeff said, then his eyes lit up. "Let me call Mike out here. He worked most of the same hours Robert did."

He glanced around the place for a second, then called out. "Mike, could you come out here?"

A short, dumpy man in his mid-fifties in a greasy apron waddled out from the kitchen, wiping his hands on a well-used dishtowel he tucked into the apron ties.

"Mike, have a seat." Jeff waved for him to pull a chair over from the table next to theirs. "These men would like to ask you some questions about Robert."

Mike looked from Danny to Connor and fear sharpened his eyes as his heart raced loud enough Connor could hear it pounding as the stink of sweat overrode the odor of grease that clung to the cook. "You cops? I don't know anything."

"You aren't in trouble, Mike." Connor held up a hand to quiet him and hopefully still his fears. Another thing he was used to people doing was jumping to conclusions; sometimes even people who weren't guilty of anything acted guilty when they were scared. "We just want to know what kind of person Robert seemed to be to you. Was he a quiet person? Did he appear to have a temper?"

Danny broke in, "Did he like the ladies? Did he hang out after hours with other employees?"

His questions were good enough, Connor didn't even glare at him for interrupting. He was used to Lisa or Kennedy doing the same thing when they were working a case. There were other officers who didn't like him taking the lead in questioning people. They said he wasn't a cop, just a consultant. Kennedy liked him, and gave him a lot more leeway than some of the other police chiefs he'd worked with over the years.

"Well," Mike looked thoughtful for a moment, "he was always making remarks about women. You know, 'She's hot.' 'She's dressed like a hooker.' 'She's asking for it.' That sort of thing. He was pretty much a loner. After work, he'd get in his car and take off. We invited him for a beer a couple of times, but he never went with us. None of us even knew where he lived or exchanged phone numbers with him."

"Anything you can think of that would help identify him?" Danny asked as he made notes on his pad.

"He's Hispanic descent and speaks with a bit of an accent," Mike continued. "Not real strong. When he gets mad, he lapses into Spanish. I know enough Spanish to know it's mostly profanity. Especially anti-woman. Also when he got mad, he was really strong, but he looked like he might've worked out in the past. I wouldn't be surprised if he'd been in prison."

"No." Jeff shook his head. "I run background checks on everyone I hire. Robert hadn't been in prison."

Mike frowned. "I've known people who were in prison, Jeff. They get a wary look. Robert had that, especially when he got mad."

Connor knew the look Mike was talking about it. He'd seen it in people too. But if it hadn't shown up in a background check, there might be a reason for it. People who'd been abused as children often had that same look. More than a few serial killers had troubled pasts.

"You've been very helpful." Connor stood and walked toward the kitchen, then decided he should ask permission before digging around too much without a warrant and involving Kennedy. He knew Kennedy wouldn't be able to get a warrant without more evidence than they had. What he really wanted was to see if he could pick up anything that would lead them to Robert, or cement him as their best possible suspect. "Jeff, may I see the kitchen?"

Jeff looked surprised, but stood and walked past Connor. "I suppose. Don't know what you'll find." He led Connor to the back of the café.

"Do the employees have lockers?" Connor asked as he looked around. From the smell of grease and Mike's appearance, the place was a lot cleaner than he expected it to be. "Someplace where they put personal stuff while they're working?"

"Not really," Jeff said. "There are some shelves over here where the women put their purses, etc."

"They don't worry about them?" He walked around touching counters and shelves. Everything was too clean for him to pick up much. Water and cleaning detergents were really good at wiping off psychic residue as well as germs.

"We've never had any problem with theft, if that's what you mean," Jeff answered. "I'm usually a good judge of character." He shook his head and sighed. "If Robert is the one who killed Lacey, I really screwed up this time."

Even though he hadn't picked up anything concrete, Connor's gut was telling him they were on the right track. "I have a feeling Robert is a good actor. He's used to fooling people. I also wouldn't worry about the background check. He could've been using an alias. It's very easy these days to steal someone's identity. It can be weeks or sometimes even months before the victim knows about it and reports it."

Connor and Jeff went back to the dining room. "We'll look for you and Mavis at the station tomorrow. Try to get a good night's sleep and let us worry about Robert."

The others were standing around. Mavis looked more together, though still tired. Mike was less scared, but continued to be nervous. Danny appeared bored, but Connor only recognized the look after spending a month around him and getting to know his moods.

Connor picked up the ticket from the table. "So do we pay at the table or the cash register?"

Jeff shook his head. "Unless you're going to think we're trying to bribe the cops, call it on the house. Find Lacey's killer. I hope it wasn't Robert, but if it was, he deserves to be locked up."

"Thanks." Connor shook his hand. "I appreciate it." He left a twenty dollar bill on the table as a tip for Maris and nodded to Danny to head back to the Bronco.

In the truck, Danny asked, "Did you feel anything back there?"

"I got a sense of anger, but I'm not sure it came from Robert. Without knowing who touched what, it's hard to tell." He closed his eyes, wishing he could get a concrete feel for something. "But I think we're on the right trail. Sometimes even without a firm lead or vision, my gut is right about what's happening around me. Right now it says we need to look for Robert Weeks, if that's his real name. If he's not the killer, he might lead us to them."

"You know, most investigations don't go this smoothly," Danny said as he pulled the Bronco out onto the street. It wasn't nearly as busy as it had been a little while earlier.

"I know." Connor kept his eyes closed. It helped him replay what they'd just learned. "But that's one of the advantages of being psychic. I have an edge over regular police detective work. But a lot of time it still isn't enough. Sometimes the bad guys stay one step ahead of me, and that's maddening."

"Yeah, I bet." Danny chuckled as he turned toward Connor's house. "I've noticed you're used to your extra senses always being right."

Connor opened his eyes and stared at Danny. "They tend to be, but sometimes they can be fooled either by what I want things to be, or by the future changing."

Danny touched Connor's leg, sending chills through him. "Is that why you were so nervous this afternoon? You really wanted me and you weren't sure if it was your desire or your visions?"

Connor laced his fingers between Danny's. "Yes." He hated admitting that, but felt like he had to. Honesty was important in a relationship and he wanted everything with Danny to be honest and open. He was fairly sure Danny was

going to be a great help with his work as his visions dragged
him around the country saving as many people as he could.

Chapter Eleven

The warm night air hit Danny as he got out of the Bronco and followed Connor into the house. It was pleasant enough he was tempted to suggest they go into the backyard and relax for a while.

"Do you want a drink before bed?" Connor asked as he strolled into the kitchen.

That hadn't been the kind of relaxing he'd had in mind, but figured he could change his idea a little bit. "Not really." Danny came up behind Connor, wrapped his arms around him, and kissed the back of his neck. Connor felt so good in his arms. He could hold him forever. "I'm ready to go to bed. Aren't you?"

Connor twisted in Danny's arms and returned the kiss. "Ready for more of what we had this afternoon?"

"Uh-uh." Danny growled deep in his throat and gently nipped at Connor's ear.

"I have something better in mind." Connor buried his face in Danny's neck and licked. The motion sent shivers through Danny. His body quickened in anticipation. Connor was so hot and could get him going so easily. It was good not having to fight his urges anymore. Even if his wolf still wasn't sure about being with a cat, it felt right.

"Better than this afternoon?" Danny threw his head back and closed his eyes. The afternoon had been incredible and he wondered how they were going to top it.

"Uh-uh." Connor kissed Danny again. "Come on. Leave it to me." Taking his hand, Connor led him to the bathroom, and turned on the bathtub taps.

Steaming water poured into the four-foot square tub. It filled faster than Danny would've expected, but then he'd never had a bathtub like it. Since it was a lot bigger than the ones he'd known, he expected it to take a while to fill.

Connor took a bottle from a shelf and poured a liquid into the water. Bubbles created a frothy foam, and a scent of Egyptian musk filled the air.

"I thought cats didn't like water. And bubbles?" He reached down and ran his fingers through the bubbles. "Egyptian musk. Are you trying to suggest I need to worship you?"

"Maybe." Connor laughed. "This cat isn't like any cat you've ever known." Connor picked up a lighter and lit several candles on a ledge over the tub and on the vanity. When Connor turned off the lights, the effect cast tiny rainbows in the bubbles. It made Danny smile. He'd never had anyone do something so romantic for him.

Connor slipped up next to Danny, and pulled the polo shirt over his head. When he rubbed his cheek against Danny's, the light stubble left tingles in its wake, but that only caused Danny to become more excited. He wanted Connor so badly.

With trembling fingers, Danny unbuttoned Connor's shirt and buried his nose in the hair on Connor's chest. He smelled sweaty, and excited. It brought the scent of mountain lion more to the forefront than ever before. This time it didn't turn Danny off, it excited him. This was his cat. He'd already claimed him once and was ready to do it again.

Connor pulled back and slipped off his pants, underwear and socks. The candlelight dancing off the hair on his chest created a soft halo when he moved just right. He turned off the water and flipped a switch on the wall. Jets in the sides and bottom of the tub started and stirred up more bubbles. He stepped into the tub and held his hand out to Danny.

Danny took off his pants, underwear, shoes, and socks faster than he had since he was a teenager and had been fooling around with one of the boys at school. Then he stepped into the tub so he was facing Connor.

Connor pulled him close and gave him a long passionate kiss. "Sit down."

Danny did as he was told; somehow it felt good following Connor's lead in things. He didn't like being dominant in anything besides his police work. Connor turned his back to him and sat between his legs. He leaned back against Danny's chest and began to hum.

Danny put his arms around Connor and pulled him close. "What's that noise?" He rested his head against the side of Connor's he couldn't deny that despite his arousal, he was starting to relax. After a long day of delivering bad news, it felt good.

"It's called purring. It's sorta automatic. I normally can't help it."

They sat in the tub and relaxed for close to an hour. Danny couldn't remember the last time he'd taken an hour-long bath, let alone just held a man for that long, but with Connor it was perfect. He couldn't ask for a better ending to his day.

When he held up his hand and looked at his wrinkled fingers, he sighed. "I think the water's getting cold, and my fingers look like prunes. And if I don't get out of here soon, I'm going to fall asleep."

With a slight nod, Connor brought Danny's other hand up to his lips and kissed it. "Me too." He sighed contentedly. "You know, I don't think I've ever had a vision when I've been in water. Maybe that's why I love it so much. Well, that and I spent a lot of time with Mom swimming."

"So your quiet places have always been in and around water," Danny stretched.

Connor pulled the plug and stood. "Yeah, they have been."

He offered Danny a hand up. Danny stood easily, then caught Connor in a big hug. Their wet bodies were slightly cool but warmed as their embrace and kisses lingered.

"Okay. We need to get dry." Connor stepped away from Danny and pulled two towels from a rod that hung several feet over the faucet. He handed one to Danny, and climbed out of the tub.

After watching his slick sexy body move, Danny followed. "I guess the cat can't handle being wet for too long."

Connor laughed. "Don't make me pop you with this towel again."

Danny stepped close enough that it wouldn't be effective. "I can think of something else you can do with that towel."

"I can too." Connor kissed him again, then began rubbing the towel across his chest. "You do have a nice body, Dawg."

"You do too, Cat." Danny returned the action, enjoying the way Connor's body felt under the towel and his fingers.

Once they were lounging in the bed, Danny nuzzled Connor's ear. "Remember what I said I liked at the café tonight?"

"What?" Connor arched his back and moved closer into Danny. His warmth felt good against Danny's bare skin.

"When you called me Danny. I like the way you said my name." It took the edge off their teasing. Although he enjoyed the way they played with each other, knowing it could stop when they needed to, made him happy. It told him whatever it was that was developing between them was serious, or could become so very quickly.

"I'll try when we're alone." Connor paused and kissed him. "But like I said, don't get used to it. In front of Sheriff Callaway and Kennedy, you'll still be Dawg."

Danny returned the kiss and ran his fingers across Connor's chest, enjoying the play of the firm hairy muscles under his fingers. "I think I can live with that . . ., Connor."

Connor relaxed and started purring.

"There you go making that noise again." He pushed away from Connor, but chuckled.

A deep, sexy laugh came out of Connor. "Better get used to it if you're going to stay around."

"I'll try." Danny snuggled his face into Connor's neck. He tried to stifle a yawn, but failed. Between the long bath, and just being with Connor, he was more relaxed than he'd been in a very long time.

Connor was about to fall asleep with Danny on his shoulder when there was a crash in his back yard.

Danny rolled over, also instantly full awake. "What was that?"

"No idea." Connor threw off the sheet he'd pulled over them. He rushed to the French doors that opened onto his patio.

The smell of bear hit him as he stepped out onto the cool tile.

Wolf hair brushed against his bare leg reminding him how quickly Danny could shift. *"I smell bear."*

"Me to, but we get bears in the area from time to time."

Something crashed on the other side of the short adobe wall that fenced in his yard. Connor's heart pounded. He remembered his grandmother's mistrust of coincidences. He'd never had a problem with animals of any sort in Santa Fe. But that might have been because he made sure to mark his yard on a regular basis. Most critters didn't dare invade a mountain lion's territory.

Danny shot across the yard, a shadowy blur in the fading moon light. *"Be right back."*

"Dawg, be careful." Connor thought about shifting and going with him, but he stayed human. He closed the door. Something was nagging at him. There was a sense of curiosity in the yard. Someone had been watching them, but it hadn't been a bear. There was a human level of interest. There was also a touch of hate and anger there. It was jumbled.

He walked over to the wall and ran his hand along it. The smell of bear was heavier there. It was a large male black bear. It had leaned against the wall. There weren't any marks or hair caught on the rough surface, but the feelings were there. Connor slowly walked along the wall, letting his fingers ride the sharp points in the cold surface. There were spots where the feelings were stronger than others. He went along the whole distance of the wall, then went back to where he'd started.

There was a sense of excitement. Someone had been standing there for a while, or leaning there, it wasn't clear. The thoughts and feelings were an incoherent mess. He couldn't get a clear image; it was like he was trying to see through eyes that weren't working right, or trying to touch a mind that was deeply disturbed.

Connor shivered when he thought that something…someone had managed to follow him home. And worse, it was at a time when his guard was down. He'd been so wrapped up in Danny, someone had managed to get within feet of them and neither of them had noticed until whoever it had been had made a misstep and knocked something over.

Glancing around the back yard, he spotted a large pot that had held a huge decorative cactus. It was on its side, the dirt half covering the cactus and the shattered terracotta pot. Connor frowned. He'd enjoyed that cactus. It was such a quiet and sensible soul. He'd call the gardener before he left the house in the morning and have the man come by and fix it.

When he touched the broken pot, there was a touch of fear. Whoever had knocked it over had been worried about being spotted. Then the impressions were cluttered. It was like another personality was taking over and urging the first to run.

Connor wrapped his arms around his chest and wished Danny was there to hug him. If he was right, that might explain why he was having such a hard time getting feelings on their killer. If he was a split personality, he'd be difficult to get a good reading on. He'd never dealt with a multiple personality before, but knew some serial killers had them. It made killing easier, particularly when only one side of the person was doing the killing.

He stopped cold at the realization that Danny was out there chasing someone potentially deadly. Even as a trained police officer, Danny didn't have anything beyond his teeth and claws. His gun was in Connor's bedroom in a pile of discarded clothes. And he hadn't heard anything from him since he jumped the wall and took off running.

"Danny, are you okay?" Connor reached through their growing mental link. It was stronger than it had been. Suddenly more intimate than any mental contact he'd ever had.

"Fine, Connor. Just trying to find the trail again. Lost it about two blocks down." He sounded very put out by the situation. *"Smells like he might've gotten into a car, but how does a bear get into a car?"*

"How does a wolf get into a car?" Connor sat on the wall and tried to make sure nothing was sneaking up on them.

"If he's a shifter." Through the link, Connor watched as Danny turned and started trotting back to the yard.

"Maybe, or if he's working with someone." Connor shook his head and tried to sort out his thoughts. Shifters normally had a particular scent that was a mix between their animal self and their human side. But this didn't smell like that, it smelled like a bear. But the scattered thoughts and feelings he'd picked up were human.

"Do you think it's Robert Weeks?" Danny jumped the wall and rubbed against Connor's leg.

Connor pursed his lips and shook his head. "I don't really know. Nobody's said anything about thinking he's a shifter. I haven't picked up on our killer being a shifter, but whatever was in the yard tonight wasn't fully human or fully bear, and I think it might be a multiple personality."

Danny shifted and stood there frowning in the moonlight. "Dude, shifters don't let multiple personalities live. They're too dangerous."

"Yeah." Connor hugged him tight. "And he was watching us for a couple of hours tonight. This isn't good."

"Do you think we're safe here?" Danny kissed him quickly.

The kiss warmed Connor and made him smile. "I don't think he'll be brave enough to come back tonight." He hoped his gut was right. Danger had been so close to them, and he hadn't gotten a feeling for it. That worried him, but he didn't want Danny to worry too much about it. "Besides if he tries anything again, I'll know. I'm a cat, I'm a really light sleeper, and now that I know he's been here, he won't get in again while I'm home."

"And I'll sleep with my gun close." Danny took his hand and started for the house. "Now, we'd better get in before any of your neighbors spot us and report us for being naked in your back yard. We're not as isolated as you were at the cabin."

"Probably a good idea." Connor squeezed Danny's hand. As they went through the door, he glanced over his shoulder at the wall and the shattered pot. Someone had been watching them. If it wasn't Robert Weeks, it was someone else who was most likely their killer. He was definitely going to sleep with one eye open.

Chapter Twelve

"Are you sure we don't want to stop for lunch on our way in?" Danny asked as they pulled into Connor's parking spot at the station.

Connor chuckled as he undid his seat belt. "Dawg, I just fed you breakfast in bed not two hours ago. Don't tell me you're hungry again."

Danny shrugged. He wasn't about to claim to be hungry, but it was lunch time and they'd had a busy day and a long night, even if they had slept in. He couldn't remember the last time he'd slept as well as he did curled up next to Connor. And he'd never had anyone make him breakfast in bed.

"Tell you what, if Lisa and Kennedy haven't had lunch yet, we'll get them to go with us and make it look like we're all having a work lunch." Connor opened the door and got out before Danny could reply.

"Sounds like a plan, Cat." Danny said as he stepped onto the curb next to Connor. He was trying hard to not let on that anything had changed between them. They'd talked about it as they fell asleep and they wanted to keep their friends and coworkers in the dark about their budding relationship. The case came first, and once it was solved they could spread their joy. They also weren't going to mention the bear they'd smelled around Connor's place the night before. They'd both agreed it may be nothing, and if it was, Connor wasn't getting a good read on it. They needed a lot more to go on before saying anything.

Danny tugged at the seat of the new jeans he had on. Connor had insisted he get a size smaller than usual, and he wasn't comfortable. They were a lot tighter than he was used to and he felt slightly on display

"Will you stop that?" Connor swatted his arm. "You look great."

"I may look great, but I'm not sure I can sit down in these." He didn't like the way they felt like a second skin. He was fairly sure everyone could see the seams of his underwear.

"Dawg, you just got out of the car where you were sitting fine."

"I know." He sighed and followed Connor into the building.

The squad room was busy as they walked in. There was a fair number more people than the previous day. It was almost like everyone had been out on calls except Officer Collins and Kennedy and things had become a lot slower.

Connor sat in a chair next to Officer Collin's desk. "Hi, lovely lady. Did you miss me?"

"Where have you guys been?" Officer Collins asked glancing between them. "Kennedy's looking for you. He tried your cell, but you didn't answer."

He pulled his phone from his pocket. "Damn. I forgot to charge it up last night. The battery's dead." A universal charger lay on her desk, and Connor plugged his phone in.

"I had to take the Dawg shopping," he said. "That uniform was looking kind of grungy, and my pants are too big for him." He walked over to the coffee pot and poured a cup. "Besides, uniforms sometimes make people not want to talk."

Danny tried to decide what he should do with himself, and opted to sit on the corner of Officer Collin's desk with one foot on the floor and hope she didn't mind. It was strange feeling slightly out of place in a police station, but he did. This wasn't the small office he was used to, and being in civvies just made it worse. He was an outsider. He wondered if that was how Connor had felt the first few times he came into the station in Jemez Springs.

"I know it takes a big guy to fill your shoes, but I didn't think your butt was that big," Officer Collins said. "I must say, Lupan, I like the look. The color of the shirt goes well with your coloring."

Danny ducked his head. "Thanks."

Connor glared as he came back with two cups of coffee. He handed one to Danny without saying a word. "Did Alma, Jeff, and Mavis come in?"

"Jeff and Mavis did. I haven't seen Alma," Officer Collins pointed to the closed door across the room where the sketch artist normally worked. "Jeff's with the artist now. He mentioned something about not being able to find any pictures of Robert Weeks. I think Mavis went to the ladies' room."

"Did you find anything in the employee file?" Connor took the chair he'd vacated to get coffee.

"I found out there's no such person as Robert Weeks." Officer Collins tapped the file in front of her. "The Social Security number he gave belonged to someone named Robert Weeks, but he died two years ago. He was ninety-two."

"Doesn't sound like our guy then," Connor said. "Lisa, if you could call all the car rental places and see if any of them rent black Escorts. When the artist is finished with the sketches, take one around to the rental agencies."

"Why rentals?" Danny asked. It didn't make a whole lot of sense. Extended rentals were expensive.

"Unless he's towing that Escort behind the camper, he can't drive two vehicles at once. He'd have to leave it somewhere or it isn't his." Connor took a sip of his coffee.

"Good thinking." Danny said, wanting to make Connor feel like he was accomplishing something, but realizing that a lot of people owned multiple vehicles, even if it didn't make sense to Connor.

"I thought so," Connor said.

"I've asked DMV to check on any black Escorts registered in the state," Officer Collins said. "And I also checked the address he gave." She flipped the file open. "It's an empty lot over on the east side of town."

Kennedy came to the door of his office. "In here, McGriffin, Lupan."

Connor walked in and sat facing Kennedy's desk.

Danny pulled up another chair and settled beside him. He wished he had on his uniform, it would make him feel more official sitting there facing the Santa Fe Police Chief.

"I sent out an inquiry to departments in other cities and asked if they'd had any similar cases," Kennedy said. "I got some answers." He handed a sheet of paper to Connor.

"Two reports from Colorado Springs and one from Pueblo. Hikers found a young woman's body in Chipita Park about a year ago, and another one a couple of months later in Cameron Cone Campground. Pueblo found theirs in November in Lake Pueblo State Park. Two more showed up around Taos in January and March."

"Did they have any descriptions?" Connor asked as he handed the paper to Danny.

Danny scanned the paper, but nothing hopped out at him.

"Not much," Kennedy replied. "The first body had been partially eaten by wildlife. They had a hard time identifying her. All five were hookers, and all five were Hispanic."

"So, Lacey Simmons doesn't fit the profile. She wasn't a hooker," Danny said. He hoped there was a pattern. Serial killers normally worked off a pattern of some kind. Either Lacey was someone special, or they were dealing with two different killers. A copycat would be bad, but copycats didn't normally show up until after the case had been revealed to the news and that hadn't happened.

"And she wasn't Hispanic," Connor added.

"She may have turned him on and then spurned him. That would make him angry," Kennedy said.

Connor nodded. "That fits with what Mavis said about her laughing because he was interested in her." He leaned close to Danny and restudied the list of victims over his shoulder. "It looks like he may be heading south and just stopping along the way occasionally. He may have started further north than Colorado Springs."

Connor closed his eyes and placed his fingertips together against his lips.

"What are . . ." Danny started, then realized Connor must be trying to get some kind of reading from the list. He was still getting used to Connor's tells. The few times he'd been exposed to psychics in the past they'd all had different tells when they were trying to use their powers.

"Sh-h-h," Kennedy said.

Minutes later, Connor opened his eyes. "Send the sketches to the State Penitentiary at Cañon City."

"Will do," Kennedy said as he began typing on the keyboard of the laptop on the desk in front of him.

"Why Cañon City?" Danny asked. He wasn't real up on Colorado and couldn't remember where Cañon City fit into the landscape.

"Because that's where the state pen is, and it's also where our first victim was from," Connor said a bit impatiently as he finished off his coffee and crumpled the cup a little more forcefully than he needed to.

"Okay," Danny said. "Don't growl at me. I was just asking." He focused on Kennedy, temporarily giving Connor the cold shoulder. If they were going to make a relationship work, Connor was going to need to relax a bit more and not be snappy with him. "Is he always so touchy?"

"Pretty much so," Kennedy replied. "Especially when you question something he sees."

Connor stood and stomped out to the squad room. Danny glanced at Chief Kennedy who stood and waved Danny out of the room, indicating they should follow Connor. The way he did it said he was used to following Connor around. Danny wasn't sure how hard it was going to be to get used to Connor suddenly acting like a brat. They were going to need to talk about that. He must be good about providing Kennedy information, if a hardened police chief like he appeared to be to put up with it. Most consultants he'd ever heard about tended to follow the procedures the police department followed and didn't just try and take control of everything unless they were being dramatized on TV.

Mavis sat in a chair next to Officer Collin's desk. She looked just as tired as she had the previous night. Bags under her eyes indicated a sleepless night.

"Hello, Mavis. Thanks for coming in," Connor said. "Lisa, I need a map of the U.S. Put it on an easel, please." After picking up the file from Lisa's desk, he walked over to a large white board and made a list. As he wrote the information, he taped pictures of the victims beside it.

Danny walked up next to him and offered to hold the file. "Here. It'll be easier than trying to juggle all that."

Lisa appeared with a roll of scotch tape. "You'll get used to this. It's like he's still partially in the vision. It's the only time he gets like this."

Danny just nodded and watched as Connor laid out their timeline and victims.

Chipita Park – July 30 – date of death a week earlier - hooker from Colorado Springs.

Cameron Cone Campground – September 17 – date of death, September 16 – hooker from Colorado Springs.

Lake Pueblo State Park – November 13 – date of death, November 12 – hooker from Pueblo.

Mavis gasped. "He's a serial killer?"

Connor turned. "Looks like it." He continued with the list.

Cruz Canyon – January 10 – date of death, January 8 – hooker from Taos

Cruz Canyon – March 7 – date of death, March 4 – hooker from Taos

Jemez Springs – May 27 – Consuela Sanchez – date of death, May 27 – hooker from Santa Fe.

Jemez Springs – June 25 – Lacey Simmons – date of death, June 24 – waitress from Santa Fe.

Similarities: Hooker, Hispanic

Exception: Lacey Simmons

Lisa brought in an easel with a map and stood it next to the board.

Connor marked the locations of the bodies. "It looks like he wants the bodies found. He leaves them where hikers or campers will stumble on them."

Danny tapped the spot between March and May. "I wonder if this is when the skeleton we found was killed. It would fit the pattern. There might be others in the empty months that haven't been found."

"Months." Connor hummed and put his finger on his lips. "There does seem to be a pattern here of one a month."

A commotion in the hall caught Danny's attention.

An officer came in holding the arm of a woman. She didn't look or sound happy to be there.

"Let me go!" She jerked her arm out of the officer's hand. "McGriffin knows I'm coming. He told me to see Kennedy."

"It's okay, Jones," Connor said as he turned toward the two. "I thought you were coming yesterday, Alma."

She glared at Officer Jones as she ran her hands down the front of her sleek black dress. "You wanted me to talk to some of the girls. I had to wait until last night."

Connor put the cap on the marker he'd been using. "Did you get anything from them?"

"Yeah," Alma answered. "Louisa said he has a tattoo of an eagle on his back. Huge thing."

Mavis spoke up, "Robert has a tattoo like that. I saw it when he changed shirts one night after he spilled grease on himself."

Alma walked over to the list. "Humph. Six hookers dead, and you don't start looking for him until he kills a waitress?" She frowned as she looked from the board to Connor.

Danny couldn't blame her for being pissed off. Although he hadn't dealt with a lot of hookers in Jemez Springs, from what he knew of the few he'd run across in Albuquerque during his time in the police academy, they were a tight bunch, and quick to call foul when they felt they'd been wronged. He could see her point when she wasn't looking at all the information.

"We started looking for him as soon as he killed Connie," Connor countered. "Lacey was killed after Connie. We didn't know about the others until today. They aren't in our jurisdiction. When you leave here, tell Louisa I'd like to talk to her."

"I can try—" Alma's frown deepened "—but you know Juan won't be happy about her talking to you during working hours."

"Tell her I'll pay for her time and yours." Connor gestured for Kennedy to come over. "It's up to you if the money comes out of department funds or my account."

Kennedy looked at Danny. "If you think Sheriff Callaway will split it with me, I'll pay it. We are working on a case that crosses our jurisdictions."

"Actually, this crosses state lines," Danny pointed to the map Connor had been marking. "Doesn't that mean we should be calling in the Feds?"

"We can let them know after we catch the guy." Captain Kennedy crossed his arms and looked a bit angry. "I've seen the Feds screw up more cases than they solve around here. Unless you've got a problem with my plan."

Danny shook his head. "As long as he doesn't get away, I'm good with it." The Feds were also something he didn't have a lot of experience with, but he'd heard horror stories about dealing with them, and he wasn't about to argue with Kennedy on something like that in his own squad room. "I can agree for Rusty on getting half of the money on this."

"Good." Kennedy looked at Alma. "When you're done with Officer Regulous, stop by and see me, and I'll cut you a voucher."

Alma frowned again. "Cash. Come on Kennedy, you know we only deal in cash."

"The voucher will get you cash at the front desk."

She shook her head. "Cash from your hands."

Kennedy sighed and nodded. "Okay. I'll get you the cash."

Jeff and a uniformed woman came from the door Lisa had pointed out earlier. Jeff's steps were dragging.

"The sketches are pretty close," the woman said.

"We have another person to describe him," Connor said, motioning Alma toward her. "Alma, please go with Officer Regulous and tell her what the man looked like."

"Okay. This better not take long. I need to get to work or Juan will have my ass." Alma fell into step with the officer, and they disappeared back into the door that was promptly closed.

Chief Kennedy said, "Jeff, Mavis, I want to thank you for your help. If you remember anything else about this Robert Weeks, please call Officer Collins, she's handling things for me."

"No matter how unimportant you think it is," Connor added, "call. Even if it's just how he likes his coffee. It could be just the information we need to nail this bastard."

Danny suppressed a chuckle. He'd read more than a few case studies over the years where the smallest detail had helped bust a killer. But it still sounded strange for Connor to be making such a request.

"I know that one," Mavis said. "Hot and black."

"Thanks," Connor said, then made a note on the white board. "Anything else that pops into your head?"

"And he smokes," Jeff added.

Both Jeff and Mavis agreed that was all they had, then claiming they needed to get to the café so they could help with the lunch rush which was probably winding down, they both hurried out of the squad room.

Connor stood in front of the board for a couple of minutes, frowning and tapping his lip with the closed marker. "Lisa, where's Lacey's car? Did they bring it in?"

"It's in the impound lot. Forensics went over it but didn't find anything."

"Come on, Dawg. Let's go." Connor headed for the door.

"Where're we going?" Danny stood and followed. He kicked himself for asking as he realized Connor wanted to check out the woman's car, otherwise he wouldn't have asked about it.

Connor confirmed. "I want to see Lacey's car, and tonight I want to talk to Louisa."

"Officer Collins said they went over the car and didn't find anything." The words were reflexive, and Danny inwardly groaned as soon as they left his lips.

"You have to learn, they aren't *me*." Connor walked to the Bronco. "Wait here a minute. I wish we'd brought my Jeep instead of a squad car."

Connor turned and went back into the squad room.

Danny was trying to figure out what he was doing as he trailed along behind him.

Officer Collins was just sitting down with a fresh cup of coffee when Connor walked up to her desk. "Lisa, can the dawg and I borrow your car? I'd rather not take a marked vehicle where we're going."

"Sure, Connor." She bent over, pulled her purse out of her desk drawer, and threw him a set of keys. "Try not to leave too much man-evidence in it to set Steve off."

"Thanks."

He went back out and went to a non-descript white Toyota Camry. He pointed the key fob at the car and it beeped open.

"Why are we driving this?" Danny asked as he opened the passenger side door. He knew Connor was up to something and really wished he'd let him in on it. If they were going to be partners, he didn't like having to constantly pump him for information.

"For the same reason I told you not to wear your uniform," Connor said as he got into the driver's side. "It'll be less conspicuous where we're going tonight."

They drove a couple of blocks to the police impound lot, parked, and got out of the car.

A guard came out of the building. "Hi, Connor, what's up?"

"Where's the Honda that belonged to Lacey Simmons?"

"Let me get the keys." He stepped back into the building and came back out carrying a tagged key. "Follow me." He led them a couple of rows back to a silver Honda Civic.

"Here you go." He handed the key to Connor. "You know the drill, don't damage the car any further than it already has been and bring me back the key when you're done." He turned and walked away, like he wasn't actually supposed to be leaving Connor alone with the car, but didn't want to be around when Connor did whatever it was he did.

The mixed way the police in the department treated Connor wasn't surprising to Danny. The police had accepted shifters a bit faster than a lot of the world had, but they were still leery of them at times. He had no doubt that a lot of the officers were more than a little disturbed by Connor's psychic abilities and didn't want to be around when he used them. Of course if he went into asshole mode when he was working a case the way he'd been since they'd gotten up that morning, Danny didn't blame them. This was a new side to Connor for him.

Connor unlocked the car, got into the driver's seat, placed his hands on the wheel, and closed his eyes. He sat for a minute, got out, walked to the gas tank door, placed his hands on it, and again closed his eyes.

"What are you doing?" Danny asked although he didn't doubt this was Connor trying to use his psychic powers to get a vision of what had happened.

"Sh-h-h," Connor said. He slowly opened his eyes. "She ran out of gas because our suspect syphoned it out. I don't know if it was while she was at work or while she and Mavis were having their beer." He frowned. "I also can't get a really good read on Robert. There's definitely something odd going on in his brain, and that oddness is blocking me from really seeing what's going on. Normally by now, I've got a motive of some kind. If Lacey had been a hooker, that would make sense, but she wasn't." Pursing his lips, he started back toward the guard shack. "I don't totally understand this, and even if it isn't really hookers, and just Hispanic women, the change there doesn't make sense either."

"And there's always a reason why serial killers kill," Danny added as he walked next to Connor. "They don't usually deviate from their patterns."

"At least not unless it's for a good reason."

"Like maybe Lacey figured out he was killing hookers?" The idea didn't sound right to Danny, but he had to voice it. It was the only thing he could come up with.

"Maybe, but I doubt it." Connor countered. "It doesn't feel right."

At the shack, Connor handed the key back to the guard. Their hands touched. "Thanks for your help."

When they got into Officer Collins's car, Connor sighed and leaned his head on the steering wheel. All the air of superiority he'd been projecting since walking into the Santa Fe Police Department that morning vanished and he looked tired and worn out.

"What's wrong?" Danny putting his hand on Connor's arm.

Connor lifted his head and stared straight ahead. "Like I said yesterday, sometimes I hate my 'gift'."

"Why?" Danny could imagine several reason why being able to perceive things others couldn't would be a royal pain. Connor had made allusions to sometimes hating what he could do, and this seemed like a time to get into it with him.

"Officer Dealy is dying. He has cancer." He blinked rapidly. "He'll be dead before the end of the year."

"Are you sure? Why didn't you say something? Does he know?" There were other things Danny wanted to ask, but he stopped and stared up at the guard shack where Officer Dealy was writing something down on a clip board, most likely recording their visit.

"He knows. He's trying to put on a brave front and has refused treatment. Doesn't want anyone to know, not even his family." He started the engine.

"And you get things like that all the time?"

Connor shrugged. "Yes and no. It depends on how important it is to the person. If they've been thinking about it like he has, it's close to the surface. Or sometimes, if it's going to impact someone soon, I'll see something. Most of the time, it's nothing I can help with. That makes things hard."

Danny squeezed Connor's leg. "I'm sorry you have to endure that."

"Me too." Connor backed the little car out of the parking place.

"Now where?" Danny asked. He hoped they were going to be able to go somewhere Connor could relax for a few minutes, but he doubted that was going to happen. They were on a case, and he was getting the impression, Connor would stay fairly keyed up until it was resolved. He'd said the last case had lasted a while. If he stayed on such a tight string the entire time, that might explain why the Santa Fe police psychologist sent him off into the mountains to relax for a while once the case was done.

"We'll get something to eat and then go see if we can find Louisa." Connor headed down the street and kept his mouth shut on where he was going to take Danny to get something to eat. But Danny was beginning to understand Connor's taste, so he wasn't too worried about that. He was more worried about getting Connor to relax for a little while.

Chapter Thirteen

After an early steak dinner, Connor drove down Taos Road looking for Alma. The meal had helped him ground and center. Food often did that for him, and Danny's easy company didn't hurt either. He was enjoying the way the two of them were meshing so well.

"You know, I didn't realize there were still spots where people risk their lives shaking their asses on corners anymore,' Danny said as they entered a seedier part of town.

"Even with modern technology, there will always be men who don't want their other halves to be able to check their phones and see who they've been calling or what sites they go to when they're looking for a hookup," Conner countered. He hadn't taken the time to tell Danny how much help his questions were being. Even though he liked having quiet when he was in the middle of getting a vision, the way so many people shut up and acted reverently as he did his thing got a little disturbing. Danny wasn't afraid to question him, and although it hit him wrong sometimes, he liked it. It helped make his mind work. He needed to tell Danny that. That and more.

Danny nodded. "Or see what apps they have installed."

"Right." Connor slowed down as they got to the area he wanted to be in.

"There." Danny pointed to a group of women by the corner of a building.

He was right on the money. Connor pulled over, but kept the car running.

Alma came up to Danny's side while he rolled down the window. "What are you doing here?" She sounded a bit nervous, making Connor think her pimp, Juan, hadn't been too happy about her visit to the police station earlier.

"She hasn't come by the station and I need to talk to Louisa," Connor said.

"Wait here." With a heavy sigh, Alma walked over to a woman in a short skirt and high boots. Her long blonde hair was an obvious wig and contrasted with her Hispanic features.

The woman shook her head and made harsh negative gestures. Alma said something else to her. With the traffic noises and the distance, it was too light for Connor to make out. Finally, Louisa nodded and she and Alma walked to the car.

Louisa leaned in Danny's window. "Alma says you'll pay. Let us in the car and drive off. Juan's watching."

"Want me in the back?" Danny asked quietly.

"Yeah, that way I can talk to Louisa easier," Connor said. It made sense to him. What he didn't understand was why Alma hadn't let Louisa know they had already been paid by Kennedy, unless she'd pocketed the money already and not told her coworker about it.

Without another word, Danny got out, and Louisa got into the front seat. Danny ran around to the driver's side and he and Alma got into the back.

Connor drove a few blocks away, making sure to take several turns in case Juan or any of his men decided to follow. He'd dealt with Juan and his girls a couple of times on the last case. He knew how they worked, and if Juan was already nervous about Alma talking with him earlier in the day, he'd probably have someone follow them to keep an eye on things. He realized that was why Louisa scooted close to him and Alma put her arms around Danny and practically sat on his lap.

Like before, he kept the motor running when he parked. Especially after their visitor the previous night, he wasn't going to take any chances of having something unexpected happen and not be able to get away.

"Tell Juan how much Kennedy gave you or not," he told them. "It's up to you."

"It isn't worth lying to him," Alma said as she pulled bills out of her bra and reached across the seat to hand a couple to Louisa. "If he finds out, there'll be hell to pay. He'll give us our percentage of it anyway."

"What can you tell me about the man with the camper?" Connor turned so he could look at Louisa as he talked to her. He hoped he could pick up something, but was about to decide his normal tactics weren't going to work on Robert Weeks, or whatever his name really was.

"He's dark. Not clean. He has a big eagle on his back," she said. "He smelled like smoke, but I didn't see him with a cigarette. When he gets really excited, he smells like a wet animal." She shook her head. "He's nasty, but he pays good."

"What about the camper? Is it a camper on a pickup, or is it like a motor home? Where was it?" Connor took a breath and tried to tell himself to not hit Louisa with so many questions at once. He doubted she'd be able to give him all the information he needed. He should know better than to ask more than one question at a time, but he got excited when he was on a trail and things were starting to heat up.

She pursed her lips and a thoughtful line appeared on her heavily powered forehead. "It kind of looks like the kind on the back of a truck, but it's one unit. It was in a park in the middle of town, over on Cerrillos Road."

"Did you notice anything special about it?" Connor asked. "Like what color was it?" He forced himself to keep it to one question.

"It was white with green accents. I didn't see a name."

"How about a license plate?"

She shook her head. "Sorry, I don't go around noticing things like license plates, makes the johns think I'm with the cops or something."

She'd been a hooker long enough to know when it was safe to see things and when it wasn't. Connor couldn't blame her for missing things someone like a policeman might not. Her focus would be on whether the man who was picking her up looked like he had enough money to pay for her time.

"Let me touch your hand, Louisa," Connor said.

Louisa frowned and glanced over the seat at Alma. "You didn't say anything about him being strange or anything."

Alma rolled her eyes. "Just do it. Trust me."

"Okay." Louisa held out her hand and it shook slightly as Connor took it.

Even though he was used to people being a little afraid of him, he wished that one day they wouldn't be. That was one of the nice things about Danny, he wasn't afraid of what Connor could do.

As his skin came in contact with hers, he opened himself up and let images flood through him. Louisa hadn't lived a quiet easy life. Drugs poured through her. Juan and her tricks often beat her. As much as he wanted to help her, Connor knew there wasn't anything he could do. He forced himself to sort through the visions that bombarded him. There was so much, almost too much. He pushed aside the stuff that wasn't relevant to their case. He had to focus. Then the RV came into focus. He had to slow the images rushing at him down. He'd gone past the important information. It took an effort to replay things slow enough so he could find what he needed, and then it still wasn't much.

The inside of the camper was cluttered. Out of focus images filled the area. None of it would sharpen enough to be clear. A few things solidified, but they were just passing flashes. Dirty clothes littered the floor and furniture. Dirty dishes filled the sink. The sheets on the bed were stained.

There wasn't any solid image of Robert Weeks. Nothing concrete that he could tie to the murders. Feeling like he'd wasted his evening, Connor released her hand. "Can you think of anything else that might help find him?"

Louisa chewed on her lower lips for a second. "He had a computer and printer set up. There were several cameras laying around, and the walls had pictures of naked women on them."

On reflex, Connor gestured to Danny. "Can you hand me the folder with the pictures in it?"

Danny took the manila folder from the seat next to him and handed it to Connor. "Good thing you thought to bring this along."

"Something told me we might need it." He opened the folder and pulled out pictures of the victims. He flipped on the dome light and slowly showed them to Louisa. "Did you see any pictures of these women?"

"Yeah." Louisa pointed to the two Colorado Springs women.

For the first time in days, Connor felt like they were really making progress on the case. He had a connection between Robert and the murdered hookers. He slipped the pictures back into the folder, then handed it back to Danny. "You've been a great help, Louisa. You, too, Alma."

"I just hope you catch the S.O.B.," Alma said.

"We're going to try," Danny assured her. "He's got too much blood on his hands to get away for long."

Connor drove back to where they picked the women up. "If either one of you thinks of anything else, or if you hear something, don't hesitate to let me know."

"Your money's always good," Alma said as they both opened their doors and slipped out into the night.

Not waiting for anything else to happen, Connor pulled away from the curb and drove away. "I think it's time to call it a night, Dawg. Tomorrow we head back to Jemez."

Danny slid over the seat to settle next to Connor. "Do we get another soak in the tub?"

Connor grinned. "I think that can be arranged." A warmth filled him at the thought that Danny enjoyed his tub as much as he did.

Connor wasn't sure what was more comforting, the warm water around them or Danny's strong arms about his chest. He leaned back and enjoyed Danny's support in the afterglow of the sex they'd just had.

Danny kissed the back of Connor's neck. "So can I ask you a few questions without totally spoiling the mood here?"

"Sure." Connor tensed. He didn't have a lot of experience with such conversations, but the couple of times he had them, it had never ended well. "What's on your mind?"

"Why are you acting different now that we're in Santa Fe than you did when we were in Jemez Springs?" Danny ran his hand down Connor's torso; the warm tingle of it helped counter the sudden stress the question caused.

"Not sure what you mean." Connor wasn't picking up anything from Danny as far as psychic impressions went. He stopped and thought about it. He didn't normally, beyond the attraction Danny had for him, and the dreams they'd both shared. The only big vision he'd had was of them in bed, and he wondered if that one hadn't been to help push them together.

"Well, you're a bit of a sexist ass here. You're pushier than normal, and you act like you're in control of everything. The only reason I can see that Captain Kennedy and Officer Collins put up with it is that you've really helped them break some cases, otherwise you wouldn't be a consultant."

"You think I'm an ass?" Connor started to turn in Danny's embrace so he could see his face, but Danny held him tight.

"Not all the time." Danny kissed the back of his neck again, sending soft warm tingles down his back. "If I thought that was how you were all the time, I wouldn't be here with you. Over the past month, I've really come to like you a lot. But today, and a little bit yesterday, I'm seeing a different side to you. A side I'm not real sure I like very much. You're driven, I get that. You want to solve the case. I'm with you there. But you need to relax. You can't just march in and start ordering people around. Collins and Kennedy aren't your peons; they're a major part of the police force here in Santa Fe. You weren't doing that in Jemez Springs, and if that was just because you didn't know us all that well, then maybe I don't want you to get to know Rusty and Jeri."

Connor sighed. He thought about Danny's words before he responded. He'd never had anyone stop and call his faults into the light. "You're right. I am driven." He shook he head, then leaned a little more heavily into Danny. Since Danny wasn't across the room making accusations, but lying there with him in the tub talking like everything was fine made things easier. "When I started having my visions back when puberty hit, it was strange. Even with my family knowing what was going on, it still set me apart from everyone. I'm the only one in my generation with the Sight. The kids at school didn't understand. It was really hard for me."

Danny nodded and kissed the top of his head. "Kids can be really evil. I'm sorry you had to go through that."

"Then realizing I was gay too, while trying to hide being a shifter, it was all almost too much to endure at times. Then I found a way to turn my gift to something useful. I could use it to fight crime. What teenager doesn't want to be a superhero? And for a while that's what I felt like. I could see things no one else could. I could change into a mountain lion. I thought that put me above everyone else, and for a while it did." Connor sighed; he'd never revealed this to anyone, but somehow it felt right to tell Danny.

"What happened?" Danny prompted quietly.

"I was too late. It was the first time I was too late. I'd had a vision of one of the boys in school killing himself. He was on the football team, and gay. In my vision he'd been down by the creek and had blown his head off. I shifted and staked out the place for a week. He ended up hanging himself half a mile from where I was." Connor shuddered at the memory. "That was when I learned that if I staked out a place, it might cause a change in the future I'd seen."

"That was why you didn't want us leaving someone where you saw Lacey killed."

Connor nodded. "Right. The night he hung himself, he'd come down to the spot where I was waiting. I must've fallen asleep 'cause I never heard him, but when I woke up I saw his shoe prints in the ground near me. He'd turned around and gone to the other spot. What I never understood was why he didn't have the gun I'd seen. But that told me I wasn't a superhero, and that I couldn't save everyone. If something was meant to happen, it would regardless of what I did. It also gave me the drive to try to do everything I can to save as many as possible." He sighed; his confession felt like he was getting a massive weight off his shoulders -- one he hadn't even realized was there. "Sometimes I get so focused on what I'm doing, I don't stop to think about what I'm saying or doing."

Danny ran his hand along Connor's jaw and turned him slightly so they could kiss. "Okay. I think I understand. But I want you to know that I'm not going to let you keep acting like an ass. I don't want the police and other law enforcement we might work with thinking of you and by extension, me, as rude. When I catch you dropping into rude, or overpowering mode, I get to shut you down. I won't do it publicly, that would be very uncool. But I think you get the point."

Connor turned so he was laying chest to chest across Danny. "Thank you for understanding. I guess you're going to be my guide dawg." He kissed Danny.

"And if we're both lucky, I'll keep you out of jail for pissing some police chief off." He combed his fingers through Connor's hair. "Not everyone is as laid back or desperate as Chief Kennedy."

"You think Kennedy is desperate?" It wasn't something Connor had ever picked up from the captain.

"Dude, you solve things no one else can. You make him look good. Yeah, he's a bit desperate for your help." Danny kissed him again, then yawned. "I'm glad we could talk about that. Let's make sure we can always talk about whatever's on our mind."

Connor nodded. "I like the sound of that. Honesty and openness. The basis for a good relationship." His earlier nervousness vanished. He must mean a lot to Danny for him to take the bull by the horns and lay everything out like he had.

"Yes it is." Danny slid his hand down the curve of Connor's ass. "Now, let's get to more of the fun parts of relationship basics."

"Definitely." Connor caught a quick flash of what Danny was wanting, and quickly moved to accommodate him. It felt good being able to be open and honest with someone and he was going to do everything he could to keep Danny happy.

Chapter Fourteen

Connor and Danny strolled into the squad room shortly after breakfast. Danny was feeling good about things, better than he had the previous day. After Connor's bathtub confession, he thought he knew him better, and that made him feel at ease the feelings growing inside him. Having an inside track on Connor made understanding what drove him easier.

Connor tossed Officer Collins' keys to her. "Thanks for the loan. I gassed it up for you. Clean up the fast food wrappers so Steve doesn't get upset." He poured Danny and himself cups of coffee. "We're heading back to Jemez Springs today. I figure we can work from there just as easily as here. That's where the latest murders happened, so the trail is fresher there."

"Probably right." Officer Collins slipped the keys into her purse. "By the way, nothing popped up on any of the car rental places. I guess our guy actually has two vehicles, and just has the spare parked somewhere."

"If we could figure out where, that would help. Danny and I have been all over this state trying to track down the RV, and haven't seen a black Ford Escort at any of them."

"Are you sure, Cat?" Danny asked as he sipped the coffee Connor gave him. "When we were driving around checking out the RV leads, we weren't looking for an Escort. We might've missed it."

Connor shook his head. "Nope. I've been over every place we looked and no black Escort. It's something else we're missing."

"You know." Officer Collins tapped her nail on her desk. "What if we did a search for someone who owns both a green and white RV and a black Escort? There can't be that many people in New Mexico that have that combination of vehicles. It might help narrow things down."

"Sure, give it a shot." Connor took up a seat at an empty desk near the white board and entered the information from the board into his laptop.

Danny walked over to the board and started a new column:

Suspect:

Dark hair

Smells of smoke

Green and white single-unit RV

Cameras, computer set-up

Pictures of naked women – some victims

Black Escort

Alias: Robert Weeks – fake

Connor stood and walked over to add the word 'messy' next to RV and drinks coffee black. "Make sure we cover all the important bases here."

"Sure." Danny nodded. He wondered if the RV smelled bad due to the messiness. It might not be something the humans would notice, but it might be an angle he and Connor could work with their more sensitive noses.

Chief Kennedy stepped out of his office. "Connor, we heard back from the pen. A man named Robert Hernandez was serving five to ten on an attempted rape charge. He was released two weeks before the first body was discovered. They sent his records." He held up a file. "He's five feet seven inches, fifty-eight years old, has an eagle tattoo on his back, and an appendectomy scar on his abdomen. He's originally from Taos, and his mother still lives there. He has one brother who lives with her."

"Lisa, can you please make a copy of that for us to take back with us?" Connor asked.

Danny added the new name and information to the list. There was something coming together and that felt good. It also felt like they were missing something. He paused and stared at the dates; there was something there. It chewed at his gut, but he wasn't sure what it was.

"Did the pen say anything about what kind of prisoner he was?" Connor asked. "How did he spend his free time?"

"They said he took an interest in photography while he was there," Kennedy said. "Mostly flowers and such."

"It's probably all he could do while locked up." Danny turned from the white board.

Officer Collin's computer beeped and she leaned forward. After a second she looked up. "Hey, Cat, might have something here. Since we failed to find anything in the car rental companies about a black Escort, I set up a database search for black Escorts being bought or sold. One of the lots down on Cerrillos Road had a black Ford Escort brought in two days ago. They just finished the paperwork on it this morning and got it into the database. It's not available for sale yet." She tapped a key on her keyboard and the printer across the room started up.

Without being told, Danny hurried over to the printer and retrieved the paper. "We'd better move quickly."

"I'll call and let them know to expect you," Officer Collin's said as she picked up the phone.

"Heading that way. Come on, Dawg, let's roll." Connor headed for the door, stopped, and turned back.

Danny hurried to follow, then stumbled to not crash into him. "Some warning, Cat."

"Sorry." Connor mumbled. "Something else to look into, Lisa. Please check the public records for the purchase and licensing of an RV in Hernandez's name. Or any other name around Colorado Springs near the time he was released. Also check New Mexico registrations for the RV. He could've had it already and stored it at his mother's place, or it might be registered in his mother's name or in the brother's."

Danny pulled the Bronco onto the used car lot. It was smaller than a lot of the others they'd passed, and he wondered if that was why their guy had chosen it, if this was even the right black Escort.

Connor jumped out and headed for the office. He left the car door open.

It was obvious he was eager to be on the trail, but if something happened to the Bronco, Connor wasn't going to have to be the one to tell Rusty about it. Danny called out, "Hey, you could close the door, you know." He got out of the car, closed both doors, and followed Connor toward the office.

"That's why I like my Jeep. Don't have to bother with doors most of the time."

"Morning, Officers." A portly man in a bad suit met them on the tiny porch of the shack that served as the lot's office. "How can I help you? The woman on the phone was fairly vague."

"You have a black Escort that was previously owned by a Robert Hernandez?" Danny asked.

"Yes. The guys are detailing it right now." The man gestured around the building toward the garage sitting in the shadow of the office.

"Stop what they're doing. I need to check it over. Was anything left in it?" Connor asked.

"Just cigarette butts in the ashtray." The manager looked confused. "That's already been emptied."

"Danny, check the trash and pull those."

"I know better than to ask why," Danny said as he followed Connor. They could get the cigarette butts in a little while. He felt like it was more important to watch over Connor, in case anything he did freaked out the people working in the car lot.

"You're learning." Connor headed for the garage behind the office.

Danny blocked the man who tried to stop them by pulling out his badge. "Sheriff's department."

"Barry, let them be," the manager trailed after them. "They think this car was involved in a crime or something."

"Oh." Barry held up his hands and backed away until he hit the wall.

"Give us a little space," Danny said as Connor opened the car door and slid in. He hoped to block the manager's view of what was going to happen.

Once Connor was seated behind the wheel, he closed his eyes.

A predatory glee settled in on him. The simple satisfaction of getting prey in his grasp was overwhelming.

But there was more.

Visions of Rage

Fear hit hard. The woman was terrified. Tears soaked her face as she struggled against the ropes binding her hands. She couldn't see anything. The darkness encompassing her was hot and stuffy, making her want to scream, but her mouth was taped shut. The car hit a bump, bouncing her up a foot and she hit her head and shoulder. Pain seared through her.

Connor hissed in her pain, and tried to force things back so he could concentrate on the vision. His head pounded but he held onto the vision.

The car jolted to a stop. She tried to move her hands to rub her head, but there wasn't enough space. Something hard and metal dug into her back. The smell of motor oil grew stronger. A car door slammed, shaking her darkness. A key slid into a lock. There was a loud click and fresh air flooded in. Somewhere nearby the river bubbled along, the sound of freedom gave her hope.

A large figure loomed over her. The smell of burger grease hit as meaty hands reached in.

She struggled, trying to kick, but her legs cramped and the pain lanced through her lower back as the man hauled her free of the trunk.

He pulled the tape from her mouth and replaced it with his mouth.

The predator pulled in the taste of her flesh and her fear. It was intoxicating, far beyond any liquor he'd ever drank. A darkness surged within him.

She jerked away. "Let me go!" In a flash, she recognized the man's profile in the waning moonlight. "Robert? What are you doing to me? Robert, I thought we were friends."

"I have no friends, Lacey." He shook her. She didn't know how he was strong enough to be able to hold her up by

one hand. Her shirt bit into her neck as he hoisted her by the fabric "But you're going to be real friendly to me tonight."

As she tried to catch her breath, her heart pounded so hard she was afraid it was going to burst. "I need to get home to my son."

"You will. We're just going for a little ride." Anger lit up his eyes. It was almost like his eyes glowed in the moonlight. "I've seen you drinking and whoring around while your little boy cries himself to sleep because you aren't there." He shook her again. He kept her feet just off the ground. "Just like my brother and I used to do while our mother was out selling herself to any man who'd pay for it."

"What do you mean? I don't whore around. You're crazy!"

The darkness surged. Robert didn't like being called crazy.

"That's what you say. But I've seen the way you flirt with every man who comes into the café." He walked slowly away from the car, still keeping her effortlessly suspended in one hand. "And I know you're putting out for Jeff. You're just like my mother. You'll spread your legs for anyone in pants as long as they pay you."

"Jeff and I aren't sleeping together." The talking helped her calm slightly. They were in a parking lot near the river. There were no lights, except those coming from a couple of semi-trucks parked nearby. "He's my boss. He's married. His wife is a friend of mine."

"Don't lie to me. Tonight, I'm going to get some of what you're passing around."

Robert stopped at a looming RV and fished a key ring out of his pocket.

The darkness felt at home in the RV. It was safer there. Like a den.

Lacey screamed and he hit her.

The vision cleared.

Connor reached down beside the driver's seat, popped the trunk and jumped out of the Escort.

It looked like a normal trunk. Recently cleaned. The gray carpet only had a few small pebbles on it. The spare tire and jack were in their proper places. The smell of car products was faint, like the cleaning products had covered up their scent. Connor leaned close to the carpet; the urge to shift and get a better smell was strong, but since he didn't know the people in the dealership, he resisted.

The feeling of fear he'd experienced when his vision started hit him again. He jerked back before the vision could take him again. It had been strong enough he could replay it as he needed to. A small jute fiber caught his attention. He leaned back in and plucked it from where it was caught in the carpet fibers. It might be nothing, but he needed every piece of evidence he could get.

"Dawg, do you have an evidence bag on you?"

Danny chuckled. "Back in the Bronco. Give me a second."

"E…e…evidence bag?" the car lot manager stammered.

Connor nodded. "I thought the woman on the phone told you this car is of interest in a series of killings." He glanced at the Escort and tried to figure out if it would do any good for a forensics team to go over it or not, then decided it probably wouldn't hurt. They needed all the hard evidence they could get. "She'll be arranging for it to be picked up shortly. We'll bring it back after we've gotten everything out of it."

Danny reappeared with a couple of evidence bags. He handed one to Connor, then went over to the trash can to fish out some of the cigarette butts. Connor put the rope fiber in the small Ziploc bag, and headed out of the detailing shop.

"Thanks for your help," he said to the manager.

As they got into the car, Connor said, "We need to get the butts and this strand of rope back to the station before we head out."

"Whatever you say, Cat," Danny said.

"Good Dawg," Connor said. "You're learning."

Danny glared at him. "Pat me on the head, and you might lose a finger," he growled.

"I'll pat you somewhere else later." Connor grinned, laid his head on the headrest, closed his eyes, and started purring.

"There's that noise again."

"It's helping me think," Connor mumbled. "A couple of things that stand out from my vision. One, Robert is really strong. He was able to hoist Lacey up by one hand. Two, he transferred her from the trunk of the car to the RV at a rest stop."

"That sounds shifter strong," Danny threw in. "But not all shifters are able to do something like that."

"Right." Connor nodded. "And we keep smelling bears."

Danny smacked the steering wheel as they turned the corner, heading back toward the police station. "I know you sniffed the carpet, but neither one of us shifted to see if we could smell bear."

Connor shook his head. "Hindsight. I'll ask Kennedy to not do any further cleaning on the car, in case we need to give it a good sniff later, but I doubt he spent much time shifted in the car."

"Probably not. But a bear might be able to steer a car."

"Probably not. Sure, their paws are more hand-like than ours, but I doubt it." Connor closed his eyes again. The moon had been waning. Not full, but almost full. "Wait a minute. We need to look at the dates again. It's been one a month, hasn't it?"

Danny nodded as he stopped for a red light. "Yeah, well, we have a couple of months where there isn't a body."

"At least not one we found." Connor wished he had his laptop with him so he could pull up the chart of the dates and compare them to the full moon.

"But he isn't killing on the full moon," Danny said. "You and I both know the pull of the moon. I think we might've noticed that pretty quickly. Plus he's shooting the women, not rending them."

"Right, but that doesn't mean he's not a shifter." Connor pulled out his phone and sent Lisa a text.

Check and see if there have been any bear shifters incarcerated in Cañon City, Colorado recently.

He put the phone away. "We'll find out. Luckily, since we've all had to come out, there's a record of shifters in prison."

"But that should've been on his employee record too," Danny added as they pulled into the police station.

"Maybe, maybe not. Bad guys don't always play by the rules." Connor unfastened his seatbelt as soon as Danny brought the Bronco to a stop.

"That's what makes them bad guys." Danny turned off the engine and got out of the Bronco. "He was using an alias and didn't say he'd been in prison either."

Connor didn't wait for him; he hurried into the station so he could get the cigarette butts and rope turned in to Kennedy for DNA testing. He paused at Lisa's desk. "You got my text?"

She nodded. "I was going to check that right after I got done with the reports from that holdup at Walmart last night. So, you're thinking he's a shifter."

"If my vision of him picking up Lacey Simmons with one hand is correct, yes, some large powerful shifter. He doesn't look big enough to be that strong otherwise." Suddenly Danny taking out after the bear at his place two nights earlier hit Connor. Even as a wolf, Danny wouldn't have been a match for a bear shifter. He'd have been in grave danger if he'd caught Robert by himself. He glanced back where Danny stood a couple of feet behind him. "Dawg, do you have any silver bullets?"

"At the house." Danny nodded slightly. "If you're right, it might be a good idea for both of us to have some."

"He's right, Cat," Lisa said. She stood from her desk and walked over to the weapon's locker near the back door. "Luckily silver ammo is standard for all departments nowadays." She entered her code into the touchpad lock, then pulled out a box of ammo. She stared into Connor's eyes as she handed him the small pack. Connor couldn't think of many people who would stare at him so intimately. She trusted him and didn't want anything to happen to him. The way she touched his hand as she handed him his defense made his throat tighten.

She glanced at Danny. "He's got a small pistol he carries in the Jeep. Make sure he keeps it on him, and loads it. I'm trusting you to keep him safe." The feistiness of her kestrel blazed through her eyes.

Danny nodded. "I'll bring Big Cat back safe and sound, or I won't come back either."

Connor wondered for a moment if Lisa had somehow figured out they were more than just friends. Like other people, she'd been pushing them together, but there was something more in the way she looked at the two of them. Then he shook his head. "Look, Dawg and I need to get going. If I'm going to get my pistol from the Jeep, we need to get to the Jeep."

"Right." She walked back toward her desk. "I'll get on all this new evidence and see what we can find. It's probably going to take a while to get DNA, but you know that."

"I do." Connor nodded toward the back door, and headed that way with Danny in tow.

"I think I'm ready for lunch," Connor said. "There's a truck stop on 285 just outside of town. They make a good cheeseburger."

"Sounds good to me as long as they don't put mushrooms on it."

Between bites of salad, Danny asked, "Do you think we should really leave Santa Fe? I feel we can do more here than at home." It wasn't the best salad he'd ever eaten, but for a truck stop salad it wasn't bad.

Connor shook his head. "He's left Santa Fe. We'll just have to wait for him to strike again."

Danny pursed his lips. "But if we're right about him being a shifter and the full moon having something to do with everything, that could be another three weeks."

"Maybe yes, maybe no." Connor chewed his burger. "Since he's not killing as a bear, then the primal animal urge to kill isn't what's driving him. He may be killing hookers to get back at his mother. That was part of the vision I saw at the car dealership."

"So, like Jack the Ripper?" Danny crunched a cucumber. "They always suspected he was killing hookers to get back at his mother."

"Probably. I think Robert has some major mother issues, but the change in pattern to Lacey Simmons does make me wonder if he's escalating things or what."

Danny had spent a lot of time going over various serial killer cases in the police academy. He'd been fascinated by them, and thinking back, it was almost funny since he'd ended up in one of the quietest towns in the state as far as violent crime went. Even with a wolf pack in the county, things stayed quiet. He also wondered how Cortez was going to react to the idea they had a bear shifter killing people in his territory. He probably wouldn't be happy. "So, how does Simmons fit into the pattern?"

"From what he said in the vision, he saw her as a whore." Connor frowned and then ate another fry. "Maybe it's a combination of things with him. Maybe if he sees a woman neglecting her child, then he thinks of her as a whore."

"But Simmons wasn't neglecting her son," Danny countered.

"We know that, but if Robert was just looking at it from his skewed viewpoint, he might've seen something else."

Danny couldn't deny that. People always had different ways of looking at things; that was one of the first rules of police investigation. See what everyone has to say about things, then figure the truth is somewhere in the middle of all of it. "Okay, but if we're lucky, we're going to get enough evidence from what we're gathering right now that we can find him and stop him before he hits again."

"I hope so." Connor ran a fry around the bottom of his plate, scooping up catsup. "I want to change vehicles. I'm more comfortable in my Jeep than in your patrol car. Then we head for Taos."

Danny crunched a crouton. "Going to see his mother?"

Connor nodded. "Exactly. We need to sniff around and see if he's been there. Also see if the family's shifters."

"I hadn't even thought of that. If he's turned and not born, he could be a lot more dangerous." Danny shivered. Cortez didn't like turned wolves in his territory. They were too unpredictable, so he chose his turned wolves carefully. The lunar cycles were also a lot more controlling in a turned shifter. He was thankful that only a few species could turn humans, but bears were one of those. He really wanted to get back to his place and get his silver bullets. The idea of going after a turned bear shifter who was killing prostitutes chilled him.

"Right, Dawg." Connor finished his food. "We need to move as fast as we can. Don't want this trail going cold. And don't forget, I can't get a clear vision of this guy. If I'm right and he's also a multiple personality, he'll be even more dangerous. He's got a lot of dark rage in him."

"Would that be the only reason you can't get a clear image of him?" Danny finished off his salad. "Couldn't him being a turned bear also cause that?"

Connor took a long drink of his tea, draining the glass. "Maybe. I hadn't thought of that. If he and his bear are fighting for dominance, it might have a similar affect as a multiple personality." He grinned. "Thanks, Danny. Having you around is great. You're opening my mind up to a lot of new options."

Danny liked feeling useful. And being able to help Connor figure out angles he'd never thought of before made him feel like he was actually going to be part of the team, as opposed to just the guy who held the evidence bag.

Chapter Fifteen

They arrived at Jemez Springs midafternoon and went straight to the Sheriff's Office. It felt like going home to Danny. He didn't like the general size and over-population of Santa Fe. It was always great getting back to the small town he was used to.

Rusty greeted them. "Kennedy called. They think they can get DNA off of the cigarette butts and have sent them to the lab. It'll probably take at least a couple of weeks. He also said they found a Dodge Brougham RV registered to Dolores Hernandez." He read off the license plate number. "They've issued an APB for it."

"Good." Connor walked over to a board. "Officer White, do you have a New Mexico map?"

"I'll get one." Danny went over to his desk, where he kept a map in his desk. It was just easier a lot of times to make notes on a paper map than using the ones online, even if he was getting pretty good at figuring out how to put the pins on the digital maps, Rusty was always going on about the lack of security when doing too much police work online.

Connor duplicated the list from Santa Fe.

Danny taped the map on the wall next to the board. He glanced at the list and noted that Connor had added some of their notes about him being a shifter to the items. There were also some question marks about Lacey Simmons and the change in quarry.

Connor marked the locations the bodies were found. "It looks like he's traveling south, possibly toward Mexico. If I'm right, the next hit may be around Albuquerque, unless he realizes we're onto him. That might make him move faster, change direction, or wait until he gets south of the border before making another kill." Connor yawned. "Dawg, get your bags packed, and be ready to roll. We're headed to Taos in the morning."

Danny looked at Connor for a second. Waiting until morning didn't make a lot of sense. Taos wasn't that far away, and they could get a hotel room. "Why wait?"

With a quick yawn, Connor sighed. "I think we can use a decent night's sleep, and this time of year, most of the hotels in Taos are going to be booked. So let's get some shut-eye and head out first thing."

"Sure." Danny couldn't really argue with him. They'd been on the go, and he had no idea how much energy Connor's visions took out of him. Although he still looked like he was up to keeping at it for a while, Connor might need the rest a lot more than he was willing to let Rusty and Jeri know about. "I can make sure I don't have any paperwork around here that needs to be done. Do you want me to drive you out to the cabin first?"

Another yawn escaped Connor. "Sure. Maybe I can squeeze in a catnap this afternoon."

Danny rolled his eyes as he gestured for Connor to head out the door. "Be back in a few." He said as he followed Connor. It felt good being back in his home station. The squad room in Santa Fe had been too busy for his taste, even if they did seem to be able to get things done in a more timely fashion.

A knock on the door jerked Danny out of the doze in his chair where he'd been watching the nightly news before going to bed.

"Cat, what are you doing here?" He looked around Connor. The street outside his place was empty. "I didn't hear you drive up. Where's the Jeep?"

Without being invited in, Connor stepped through the door, gathered Danny into his arms, and kissed him. It was a warm passionate kiss that made Danny want to melt into him. "I didn't think it would be a good idea for my Jeep to be parked outside your place all night."

"Oh," Danny swung the door closed with his foot, "are you planning to stay all night?"

Connor flashed a sheepish grin. "I was hoping to."

"I don't know." Danny gave him a hard look. It was a great opportunity to make Connor squirm a bit, and maybe actually ask for something as opposed to assuming he'd get what he wanted. "Do you think it's a good idea?"

"Do you have a better one?" Connor stepped back. He cocked his head and looked more adorable than he ever had. "I know it's crazy. We can't get along during the day, but I can't go to sleep thinking about you." He brushed a lock of hair off Danny's forehead, leaving warm tingles of excitement where his finger touched Danny's skin.

The only reason Danny had fallen asleep in front of the late-night news was that he hadn't been able to drop off when he lay down in his bed, so he had gotten up to try and do something boring. He'd been tired enough the boring had worked. When he'd been lying in the bed by himself, his mind kept going to Connor. "I know. I'm the same way." Danny shook his head, turned, took Connor's hand, and led the way to the bedroom. There was something right and perfect in having Connor's hand in his and he wanted to keep that feeling for as long as he could.

The sunlight peeking through the curtains woke Danny. The sheets next to him were still warm, but he was alone in the bed. Connor's scent filled the room. It might've been him getting out of bed that woke Danny, but he wasn't sure. He listened and couldn't hear anyone, or anything moving around the house. There was a bit of traffic on the street outside the house. Danny yawned and stretched.

"Damned Cat." He swung his legs over the side of the bed and headed for the shower. He'd thought about returning the favor of breakfast in bed Connor had given him but he'd been denied the opportunity. It was going to take him a while to get adjusted to Connor's behavior, particularly if he kept acting like some kind of idiot who was raised by crazy, inbred relatives in Arkansas.

"He couldn't leave a note or anything," Danny mumbled as he tucked his brown uniform shirt into his matching brown pants. It amazed him that Connor could be so cool and attentive one minute, then completely rude the next. Sometimes Danny wondered if it was his psychic gifts that kept people at a distance, or Connor's general behavior. If he wasn't so interesting, cute, and fun, Danny wouldn't think he was worth the assholeness that seemed to come with him. The fact that Connor had brought a good level of excitement to Jemez Springs helped a lot too.

"Maybe he ran to the office to get updates," Danny wondered aloud as he waited for a couple of sausage biscuits to warm in his microwave. Then he shook his head. "Nah, he'd have just checked his phone. If our bear shifter showed up in the middle of the night he would've woken me." He glanced at the clock. Connor had been gone for at least thirty minutes. "And if he just ran out to get both of us coffee, he should be back by now."

Eating his quick breakfast in a couple of bites, Danny made sure to turn off the lights, grab his duffel bag with several days of clothes, and his overnight kit. He locked the door and started down the steps, grinning slightly as the scent of mountain lion wafted around him.

"Mawnin', Dawg. How are you feeling this fine day?" Connor's voice rang loud in his head.

"Where are you?" Danny glanced around, trying to spot Connor somewhere close by.

"Look over your head."

Danny looked up. Connor, in his mountain lion form, lay on a branch about ten feet up the big ponderosa pine that dominated Danny's tiny front yard. "What are you doing up there?" He shook his head and frowned.

"Waiting for you to wake up. Ditch the uniform and meet me at my cabin. Good, you remembered to grab extra clothes. Don't know when we'll be back."

Connor leaped down, stretched, and trotted down the street in the direction of his rented cabin.

Danny went back inside and yanked off his uniform shirt. "I bet he thinks he's doing the smart thing and not letting people see him coming and going here." Shaking his head, Danny dropped his uniform pants. "Like there are so many mountain lions wandering the streets of Jemez Springs." He walked into his closet and grabbed a clean pair of tight jeans. He paused as he pulled them up. Connor liked him in tight jeans, even though he preferred his baggy ones. It would serve him right if he wore the ones he was comfortable in, and didn't bother with what Connor liked.

Then he grabbed one of his more form-fitting shirts, tucked it into the jeans, and went out to find his non-work boots that he was fairly sure he'd left under the bed.

He came out, got into the Bronco, and took the conventional way toward the cabin, taking time to stop and get them both coffee. It was more than Connor deserved for being stupid, but Danny needed something to wash down his breakfast, and wanted to be nice.

As Danny pulled his Bronco in beside the Jeep, Connor trotted into the clearing. He was a little winded from the run up the mountain from town to the rental cabins. The previous night, when he'd run from the cabin to Danny's, it had been cooler and dark. It had sounded like a really good idea, particularly when they didn't want everyone to figure out they were more than friends. But in the heat of the day, going uphill the whole way…it felt kinda stupid.

Connor shifted. He shook slightly, settling his clothes over his lanky frame. "Be right back." He waved at Danny as Danny opened the Bronco door and stepped onto the grass next to the Jeep. Connor went into the cabin. The place was familiar, but after being gone for a couple of days, it didn't feel as comfy as it had before he'd left. He'd taken time to get a few things together before he'd headed for Danny's the previous evening. He grabbed the overnight bag from the couch and headed back out, taking a moment to lock the door as he exited.

Danny stood next to the Jeep with his duffel bag over his shoulder and a cup of coffee in each hand. He held one out to Connor. "So how do we keep things from flying out since you didn't bring the roof and doors back from Santa Fe?"

"Back here." Connor walked to the back of the Jeep and opened up a small storage trunk he kept back there. "It's not overly secure, all things considered, but it keeps things in the vehicle while we're flying down the road." He didn't add that he'd never had any problems with things being stolen out of it. In a lot of ways, he thought it was as secure as any trunk on a car.

Danny dropped his bag into the trunk then jumped into the front passenger seat. "What are our plans in Taos?"

"Talk to Hernandez's mother and neighbors." Connor locked the trunk before getting into the driver's seat. "Friends if he has any." Connor put the key in the ignition and started the Jeep. He tried to remember if he'd ever heard of serial killers having friends. But most of them had jobs and such, even if they didn't normally hold them down for long. They were also good at putting on a front. Many times neighbors were shocked to find out they lived next to a killer.

"Let's roll." Danny clicked his seatbelt and grinned.

As he started down the driveway, Connor pulled out his cell phone and called Kennedy on speaker phone. It was a good thing the area had excellent cell phone coverage. Just over the pass toward Santa Fe was more than a little spotty. "Kennedy, the Dawg and I are headed for Taos. Call whoever's in charge there and alert them."

"Will do." Kennedy said quickly. "Watch your speed, I don't want to have to bail you out for a speeding ticket."

"I'll do my best." Connor replied as he reached the main dirt drive that would take them to the highway. He paused as he tapped off the phone and slipped it into his pocket. "Dawg, did I just-"

"Order the police captain of Santa Fe, New Mexico to do something without really stopping to think about what you were doing?" Danny grinned. "Yeah. You did. I'm proud of you for realizing what you did, but you really need to work on not doing it. Not everyone is going to be as understanding as Kennedy. They won't know you."

Connor sighed as they reached the highway. "Danny, I don't know what would happen if I couldn't follow my visions and help people." One of the reasons he hadn't been able to sleep the previous night was he'd been thinking about what Danny kept telling him about the way he treated people. He worried that if he didn't come through and try to get more things done by not exactly asking people for help, he wouldn't get as much done. He kept people off balance, but that might not be as good a thing as he thought it was.

"And it's a good thing you want to do that, but we need to work on your people skills." Danny patted Connor's leg. "Look. I'm going to help you with it. Okay?"

"Okay." Connor replied. The fact that Danny hadn't run away when things got tough made Connor want to do more for him. He wanted to do what he could to keep Danny around. He'd begun to wonder if maybe having Danny, a trained deputy, as his partner, might not help authority figures who didn't know him be more accepting. But it was obvious he was going to have to make a few changes. Life was full of changes, his grandmother had always told him. He was finally beginning to understand what she'd meant.

Chapter Sixteen

Before it was time for lunch, Connor pulled into the police lot on Paseo Del Carion in Taos. There was something profoundly relaxing about driving in the mountains, along the twisting turning road from Jemez Springs to Taos. Even though they were heading to interview the family of a killer, the drive helped set him at ease. Some of that was also due to having Danny along for the ride. In all the hours they spent on the road, even going on this same drive two weeks earlier, it just seemed they grew closer and closer. It was the first time in his life that he'd let himself get as close to anyone as he was to Danny, and that closeness felt good.

The parking lot was crowded, and they couldn't find a spot. They had to park a couple of blocks down in the last open spot in a public pay lot.

"Tourist season," Danny muttered as they started walking back toward the police station. "Too bad they don't issue licenses for them like they do elk."

"It's not that bad," Connor replied as they stopped at the corner for a light to change. "There aren't as many people here as in Santa Fe."

Danny shook his head. "Maybe not number-wise, but Taos is a much smaller city. Plus it's Pow Wow week. The town wasn't designed for this many people. I keep threatening to move out into the desert and be as far away from people as possible. It's one of the few advantages I can see in moving to pack lands, but I'd hate it."

Connor laughed as they reached the far side of the intersection. "And if you stayed on pack lands, you never would've met me. Somehow I doubt Cortez would let me on his lands without you."

"Right. He doesn't like other species." Danny dodged around a little girl walking down the sidewalk with a cone of cotton candy and not paying any attention to where she was going, while her mother meandered along with her nose in her phone.

"You know, he might have to change his attitude," Connor said as he was able to angle back to be next to Danny. It was strange the way he felt the distance between him and Danny when the girl came between them. "The world is changing, and we shifters can't stay in a primitive tribal society for much longer."

Danny rolled his eyes. "Try explaining that to some of the people like Cortez. Change doesn't come easily to the older ones in the community."

"I know." Connor laughed again. He'd found himself laughing a lot more since Danny was around. "Next thing you know dogs and cats are going to be living together and the world is going to come to an end."

"No." A huge grin spread across Danny's face. "I won't be the harbinger of the shifter apocalypse. Go find yourself another wolf."

"But I don't want another wolf." Connor opened the door into the police station, cutting their playful conversation short.

The insignia on his uniform identified the man at the front desk as a sergeant. He gave them a welcoming smile. "How can I help you guys?"

"Larry Kennedy in Santa Fe was supposed to call your chief and tell him to expect us," Connor said.

A Native American woman with classic beauty hurried out of an office a couple of feet from the main desk. "I'm Chief Sara Randall. Kennedy said to expect you. He seems to think you may be able to help with our murders."

Smiling broadly, Danny flashed his badge, then held out his hand. "I'm Deputy Danny Lupan from Jemez Springs, and this is Connor McGriffin who consults for Santa Fe. We think they may tie in with some other cases we're investigating."

Connor held his tongue. He wasn't used to anyone, not even Danny, stepping up and taking change, but he wanted to make a better impression, and Danny was right, if he worked with the police a little more as opposed to ordering them around, things might go smoother. He wasn't normally worried about making friends, but if he was going to treat Danny as the partner he wanted him to be, he needed to make an effort. He glanced around the office; it was smaller than Santa Fe, but not as diminutive as Jemez Springs. Other than the desk sergeant and the chief, there didn't appear to be anyone in right then, and Connor wondered if they were all helping with the traffic for the Pow Wow. Being able to look around made him realize something else—letting Danny take point on things would give him the opportunity to observe more, and that might work out really well in investigations.

Chief Randall shook Danny's hand. "We have two victims. Both hookers. Both found in Cruz Canyon. Both killed with a single shot to the forehead."

"Do you have any suspects?" Connor asked, finally drawing attention to himself.

"No," the chief replied. "We questioned some campers in the area, but didn't get anywhere."

"Do you know anything about a man named Robert Hernandez?" Danny asked.

"The name sounds familiar. Come into my office and let me look and see if I have anything on him. Hernandez is a common name around here." She led the way into a small office. "Can I get you anything to drink? I know it's a long drive from Jemez Springs."

"Thanks, but we just stopped at Taco Bell a couple of blocks back." Danny patted his stomach. Connor was also a bit full, but knew the fast food wasn't going to last long. Their walk from the Jeep hadn't left him overly thirsty.

Chief Randall sat at her desk and started going through computer files. "Do you have an age on Hernandez? I've got a couple."

After taking his pad and pen from his jeans pocket, Danny leaned forward. "Early forties."

She nodded and kept tapping keys. "Ah, this might be the guy. Local boy. Quite a record. Small potatoes, though. Petty theft. Shoplifting. Minor offenses as a juvenile. Oh, wait. It says here he was sent to prison in Colorado for attempted rape. Released just over a year ago." She looked up from the computer. "His mother, Tabora, and brother, Carlos, live over on Ranchitos Road."

"We have reason to believe he may be our suspect," Danny said with a slight nod. He noted something on the pad.

The chief tapped a couple of keys and kept reading her screen. "Well, it looks like his brother has a record also. Same type of petty offenses. Mother usually bails them out. Most of this was before my time as chief, but I've picked up Carlos a time or two. Got a real chip on his shoulder. I've never had the pleasure of dealing with Robert." She pursed her lips. "He's listed in the sex offender data base, but he hasn't checked in with his parole officer since his initial meeting a year ago. Sounds like they went out to his mother's place several times, and she claims he never comes there."

"What about the father?" Connor asked. He flashed back to the vision he had of Lacey Simmons being pulled from the trunk and the way Hernandez had railed at her. He didn't figure there was a father figure in his life, but wanted to be sure.

"Apparently there's no father present. Mother has never been married. According to birth records, father is unknown for both sons. May be different fathers. The mother was picked up for soliciting several times when the boys were small."

"So she *was* a hooker?" Danny asked as he made notes on his pad. He glanced at Connor, as if confirming the facts of Connor's vision.

Connor gave him a brief nod, but stayed quiet, not wanting to interrupt the Chief's flow of information.

"Looks like it," Chief Randall said. "Her last arrest was over twenty-five years ago. Looks like as soon as the boys were old enough to get jobs, she quit."

"Do you know where the victims are buried?" Connor asked. It was a long shot, but he might be able to get some impressions even after nearly a year.

"Yes." She clicked some files on her computer and printed out the names of the women and where they were buried. She handed the printouts to Danny.

"Do you still have any of their personal items?" Danny asked, obviously trying to think of the things Connor would be asking for.

"Kennedy said you might have some strange requests." She stood. "Follow me."

They followed her down a hall into a room filled with shelves of storage boxes.

Chief Randall pulled two envelopes from a box. "Here's all we have left. There wasn't much, and family never showed up to claim anything. There's Jessica Rojas, she was the first victim."

She handed the first envelope to Danny.

After opening the envelope and looking inside, Danny handed it to Connor. "Not much there."

Chief Randall shook her head. "We weren't able to get anything but the victim's blood and some soil samples from her clothing so we didn't keep that. The rings, necklace and cellphone were the only things left. We checked the contacts in her phone. They were mostly relatives who live out of town. In fact, her parents still live in Mexico. Her listed address was a cheap apartment that she shared with two other hookers. There was nothing of value that belonged to her in the apartment. Some clothes and cheap furniture. The roommates claimed it for rent she owed them."

Connor opened the envelope containing small pieces of metal and electronics. He closed his eyes as he dumped them out in his hand. With a deep breath, he opened himself up to the items, trying to see if there was anything he could pick up on. After a second the vision came in. It wasn't strong, almost like an out-of-focus movie.

The woman laughed and posed erotically, obviously having fun. The man holding the camera is even unfocused, little more than a hulking, hungry shadow. She frowns questioningly. The bullet enters her forehead. Pain ends the vision.

Chief Randall stared a bit as Connor dropped the items back into the manila envelope. After a brief pause, she handed the second one to Danny. "This was Analisa

Blanco's stuff. No family on her either. She had a little better taste, or maybe she just made more money."

"Guess that's hard to say at this point," Danny said as he looked into the envelope, then poured the contents out into Connor's waiting hands.

Two silver and turquoise rings rolled out and a gold chain. There was just a bit of dried blood on the larger of the two rings. It had seeped into the fitting and stood out against the pale blue stone.

The vision came quicker.

Analisa Blanco skipped down the trail, stopping every so often to lean against a rock or strike a pose in front of a tree.

"Do you really just want to take my pictures?" "I always wanted to be a model." "One of these days, I'm going to go to LA and make it big."

Something looked different about the camera. Analisa Blanco peered at it with a tilted head. Fear spiked through her.

Connor fumbled the rings as he stopped the vision at the moment the bullet entered her head and ended her life.

"You okay?" Danny put his hand on Connor's shoulder.

The gesture helped him center on the evidence room they were standing in. He gave the rings back to Danny. "Yeah, that one just hit a little harder than normal. She knew something was about to happen."

Chief Randall frowned. "You're Kennedy's psychic, aren't you?"

Connor nodded. "I'm the one who helped him put that priest away."

She pursed her lips. "I wish he'd have told me that instead of being all vague." Her mood was suddenly a lot colder. "Is there anything else I can do for you?"

Danny looked at Connor, who closed his eyes. Even when he was trying to be good, people reacted badly to his gifts. He really wished people would stop being afraid of him.

"I think we've got what we need right now," Danny said, handing the second evidence bag back to the sheriff. "When we find Hernandez, we'll let you know."

"If he's killing people, get him off the street," she said as she put the evidence bags back in the box they'd come out of.

"Thanks for the help." Danny gestured for Connor to lead him out of the room, down the hall and into the warm New Mexico afternoon.

They were almost back to the first corner before Danny said anything. "She got cold. I'm surprised. She looks Native American, and most of us accept psychics as normal."

Connor nodded. "She may have had a bad experience with one in the past. A lot of folks don't like psychics. I understand, but it's hard to deal with sometimes."

"Well. We're done with her for the moment, unless we find something in our search that needs her attention." Danny hit the button for the crosswalk.

"I hope we don't need it." Connor said as the light changed and they started across the street. "I doubt she'll be as helpful again."

"Probably not. So, let's hope we don't need her. Where to now?"

Eager to be away from Chief Randall and her issues with his gifts, Connor picked up his step as they got closer to the Jeep. "First to see Dolores and Carlos Hernandez, and then visit a couple of graves."

Chapter Seventeen

The neighborhood where the Hernandezes lived was filled with small ranch-style adobe homes surrounded by well-kept yards. It was far enough away from the town center and the pueblo that the event traffic hadn't impacted parking in the area.

Conner found a spot in the off-street area. "We need to be ready for anything." Connor's guts tightened as they walked. If Robert Hernandez had any contact with his family, they could be walking into a major situation. He wanted Danny and him to be safe, but they had to find Hernandez and put a stop to his killing spree. There was a reason the Sight ran in his family, and his grandmother always said it was so they could stop the bad people.

"I wonder if this is going to go better than when we came through a couple of weeks ago," Danny said as they hiked down the street to the Hernandez home.

"Just finding someone home, or finding the RV would be an improvement," Connor said. He paused as they turned up the walkway toward the house. "But I don't see the RV in the driveway."

"We can drive around back and look after we talk to them, if we need to." Danny stepped in front of Connor. "Okay, let me handle this. It's not the first time I've done this kind of thing."

Connor touched the pistol he was wearing. He didn't like carrying a gun, but Hernandez was dangerous. He didn't want Danny to be the one on the front line if something started. He had to be able to help.

Danny rang the doorbell. He stood stiffly waiting for an answer. Connor stood behind him, hoping to get an advanced warning if something went bad.

A man with a surly look on his face opened the door. "We don't want any of what you're selling."

"We aren't selling anything," Danny said. He opened his wallet to show his badge. "I'm Danny Lupan with the Jemez Springs sheriff's office, and this is Connor McGriffin. We'd like to talk about Robert Hernandez."

The man tried to shut the door, but Danny shoved his foot in the way.

A short, stout Hispanic woman stomped into view. "What do you want Robert for? He ain't done nothing since they let him out on that fake attempted-rape charge."

"You say it was a fake charge?" Danny asked. "Why do you think that?"

Connor tried to feel anything from the woman or the man, but they were like dead things. Life had hardened them past the point of caring about anything. Connor always hated meeting people like them. On reflex, he sniffed; there was no scent of bear on the small porch he stood on. Only humans had been there. The scent of unwashed bodies and beer were prominent. Someone who smelled of pepper spray, probably the postman, came frequently.

"'cause he didn't do it. That girl told him she was twenty and said she wanted to have sex with him," the woman said. "You cops always try to pin things on my boys. Just because I ain't got no husband around, you think my boys are wild."

"Do you have a warrant?" The man reached for something beside the door.

"No," Danny said. "We just wanted to ask some questions."

Something was changing in the two people. Connor wrapped his hand around the handle of his pistol. He still couldn't get a firm vision of what either of them was about to do. Danny was in front of him, but he was a good enough shot he could hit the man, who he was fairly sure was Carlos Hernandez. Movement out of the corner of his eye drew his attention for a moment. In the window of the house next door was an elderly face, then the curtains swished closed. There was the impression of someone who was trying not to draw attention to how much he saw.

"No warrant, get off my property," the woman said. Anger rolled off her, but there was little else.

The man lifted a shotgun and pointed it out the door. "Get off my porch. Now!"

Danny's shoulders tensed, but he managed to keep his voice low and steady. "Do you know where Robert is?"

Connor gripped his pistol and pulled it free of his holster, using Danny's body to block his movement. He didn't want to set Hernandez off, but he didn't want them to be sitting ducks either if the man fired.

"No, and if I did, I wouldn't tell you," she answered. Her jaw was hard set, her dark eyes blazed with hate. She put her hand on the man's arm, just below the wrist connected to the finger on the trigger. "Now, leave. And don't bother coming back with a warrant. We still won't know anything."

The man glared at them across the shotgun's muzzle. "I ain't killed nobody yet. But there's always a first time. I can even claim self-defense."

A chill went through Connor. He thought he'd been smooth getting his gun out and ready, but the man who was probably Carlos Hernandez had seen him or had the street smarts to know what the move had been.

"Come on, Connor." Danny backed slowly away from the door. "We aren't going to find out anything here."

Connor followed his lead, finally re-holstering his pistol halfway down the walk to the curb. His heart pounded rapidly right up until Carlos Hernandez lowered the shotgun and closed the door.

They reached the sidewalk and turned back toward the Jeep. The whole neighborhood suddenly felt like it was breathing again after holding its breath. Somewhere nearby a bird sang, and there were street noises from the horrendous tourist traffic a couple of blocks away. When he'd had his hand on the pistol, Connor hadn't heard any of that. In all the cases he'd worked, he'd never had a gun pulled on him. He'd always been lucky and his visions had showed him options. The fact his visions weren't working like that with the current case bothered him. He wished he could see what was going to happen so he could make the choices he needed to so he keep Danny and him alive.

"Stay here." Connor stopped at the start of the driveway next door. "I'll be right back. By the way, good move with the foot in the door."

"Thanks. Where you going?" Danny sounded more than a little concerned and a whole lot stressed.

"Questions, questions. I'll be right back."

"I'm coming with you." Danny fell into step with Connor. The way he did it made Connor feel at least a little protected. The short adobe wall between the properties wasn't tall enough to shield either of them from anything if someone in the Hernandez house started shooting.

He walked up the sidewalk to the house next door to the Hernandezes. It was nearly identical, a lot of the adobe houses looked similar, just slight changes in the paint, arches, or decorative designs of the places.

An elderly man leaning on a cane opened the door. His wrinkled face was weather-beaten and his brown eyes glassy.

"I'm sorry to trouble you." Connor kept his voice calm and even, hoping to get the most out of the old man. "I'm trying to find Robert Hernandez. He borrowed some money from me a couple of months ago. I thought I'd look him up since I'm in Taos for the Pow Wow. You haven't seen him have you?"

"Bet you asked Tambora, didn't you?" The man glanced over Connor's shoulder, looking at the Hernandez house. "He could be in the bedroom, and she'd lie and say he wasn't around. Not one of them will tell you the truth." He opened the door. "Come on in and have a seat, before they come out and have more to say to you. Or even start shooting that shotgun he keeps by the door."

Connor and Danny followed him into a modest living room that had some of the clutter to be expected of someone who didn't get around real well. It was obvious he kept his recliner pointed so he could see out and watch the neighborhood. There were piles of mail next to the recliner, and a small wooden folding table with a couple of glasses and a bowl on it that were probably waiting to go back to the kitchen.

"Well now, it was about four or five months ago I last saw Robert." The man settled into the recliner with a soft sigh, then waved at the couch in a clear indication that Connor and Danny should sit.

Connor sat facing him while Danny took out his ever-present pad. Having Danny take notes was good. It helped free Connor up to question people. He just hoped Danny got the information he needed recorded.

"He came home about Christmas time," the man continued. "And left sometime around Easter. I was glad to see him leave and take that eyesore of an RV with him."

"Can you describe the RV for me? I might be able to locate it," Connor said.

"It's about ten years old, green and white, it's like a pickup camper, but it's all one piece. The camper doesn't come off the truck."

Danny wrote down the description. But Connor didn't think he needed to. It matched the other descriptions they had, but at least they were making it look like they were taking everything seriously.

"You've been a big help. Is there anything else you can tell me about the Hernandez boys?"

"Whatever you think he's done, he did it. Tambora will swear he was home when it happened, but he's guilty sure as shootin'. And just so you know, I didn't buy that part about him owing you money. You're cops. I can tell. I was always amazed that, when he was here, he seemed to leave the house right before his parole officer showed up. To tell the truth, I'm surprised that the sheriff hasn't hauled his mother and brother in for obstruction of justice or something like that. He's a sex offender. We all got the notice when he got out of jail."

"The next time you see the parole officer, you might want to let them know what you know about both of them," Connor said. "They have a hard job. It isn't easy to keep track of everyone they have to. I know they're like the rest of us, happy to take whatever help they can get. "

The old man nodded. "I'll keep that in mind. A lot depends on her attitude." He jerked his head in the direction of the Hernandez's house "I'm sure one of these days, she or crazy Carlos are going to start shooting people and I'd really rather it not be me."

"We understand." Connor stood and Danny followed his lead. "Don't bother getting up, we can let ourselves out." They walked toward the door. "Thanks again."

"Whatever he did, I hope you catch him and put him away for good this time. And take the other one and the mother with him."

Connor grinned. "Don't have anything on Carlos right now, but I'll keep it in mind."

They walked out the door and down the walk in silence. Once they were on the sidewalk, Connor pulled out his phone and opened a browser.

"What are you doing now?" Danny asked at his side.

Connor just turned and sighed, then regretted it.

Danny held up his hands in a defensive manner. "I know. No questions. Look, if we're going to be partners, in all senses of the word, you're going to have to lighten up a bit on the no questions. I deserve to know what's going on. Don't keep me at arm's length with things. I deserve to know so I can be prepared."

They reached the Jeep and Connor leaned against the back of it for a moment. "You're right. I'm sorry. I'm not used to working with someone who's not scared of me. I really appreciate the fact that you're willing to call me out on things. I like it."

"Good." Danny grinned and kissed him quickly. "'cause you're not getting rid of me easily. You're too cute, and good in bed."

Connor laughed. "Okay. Both good points. Let's go get some flowers and hit the cemetery. See if there are any ghosts wandering around who might give us a hand."

The first cemetery was about a mile from the flower shop. It was small, and from the looks of it, had been in use since the frontier days. Some of the headstones were weathered wood that looked like they were ready to blow over in a strong wind. They walked around the place for almost an hour before they found the right grave. There was a simple metal rod with a ceramic plaque on it with her name, date of birth and date of death on it. Chief Randall had said that neither victim had family to claim them. Connor wondered who had her buried. Pimps didn't normally care that much. If she'd been part of the local tribe, they might've given her a proper internment. But the who really didn't matter.

Connor took one of the bunches of roses and knelt beside a grave. Opening himself up in a cemetery was risky, but Connor hoped that by being there in the middle of the day he wouldn't be at risk of any of the ghosts there latching on to him. Ghosts loved getting hold of psychics and leading them around. It was worse than some of the visions he had.

The daylight worked its magic. Nothing came at Connor. He touched the plaque. Nothing. He traced the name and dates with his fingers. It was one of the things he hated about the way the visions dragged him around to stop the bad guys. When he was too late to save people it tore at him.

Danny placed his hand on Connor's arm. "Are you okay?"

He shook his head and sighed. "She was just a kid." He realized he needed Danny more than ever. The stakes were rising in the people the visions sent him after. There were going to be a lot more deaths. Danny could be his strength. He was giving him strength without asking.

"Do we have to go to the other grave?" Danny helped him stand, then gave him a nice strong hug.

"Yes." Connor laid his head on Danny's shoulder. His wished more than anything they could just retreat to the cabin in the mountains and hide from the darkness he was always seeing, but he had the family gift for a reason. He had to go on. "There may be something there."

The second cemetery was as empty as the first one. In a lot of ways, Connor was thankful for that.

He walked back to the Jeep. "Let's get a room for tonight and head back to Jemez Springs in the morning."

Danny chuckled. "That might be a feat, considering the Pow Wow's going on, but sure, let's see what we can find. If nothing else, Santa Fe's not too far away, and I think you could use a soak in your tub."

The idea made Connor smile. "Done. And I know just where to stop for dinner. How do you feel about Mediterranean?"

"Sure." Danny clipped his seatbelt closed. "As long as you're buying."

"Always when we're on a case." Connor latched his own seatbelt, then started the jeep.

"I know consultants don't make a ton of money from the police, do you mind me asking where your money comes from?" Danny grabbed the bar on the dash as they bounced onto the road outside the cemetery.

"Family funding," Connor said. "My gifts are hereditary. A few generations back one of my grandmothers decided she didn't want to be poor and wandering all over the world following the visions. She set up a couple of her kids who didn't have visions in the stocks and bonds markets. For some reason the visions helped her get started. Since then, my family's been wealthy and the members born with the Sight don't have to charge for their services. I've never charged any police department or despondent family for the things my powers see, although I will accept expenses from the state or county when they're offered."

"Ah. Sounds like the universe wants you out here taking care of problems."

After dropping the Jeep into fifth gear as they barreled down the highway toward Santa Fe, Connor put his hand on Danny's leg. "And now I've got you to help out too."

Danny turned and smiled. "Right. We're going to stop Hernandez and then see where the visions lead us."

Connor liked the sound of "us". As the mountain twilight grew deeper, his personal light brightened.

Chapter Eighteen

Connor's phone rang as he walked out of the rented mountain cabin. His brain was still fuzzy from the vision. Caller ID showed it was Kennedy. Not that there were any easy visions, but the one he'd just endured had been hard. It had woken him up screaming in the woman's voice. Even Danny's strong arms around him hadn't been enough to help him calm down enough to sleep.

"What do you want, Kennedy?" As soon as his words came out snappy, he mentally kicked himself. He was trying to make some of the changes Danny asked so he'd get along better with the police. With it being Kennedy, he'd reverted to his normal tone, the one Kennedy was used to. "I'm just headed out the door for Albuquerque."

"Somehow I knew you'd already know about it," Kennedy said. "What did you see?"

"Female. Hispanic. And I saw a sign that said South Sandia Peak." Connor left out the screaming. Kennedy didn't really care about the gritty parts of his visions. He was a police officer and was only concerned with the facts.

"Chief Ellis is expecting you." There was the sound of a phone ringing. "Gotta go. Call me when you get there."

"On our way." He hung up and glanced back into the cabin. There were the soft sounds of a shower running.

Connor had already had one before the sun was up, right after the vision, while Danny had fixed the coffee.

"We need to get moving, Dawg." He called as he walked inside finishing his coffee.

The water shut off. "Who was that on the phone?"

"Kennedy. He got a call from Chief Ellis in Albuquerque and told him we'd be there in a little while." He took a deep breath. The cabin smelled a lot homier with the scent of Danny getting out of the shower and the aroma of fresh-brewed coffee. "No uniform. You're with me today, not the sheriff's office."

Danny stepped out of the bathroom with the towel over his shoulders. "So I can come like this?"

Connor sighed. He loved the way Danny was playful when it was just them, but they both understood how they had to act when things got professional. "I wish. Look casual."

"Okay." Danny turned back into the bathroom. "Any new info from what you saw a little while ago?"

"Not that Kennedy said." Connor put his coffee cup in the sink. "You know, just because I have these visions, a lot of people seem to think I know everything. Sometimes it's nice when folks don't do that."

"And that's where I come in." Danny walked into the living room in jeans and socks carrying a shirt and his boots. "I know you don't know everything."

"Thanks, Dawg." He poured a couple of travel mugs of coffee. "We'll call the diner and get some breakfast burritos to go."

"Sounds good. While you get those, I can go let Rusty know I'm heading out again." Danny sighed as he pulled on his shirt. "So how long are we going to keep me just taking vacation time and leaving Rusty and Jeri shorthanded? One of these days I'm going to need to quit so they can hire a new deputy."

It was something Connor hadn't thought about. Things with Danny were moving quickly, more so than the case. They still hadn't officially told any of their friends and coworkers about their relationship, but both Lisa and Officer White had dropped knowing glances and such. They were police officers, they weren't stupid, and being women meant they'd caught on faster than the men.

"Let's get Hernandez, and then we can see." Connor picked up the travel mugs. "Plus won't you have to clear that with Cortez? I thought the local alpha liked having one of his wolves on the police force."

"That was part of what I had to do last night." Danny stomped his foot hard to settle it in his boot. "Cortez says we'll see what he can work out with Rusty."

With the vision, Connor had forgotten about Danny running off for a couple of hours the previous night. He'd had a few ideas to try to work through on how to track Hernandez, and had welcomed the solitude. "Okay." Connor headed for the door. "Let's get rolling. Our bags are still in the Jeep from Taos."

While Connor locked up the cabin, Danny jumped into the Jeep and fastened his seat belt. "Come on, Cat, you're getting slow."

Connor jumped from the porch, over the hood of the Jeep and landed standing in the driver's seat. Although he didn't use it very often, he so loved the flexibility his shifter nature gave him. He handed Danny the coffee mugs and dropped into his seat. He started the engine and pulled out before he said, "Let's roll, Dawg." The trail was fresh again, and he was ready to close in on Hernandez.

The mid-morning traffic was light as they turned off Interstate 25 onto Paseo Del Norte Boulevard. After a few minutes, they pulled up in front of the police department and jumped out of the Jeep.

Connor opened the front door, and Danny walked in ahead of him. He led the way to the reception desk, confident in his new role as buffer between Connor and the police. "We're looking for Chief Ellis. Larry Kennedy in Santa Fe sent us."

"You must be McGriffin," said a tall gray-haired man, who looked up from where he was leaning over a desk talking with another officer.

"That's me." Connor raised his hand from beside Danny. "This is my associate, Deputy Lupan."

"I'm Ellis." The man walked over to the reception desk. "Don't know how you can help, but Kennedy said you have your ways."

Danny suddenly realized that Kennedy understood how a lot of the other police forces wouldn't be as open to Connor and his gifts as the Santa Fe force was. So he didn't elaborate on Connor's 'ways' and left it to Connor to explain. "Right. We've got similar killings across the state and into Colorado."

Ellis frowned. "Across state lines? Why aren't the Feds involved?"

"We're close on his trail," Danny had been expecting that question. "Hoping to get him before he kills again. We let the higher ups deal with notifying the Feds."

"Well, you aren't doing too great if he killed again last night and you were far enough away that you didn't get here until now." Ellis sighed.

"He's changing his MO," Danny kept his voice level even as he felt Connor stiffen beside him. "We weren't expecting him to kill again so soon."

"If he's a serial killer changing his MO, then you might be over your head, *deputy*." Ellis' frown deepened.

"We're pretty good." Danny didn't rise to his needling. "McGriffin is the one who busted the priest killer in Santa Fe a few months back."

That eased Ellis' harsh face a little. "I heard about that one. It took a while."

"Too long," Connor said through gritted teeth.

The way Connor was acting, Danny knew the basic civil decency he was trying to use with Ellis was getting on his nerves. He remembered how Connor acted the first week or so in Jemez Springs. They were going to have a lot of work to do to mellow him out with the authorities.

"So, what do you know so far about your dead hooker?" Danny asked.

"How do you know she's a hooker?" Ellis asked.

"Kennedy told us." Danny suddenly wished they'd used some of Connor's shock and awe tactics as opposed to treating Ellis as an equal, either that or that Kennedy had told Ellis more about the way Connor worked.

Ellis nodded. "Not much to know, other than she was a hooker. Still trying to find her family. Natasha Alvarez had a fairly long rap sheet, but it was all prostitution. The couple of petty theft charges she's had over the years were dropped due to lack of evidence from the men claiming she'd robbed them."

"Sounds like most of the other vics." Danny put his hands behind his back and forced himself not to pace. It would be nice if Ellis would offer to let them into his office as opposed to standing there at the reception desk discussing the delicate subject of murder. "Is the body already in the morgue?"

"Not sure where else it would be," Ellis said. "The coroner hasn't made it in yet today. She should be just like we left her, with a single shot in the forehead. She's not going anywhere."

"Which way's the morgue?" Danny asked. He couldn't remember where Albuquerque kept theirs. Santa Fe had theirs in the basement of the hospital. If he got lucky, maybe the chief would call ahead for them and stay in the office to do whatever paperwork he had to do.

"Downstairs." Chief Ellis came onto the other side of the reception desk, then started down the hall to the elevator. "Hope you're both used to dealing with dead bodies."

"Seen a few." Danny followed Chief Ellis, and he and Connor waited for the steel doors to open.

"Can't always be sure with you small-town guys," Ellis said, then stayed quiet on the ride down.

Danny didn't say anything either. He wondered what Connor was thinking as they descended toward the morgue, but opted to wait until the police chief wasn't right there with them.

Chief Ellis moved like he owned the morgue, walking over to the bank of cold drawers and pulling one open.

"Here she is." He yanked the tray out.

Connor stepped up to the sheet-covered form. He pursed his lips and took a deep breath, then uncovered the body. He touched her naked shoulder and shivered.

"Wait a minute," Ellis said. "What's he doing?"

"Getting a feel for the situation," Danny replied. "It's how he works".

Connor closed his eyes as his fingers touched the cold shoulder of Natasha Alverez. The last minutes of the woman's life came rushing in on him. He gasped as the vision took shape.

She posed provocatively. He'd told her how pretty she was and he was working for a talent agency.

The flash from his camera blinded her for a second.

The lights from Albuquerque were behind him, masking his face. The man raised a different camera.

A shot rang out.

The woman screamed and fell.

It was the same scream that woke Connor before dawn.

Connor opened his eyes. "It's our guy. I know how he gets the women to go along with him. He has a camera with a small caliber gun hidden inside. They think they're posing for a picture."

"Small caliber matches ballistics reports," Danny said, making a note in his pad.

"We've got ballistics reports?" Connor blurted out before he realized Ellis was staring at him.

"Came in yesterday. If you'd gone to the office with me, you'd have seen them. All the women were killed with the same small caliber pistol at close range." Danny bent over and stared down at the hole in Natasha Alverez's forehead. "Once the coroner digs that one out, I bet it matches."

"I'll send the results to Kennedy up in Santa Fe when I get them," Chief Ellis said.

"We've still got lots of questions," Connor said stepping away from Natasha Alverez's body.

"Like why Lacey ran from him," Danny said.

"She's the only one he tied up," Connor said as Ellis covered the body and slid the tray back into the cooler. "She was scared. When he untied her, she ran."

"But she was naked when we found her," Danny said, putting away his pad. "He undressed her and took her clothes after he shot her."

"It wouldn't surprise me to find he raped her after he shot her." Connor frowned. "He had sex with the others before he shot them. Lacey resisted and ran. He still wanted her."

"Yuck." Danny swallowed hard. His wrinkled forehead and frown conveyed his distaste at something they'd never discussed before. "Bad enough raping her, but dead?" He curled his lip disgustedly.

"Some men will do anything for a thrill." Connor walked toward the door, then stopped. "Ellis, I'd like to see where they found her."

"Sure." Ellis gestured for them to leave the morgue and head to the elevator. "I'll get Officer Jackson to take you."

"Sounds good," Danny said.

Following the police chief, Connor picked up on a bit of the strangeness that often came from humans who didn't understand his gifts. He wondered how the man would react if he found out he and Danny were shifters. Too many things that were out of his norm would probably upset him even more. But keeping his tone with humans was often a challenge. With any luck, Danny would stay one step ahead of him in that situation and cover him.

Connor followed as Office Jackson pulled onto the side the road next to a sign indicating the way to South Sandia Peak. It was the sign he'd seen in his vision last night.

Jackson got out of his patrol car and pointed. "Hikers found her right over there."

Connor walked over to where dried blood caked the trampled grass. He looked out over the hills. The scent of bear was all over the place. It was fresh, and since he was getting used to smelling it, he was pretty sure it was Hernandez. He wasn't an expert in the smell of individual bear shifters, but this time it didn't matter. Connor didn't think there were a lot of bear shifters out killing streetwalkers in the area. Connor opened himself up to the impressions of the area, but did his best to not get wrapped up in the vision from the night before. He'd seen Natasha Alverez die twice, he could do without reliving it again.

No vision came rushing in on Connor, instead is was more senstaitons…emotions. The predatory feel was stronger than before. He still couldn't see Hernandez, other than the vague shape he perceived resembled the picture they'd gotten from the Federal penitentiary from Cañon City, Colorado. Hernandez had hungers he was trying to satisfy. That hunger was growing. Connor could feel the conflict between the man and the bear becoming stronger. That might account for the increasing body count and shortening of the time between killings. It also meant he was going to strike again, soon. Connor shivered as he felt like someone was watching him as he searched for Hernandez. "He's still in Albuquerque. We can expect another hit before he leaves. Officer Jackson, where did Alverez work out of?"

"I'd have to check." Officer Jackson walked back to his car. "Can I get that when we get to the station?"

"Sure," Danny added as they approached the Jeep. "We'll follow you." He got into the Jeep and waited.

Connor settled into the driver's seat and started the engine.

"So what did you see that time?" Danny asked as they pulled away from the scene.

"Not see as much as felt." Connor followed Officer Jackson's car down the mountain. "It was like he was watching us."

"You mean like when he was at your place in Santa Fe?"

"Yeah." Connor suppressed another shiver. He'd never had a killer tracking him. "I also think he's having more conflict with his bear side. That's probably why he's killing more. Maybe something in the killing helps push the bear back down. That's why he's doing it with a gun as opposed to with his claws and teeth." Connor shook his head, trying to get his thoughts to organize into something less chaotic, but they were all over the place. He kept seeing the dead hookers, but there was a pair of eyes that flowed from human to bear staring at him.

Danny sighed. "This is why turning humans into shifters is never a good idea. You and I were both born this way. We learned to work with our beasts so there isn't any conflict between us. Shifters who are born fully human don't have that. They struggle to find a balance between them. It makes them more dangerous."

"I can't argue with you on this. But we need to be on our guard. He might be mad we visited his mother. He might use the next one to try and draw us out." Connor hoped he wasn't grasping at straws, but his gut said he wasn't.

"And if that's the case, we've both got silver bullets and we aren't afraid to use them." Danny patted his leg. "We've got this, Cat. Don't worry. Together, we'll find him and take him down."

Connor nodded as they pulled off the highway and turned toward the police station. "I know." He didn't think he'd be able to express the way having Danny next to him and covering his back made him feel. But if Hernandez's target was going to shift, he wanted to be ready for it.

Connor conference called Lisa and Officer White and put it on speaker to make it easier for Danny to throw in comments. "Ladies, add this to the list. South Sandia Park - Natasha Alverez – July 6 – date of death – July 5 – hooker from Albuquerque. I have a feeling he isn't done here yet. Also make a note of the fact that all of the victims except Lacey are Hispanic. This latest one is also a change in his pattern as far as the length of time between victims goes. He's killing more frequently."

"More isn't good," Lisa said right before the sound of a marker on a white board carried through the connection. "Oh, we finally got a response from Cañon City. Turns out they don't segregate their shifters like a lot of places do. As long as the shifter is non-violent, they are housed in the general population. Turns out Hernandez's cellmate was one. Want to take a guess as to what kind?"

"Bear," Connor replied through clinched teeth.

"Right in one," Lisa said.

"So… you guys have already been thinking he's a bear shifter?" Officer White asked.

"Yeah," Danny said. "This one just gets more dangerous by the minute."

"You two be safe," Lisa said. "If you need me, call. I might be some help as you get closer to catching him."

Connor nodded. "Don't worry about it. If I need extra surveillance, I'll call."

Danny raised an eyebrow, obviously still trying to put together what kind of shifter Lisa was.

"You do that." There was a squeak in the background, it sounded a lot like Lisa's desk chair.

"Call you when I get more. Lisa, if you could update Kennedy." Connor reached for his phone.

"Jeri, do the same for Rusty," Danny called before Connor hit the End button. He looked at Connor and pursed his lips. "Surveillance?"

Ignoring Danny, Connor turned to Officer Jackson. "We need to talk to some of Natasha Alverez's friends, and find a place to stay."

Officer Jackson looked up from his computer. "Well, if you take 556 out front and go south, you'll hit I-40. Turn right and you'll find a whole bunch of motels. As to finding friends of Alverez, I'd suggest staying on I-40 over to I-25. There're several truck stops over there where a lot of the girls hang out." He tapped his computer screen. "You might look for Lola Garcia. They've been arrested together a couple of times."

"Thanks. We'll touch base with you tomorrow," Connor said. "In the meantime, have your guys check out RV parks for a green and white Dodge camper."

Danny frowned at him.

Understanding the look and realizing he was taking the police for granted again, Connor sighed. "Sorry. If you could spare a man or two to check through the local RV parks for a green and white Dodge camper with this license plate—" he scribbled down the number of Hernandez's RV and handed it to Officer Jackson. "—that would be greatly appreciated. We don't know for sure where he likes to park when he's not killing people. If we knew that, we'd have him already."

Officer Jackson took the paper. "I'll get this out as an APB. If he's driving it around, we'll spot him. Chief Ellis said we have to get this guy off the streets."

Connor smiled. "Thanks."

Danny patted his shoulder as they headed out the door. "That wasn't too hard was it, Cat."

It was all Connor could do not to scowl. "I'm trying, Dawg. I'm trying." He wondered how he'd managed to solve the cases he had over the years without Danny there to make things a little smoother with the local authorities. Up until then, most of the departments had always been welcoming for his help, and he hadn't even realized he'd taken to being pushy with people until Danny pointed it out. He'd gotten comfortable working with people who needed him.

They checked into a Best Western motel, in the area Officer Jackson had recommended, so they could clean up and call Kennedy. "I'd like to have someone undercover down here." Connor said. "With a bit of hair color, Lisa could pass for Hispanic, but it might be dangerous. Feel her out and let me know. Don't pressure her. I want it to be her call, not yours."

"I'll talk to her and let you know," Kennedy said. "It won't be the first time she's worked the streets for a case."

"I know."

"Any progress?" Kennedy asked.

"Not other than having a feel for where the latest victim worked the streets. If we're lucky, he'll strike there again." Connor hated having to wait on someone else to die, or at least be kidnapped before they could make any more headway in the case, but the way his visions worked and didn't work, that had happened before and was likely to happen again.

Kennedy sighed. "You know, with your gifts, I wouldn't think we'd be relying on luck so much."

"Sometimes luck is our best tool," Connor said.

"You're right. I'll call you back after I talk to Lisa."

"Thanks." Connor ended the call and started for the bathroom.

Danny frowned. "Are you sure you want to put Officer Collins into harm's way?"

"Don't worry about Lisa." Connor paused and looked at Danny where he lounged on the bed with his shirt off and his arms behind his head, looking sexy. He wanted to stay focused. They were getting close, he could feel it. "First of all, she's a cop. Secondly, you picked up on the fact she's a shifter. She can handle herself."

"But I still don't know what she is. Is she big and strong enough to take down a bear?"

"Size and strength aren't always the only factors. I heard of a hummingbird shifter who took down a guy by piercing his eyeball with his beak."

When he came out of the bathroom wearing only a towel, he went over to his duffel bag and pulled out a clean pair of jeans and t-shirt. "Remember, no uniform, Dawg. We're going in incognito on this one. You can carry the badge, but keep it hidden unless you need it."

Danny sat up from the bed; he looked like he'd fallen asleep. "What about my gun?"

"Open carry is legal in New Mexico with a permit." Connor pulled on his shirt. "I assume your badge will act as a permit if you don't have paperwork."

"I took care of that years ago." Danny got off the bed and went over to his own bag. "Rusty wanted to make sure we all had everything in order, even when we aren't on duty. So he made everyone, even Mary on the front desk, get open carry permits as soon as it became legal. I have a card in my wallet."

Connor smiled as he sat down to pull on his boots. "I like Callaway. He's a good guy."

"The best." Danny put on a fresh shirt. "When Sam was alive, Rusty never treated me any differently from his other friends, even though he knew I was gay and a shifter."

For a second, Connor stared at his phone. He had expected Kennedy to call back by the time he'd gotten out of the shower, and had hopes that Chief Ellis' people had uncovered something. He didn't think there were that many RV parks in the Albuquerque area.

Danny's phone rang before they could start out the door. Danny didn't even glance at it as he answered it. "Hey, Rusty, what's up?" He tapped the screen and the speaker came on.

"Danny, got some information for you. Got DNA and ID back from your skeleton. I'm really amazed at how fast that came in."

Connor stepped closer to make sure he didn't miss anything.

"Good," Danny said. "So who is it?"

"Phillipa Gomez."

"Wait a minute. I know that name." Danny pursed his lips.

"Yeah." Connor nodded. "I've heard it too. But I can't put my finger on it."

Rusty chuckled. "Yeah, I can tell you two are gay. I think every straight man in northern New Mexico knows who Phillipa Gomez is. Up until a month ago, she was on a series of burlesque billboards. She was not only a cabaret singer, but the highest rated call girl in the area. She's been missing for four months."

Danny nodded to Connor. "That would fill in one of the months where we didn't have a body."

"Right." Connor liked having holes filled in. "So, Sheriff Callaway, if you could add her name to the list, do we have an estimated time of death?"

"Three to four months ago, based on the rate of decay."

"That fits." Connor tapped his fingers against his leg. He wondered where Hernandez was getting the money for the hookers, but then he realized they weren't getting paid for their last services rendered. "I don't know about the rifling marks, but the hole in her head is consistent with a small caliber weapon. I don't see any reason to exclude her from our list at this point."

"I don't either," Rusty agreed. "She's been listed as a missing person. I guess I can send an official notification that she's no longer missing."

"Now, we just have to catch her killer," Connor said. He was getting impatient to get moving.

"You two keep working on that. I'll let you know if we get anything more through the official channels."

"Thanks, Rusty," Danny said as he tapped the phone to end the call. "Well, at least we don't have a Jane Doe skeleton anymore."

"There is that." Connor turned back to the door. "Now, let's go get some dinner and see about talking to some hookers."

Danny laughed. "You take me on the nicest dates, Kitty Kat."

His comment made Connor wonder what it was going to be like when they had time to actually go on a date. Sure they'd been out to dinner numerous times, but they hadn't had a real date. It would be really nice to go catch a movie and have dinner without fear of the phone ringing, or the latest vision coming rushing in on him.

Chapter Nineteen

A bit north of their hotel, on I-25, heading back toward Jemez Springs, Connor pulled into a large truck stop. The place was packed full of semis, cars, trucks, and all other description of vehicle. The place was large enough it had several restaurants attached to it, including a small Americana diner.

The dinner rush hadn't started yet, and they had their choice of tables. They selected a table close to the door. Connor sat where he could see the other tables and also the door. There were only a few other occupants of the diner.

Five truckers sat at the counter. They sat with at least one stool between them, telling him none of them had come in with any of the others. Three tables were occupied by other truckers — two singles and one with two men. A mother, father, and two children sat in a booth. A second booth held two young women dressed rather provocatively.

A cheerful waitress approached. "What can I get you guys?"

"Iced tea to start, and bring a dish of lemon wedges," Connor said after a quick glance at the menu. "Then I'll have your largest steak, medium rare, with a baked potato, and a Caesar salad."

Danny nodded. "Same here, but make my steak rare, and my salad a large house salad with ranch dressing."

The waitress made notes on her pad, then left.

"Looks fairly quiet in here." Danny unrolled his silverware.

"Yeah. Let's just hope Officer Jackson was right and we can get some info here." Connor sniffed and wrinkled his nose. When he and Danny had time for a date, it was going to be to the best steakhouse he could find. "I'm getting tired of subpar steaks on this job."

Danny pursed his lips and nodded. "Okay. So I was beginning to think you had major food preferences, now I know for sure. But then you *do* have the family money to fund your eating."

"And your eating when we're working a case." He sighed and looked across the table at Danny. His wolf was so handsome. "I promise you, when we're done with this, we're going out for some really awesome steaks."

"I'll hold you to that."

Their waitress came back with the tea. "Order's in. Since you don't want anything well done, it won't take too long. Salad will be ready in just a minute."

"Tell me," Connor said as she put his glass down in front of him, "is there any chance of finding some female company and somewhere to dance around here?"

"Maybe." She raised her eyebrows as she put the small bowl of lemon wedges down. "Is dancing all you want?"

"Yeah. We like to dance and unwind. We just came down from Jemez Springs to visit the big city." He did his best to sound a bit mountain by accenting his Tennessee drawl.

"Let me see what I can do. As long as it's just dancing." She walked away.

"Yeah, that was smooth," Danny mumbled. "You do realize there are gay bars in Albuquerque we could go dancing."

"Time for that later. Just watch her," Connor said. "If Officer Jackson is right, they're not going to ask too many questions, and in a few minutes we'll be the ones asking questions." He took a deep breath, getting a good whiff of the air in the diner. There hadn't been a shifter in there in a day or so. It had been long enough, the bleach and other cleaning products, dulled the faint muskiness of a couple of preditors who'd sat in the same booth as he and Danny.

The waitress picked up some plates from the kitchen and carried them to the family. Then she took a coffee pot over to the table with the two young women.

One of the women looked over at Connor and Danny. She caught Connor's gaze and nodded.

Connor nodded and smiled. "Come on, Dawg." He stood, picked up his tea and lemons and walked over to the booth. "Good evening, ladies. Mind if my friend and I sit down?"

The women scooted further into the booth.

"Barbara said you're looking for dancing partners," the woman next to Danny said.

Connor nodded again, then offered his hand to the woman next to him. "I'm Connor, and this is Danny."

The woman next to Connor said, "I'm Lola, and this is Susan."

A closer look revealed she was older than he first thought. Connor sighed. He loved it when his gut got him on the right track easily. He'd have hated it if he had to work all the hookers in that part of town to find the one he was looking for. He decided to cut right to the chase and hopefully save them all some time. "What we really want is some information. Do you know Natasha Alverez?"

The two women looked at each other. The slight musk of fear overrode the strong floral smell of their perfume.

"Are you cops?" Lola asked, looking like she would've run if Connor hadn't been sitting between her and the door.

"Yes, but you aren't in trouble," Danny told her in his easy gentle voice. "We're investigating Natasha's murder."

"She's dead," Susan gasped as her hand went to her throat. "When?"

"They found her body this morning," Connor said, keeping the information to a minimum. Until they had Hernandez in custody, he knew the local police would frown on him giving out too much info. "We believe she was killed by a man the police have been chasing for over a year. She's his eighth confirmed victim. When was the last time you saw her?"

Susan glanced at Lola who nodded. "I saw her get into a gray Honda last night."

"Where was this?" Danny asked as he pulled out his pad and began taking notes.

"Over by the truck stop on Sixth Street," Susan continued

"Did you get a good look at the driver?" Connor asked.

"He had dark longish hair is all I can tell you," Susan answered.

Barbara brought two bowls of salad and set them down in front of Connor and Danny. "So, you guys are going dancing? That's good."

"Do you ladies want anything to eat?" Danny asked before Barbara could walk away

"Now that you mention it, food sounds mighty good," Lola said. She and Susan ordered.

Connor and Danny finished their salads just as Barbara brought the women's salads, and their steaks.

"I'll take the ticket, Barbara." Connor moved his salad bowl over to make room for his plate.

"Not going to get dessert?" Barbara wiped her hands on the rag in her apron.

"I think all of this will be more than enough." Connor made the first cut into his steak. There was just a little bit of pink, the way he liked it.

"I'll be back with your check in a moment." She hurried away.

"You know their pie here is really good," Lola said.

Danny shook his head. "We're not really into pie."

Connor nearly choked on the piece of steak he was chewing and then glared at Danny, but they hadn't kept up the ruse they'd told Barbara, so he didn't care what the two women at the table knew and didn't know.

Barbara came back as Connor and Danny were finishing their meal and handed Connor the bill. "Pay at the register."

Danny placed Hernandez's prison mug shot on the table. "Watch out for this guy. He's the man we're looking for. Tell your friends about him."

Lola nodded. "I think I've seen him around." She made the picture disappear into her purse. "I'll warn everyone not to do anything with him. We'll also let Saul, our talent coordinator, know. Natasha was one of our best. He'll want a piece of the guy."

"We don't know what he says to his victims, but apparently he offers to take pictures of them for something." Connor slipped out of the booth. "Just be careful. We don't want to see either of you in the morgue. We think he's a bear shifter. Warn Saul to use silver bullets if he goes after him."

"You ladies have a nice evening," Danny said as he tipped an imaginary hat. "After that dinner, I think I'm too tired to go dancing."

"Thanks for the dinner company." Connor laid two fifties on the table, then walked out.

As they got into the Jeep, Danny frowned a little. "Do you think it was a smart thing to do to tell them Hernandez is a bear shifter?"

"I figured once she announced she was going to tell the pimp it might be a good idea. Most humans are still wary of our kind, and he'll be less likely to do something stupid like try and have Hernandez roughed up. We don't need a bear shifter pimp popping up." Connor started the Jeep.

"Yeah, Cortez would really be pissed, even if this isn't really pack territory."

Connor drove around the building to the truck stop proper, parked, and they went inside.

Connor walked around the store area. He stopped a few times and closed his eyes. He didn't pick up anything that caught his attention.

Danny approached the cashier and showed his badge and a photo of Hernandez from the prison. "Have you ever seen this man?"

The cashier glanced at Danny, then back at the picture. "I think so. Yeah. He was in here last night. What's he done?"

"We just need to talk to him. Did you see what kind of car he was driving?"

"He was in a gray Honda. He filled up over at pump number three."

"Did he pay cash or use a card?"

"He used a card at the pump." The cashier pointed to the TV screen behind him. "He looked right at the camera, and then ducked his head like he was surprised it was there. I wondered if he'd just gotten out of jail or something. Everyone knows there's cameras at gas stations."

Without a word to either Danny or the clerk, Connor went back out the door and over to pump three. He opened himself up to the energies around the pump. There was a rush of sensations.

People angry because the pump was slow.

A man and woman fighting over the cost of a pack of cigarettes and which one of them smoked more.

Then the vision he was looking for came to him. *The man from the picture was still out of focus but he held the gas pump in the tank.*

The license plate was visible.

The woman from the morgue approached the car. 'Hi, handsome. Are you looking for some company?'

Hunger rose up, and rage. The two sensations were nearly overpowering.

The vision shattered before Connor could see anything more. It was like something abruptly blocked him. He was getting tired of not getting all the information he needed on Hernandez.

On the way back to the Jeep, Connor called Chief Ellis. "We're looking for a gray Honda Civic. Here's the license plate number." He read off what he'd seen in the vision and hoped he was right. "See if you can find where he rented it and have them notify you as soon as he turns it in. If possible keep him there."

"Is this McGriffin?" Chief Ellis sounded a little gruff.

"Yes." Connor inwardly groaned. Danny had been trying so hard to get him to play nice with the authorities. "Sorry, Chief Ellis. I should know to lead with my name. I just get excited when the leads are starting to flow, and I'm used to Chief Kennedy knowing my voice."

"Right," Chief Ellis grumbled. "Look. I've got your APB out on the RV. So far nothing. Now you want me to check rental agencies for a Honda Civic. You know there's also the chance it's been stolen. Didn't think of that, did you?"

Being stolen didn't feel right, but Connor didn't say that. "No, that hadn't crossed my mind."

"I'll let you know if I turn up something." Ellis hung up before Connor could.

"Really need to work on your people skills," Danny said as he clicked his seat belt.

He turned to Danny. "I think it's time to call it a night. I hope you brought a swimsuit. That indoor pool looked inviting."

"Yeah, I did." Danny grinned. "I was a Cub Scout. 'Always Be Prepared.'"

Connor had no doubt Danny was going to be ready for the night he wanted them to have. It would be great to relax for a little while, as they waited for Hernandez to make the next move.

Chapter Twenty

Connor stared at Danny. "Dawg, I thought you were prepared."

Feeling a little less than observant, Danny held up the hand towel he'd grabbed in the hotel room instead of the bath sheet he should've grabbed. "Hey, it's not my fault the maid folded it funny and I grabbed the wrong one. My mistake."

"Fine. You can go back and get the proper one, unless you want to drip all the way down the hall when we get through swimming."

Danny pursed his lips and glared at Connor. "It's been a long day, Cat. I'll run get the right towel. You go ahead and splash around a bit." He shook his head. "You know, the way you enjoy water, I'd swear you were a tiger, or a jaguar, not a mountain lion."

Slipping into the pool, Connor shrugged. "My mom was human and took me swimming as much as possible when I was a kid. Dad didn't like water as much, so I think she was doing it to be passive aggressive to get more time alone with me."

"Could be, or could be you're just weird." Danny turned toward the door leading back to the hallway. "I'll be right back." He didn't wait for Connor to reply before he walked through the door. The coolness of the hallway hit him, making goosebumps along his arms. He really wished he'd been paying more attention to grabbing the right towel and not so much to Connor's furry ass as he put on his bathing suit. He could be in the pool with Connor and not waiting for the elevator and trying not to freeze as the air-conditioned breeze blew around him.

A brief whiff of musk hit him as the elevator dinged. Danny glanced around, but didn't spot anything odd. There was an old couple at the check-in desk. A young woman pushed past him before the elevator doors were even open all the way. She had an ice bucket in her hands and was heading for the vending room area near the check-in desk. He shook his head and put his arm out to stop the elevator doors from closing.

When the door closed, the musky smell grew stronger. It reminded Danny of the bear, probably Hernandez, that he'd chased from Connor's place in Santa Fe. He suddenly wished he had his pistol, but he'd left it in his duffel bag on the extra bed in the motel room.

The scent of fresh blood hit him hard as the elevator opened.

"Damn." Danny ran down the hall toward their room. When he turned the corner, he skidded to a stop.

A burly man stood over a woman in the middle of the hallway in front of their door.

A growing pool of blood seeped from under the woman's body.

"Stop right there and put your hands on the wall!" Danny shouted, in his loudest cop voice. He tried to reach out telepathically to Connor and it felt like something was blocking him. He could barely feel Connor, let alone touch his mind.

"You're trespassing." The man straightened and glared at Danny. His eyes weren't human. The cold darkness of a bear stared out of Robert Hernandez's human face. It looked like his bear was in charge, but he didn't know if it was possible to tell for sure with a serial killer.

Cold sweat broke out on Danny's brow. He didn't have anything more than a towel and a hotel room key card. "Hernandez, you're under arrest for murder. Step away from the girl, and put your hands on the wall." Danny didn't expect him to comply, but he hoped by using his most commanding tone, Hernandez, who'd spent years in prison would obey, if only on default behavior.

Hernandez lumbered over the body and charged Danny.

Danny backed up. He didn't want to run, but Hernandez was a bear. Danny was a wolf. Alone. Unarmed.

Leaping over Hernandez, Danny shifted. He went too high and hit his head on the popcorn ceiling, clipping one of the sprinkler heads embedded there for safety. His head pounded as he stumbled to a four-footed landing next to the body in front of their door. It was Lola.

"You don't get to sniff her." Hernandez grabbed Danny's tail and swung him hard into the wall. "They're all my prey, not yours."

Stars filled Danny's vision. He tried to turn and snap at Hernandez, but the murderer still had hold of his tail. He had to get free. He hoped Connor would have one of his visions and know he was in danger. Maybe together they'd be enough to bring Hernandez down.

Danny twisted far enough around and snapped at Hernandez, getting his teeth deep into the man's meaty hand.

"No." Hernandez slammed his hand into Danny's head.

Yelping in pain, Danny dropped to the floor.

"Stop." Hernandez's voice changed slightly. "He's a cop. They'll care if we kill a cop."

Danny tried to focus, but his head pounded so hard he could barely open his eyes.

Hernandez hit him again and even the smell of Lola's blood was gone as darkness engulfed Danny.

Connor swam to the far side of the pool and wondered what was taking Danny so long.

"Dawg, you need to hurry up before I get all shriveled up and need to get out of the pool." He reached out mentally, but there wasn't a snarky reply. He hit himself for forgetting he was in water and water blocked his visions, so it only made sense that it would block his telepathy too. Before Danny came along, he'd never had a reason to trying reaching out to another mind while he was in water.

"Five minutes," he mumbled as he started back across the pool. "I'm giving him five minutes then I'll go looking for him and give him hell for interrupting our swim with his lack of observational skills."

A police siren wailed in the parking lot before the five minutes was up. Connor looked out the thick glass that enclosed the pool. Three police cars whipped into the parking lot, heading toward the front of the hotel. He jumped out of the pool and ran to where he'd left his towel and room key. *"Dawg, we've got an issue."*

There was something wrong with Danny. Connor pushed through their link, trying to get more. Pain lanced through him, dropping him to his knees on the rough cobblestone floor.

Lola stood and walked out of the restaurant after enjoying her steak. She'd left Susan there after getting a call from Saul about a client specifically asking for her. As she walked to the bus stop on the curb, a large truck with a camper on it roared out of the night heading straight toward her.

She tried to run, but she stumbled.

A big hand picked her up off the ground by her neck, cracking it. He threw her into the back of the truck and slammed the door.

Pain radiated up and down her back. Her head pounded. She felt like a bunch of people were staring at her.

The truck stopped somewhere. The door opened, and the big man leaned over her.

"Still alive. Good." His voice was gruff, like he was having trouble getting the words out.

He grabbed her and hauled her out of the truck. After he slammed the door again, he tossed her over his shoulder like she didn't weigh anything.

The fear was almost too much.

Pain lanced out again. She couldn't focus as the man climbed a flight of stairs and entered a motel hallway.

Connor fought to get out of the vision. He knew the hallway. He had to move, but the pain in his own knees and the pain emanating from Lola was too much. He sank to the floor and moaned as he watched Hernandez carry Lola to their motel-room door, rip her throat out, and leave her lying on the brown patterned carpet.

The door to the pool area opened. "Hey, are you okay?" a man asked. "Looks like we've got another vic."

There was a bit of static coming from somewhere close by.

"Help me up." Connor forced himself to roll over. He stared at the police officer standing above him.

"Are you okay, sir?" The police officer bent over and offered Connor a hand up.

Ignoring the pain lancing through his legs, Connor shook his head. "Not really. Call Chief Ellis. Tell him Connor McGriffin told you to. There's been another hooker killed."

"Connor McGriffin?" The officer looked dubiously at him. "Do you have any ID?"

Connor sighed. He didn't have time for police procedures. "In my room. If we must we can go up there, or you can just get Chief Ellis on the line. He'll recognize my voice."

The officer pushed the button on the mic on his shoulder and asked. "Dispatch, is Chief Ellis available?"

"Chief Ellis is in route to your location, Landes, I'll put you through to him." The dispatcher sounded frantic.

"This is Ellis, Landes, what's the problem that can't wait until I get there?" Ellis didn't sound like he was having a good day either.

"I've got a Connor McGriffin here who wants to talk to you. Says there's been another murder." Officer Landes replied, looking Connor over as if he was trying to asses a threat.

Another voice came over the radio before Ellis could answer. "Dispatch, we've got a body on the second floor, her throat's been ripped out."

"I guess that answers that," Ellis said. "Keep McGriffin there, Landes."

Connor lurched for the mic, then backed off when Landes' hand went for his pistol. "Danny's missing. I can't reach him." Connor's wanted to give into the pain in his heart and his knees and sink down to the floor. Without being able to sense either Danny's thoughts, or his future, he wasn't sure how he was going to rescue him before Hernandez killed him.

"Danny?" Landes looked confused. "Do we know a Danny, Chief?" He asked into the mic.

"Does he mean Deputy Lupan?" Ellis replied. "Never mind, I'll be there in just a second, I'm pulling into the motel now."

"Yes, I mean Deputy Lupan." Connor muttered. He wanted to grab Landes and shake him. Then he remembered Danny telling him to treat the police better and he'd get better results. "Officer Landes, can I please go to my room and get my cell phone? I need to make some calls and get us some help down here."

Officer Landes looked down his long nose at Connor. "Are you implying that the Albuquerque Police Department isn't going to be able to handle this situation?"

Connor started to say something, then a vision filled his head.

Danny lay still in the desert while metal bars kept Connor from getting to him.

"No." Connor folded his arms and did his best not to look angry. "I just need a bit of personal support in this."

Chief Ellis marched into the pool area. "All right, Landes, I'll take McGriffin from here."

A look of relief crossed Officer Landes' rugged face. "What do we need here, Captain?"

"Room by room search." The captain's steely gaze settled on Connor. "We need everyone who was in the motel at the time to give a statement. Hopefully someone saw or heard something."

As Landes hurried off to comply, the Chief gestured for Connor to walk over to one of the tables and have a seat in the metal chairs there. "All right, McGriffin, what's going on? I get a call that somebody found a woman with her throat ripped out in front of what turns out to be the room you and Deputy Lupan are in, and you're down here in the pool."

"Look." Connor rubbed the bridge of his nose. He had to stay calm and stop the vision of Danny's death from coming true. To do that, he had to stay out of jail, and that meant he had to cooperate with the police. "All I know at this point is there's a dead woman in the hall and Danny, Deputy Lupan, is missing."

"If you were down here in the pool, how do you know there's a dead woman up there?" Chief Ellis pointed in the direction of Connor and Danny's room.

Connor took a deep breath, there was a slight hint of blood on the air. "I can smell the blood."

Chief Ellis' frown deepened. "You're a shifter. Why didn't you tell me that before?"

"I didn't think it was important. It's just part of who we are." Connor was used to encountering prejudice against his psychic gifts more than his race, but he knew it was still out there.

"I suppose since you two say we're chasing a bear shifter, having shifters to help catch him is a good idea." Chief Ellis seemed to ignore the chatter on his radio as he talked with Connor.

It was all Connor could do to sit there and talk to the police chief like there wasn't anything major wrong. Danny was missing. Hurt and missing, but he had to sit there and endure the pain in his heart. He couldn't let his vision come to pass. "We didn't realize Hernandez was a shifter until we'd been on the case for several weeks. If you call Chief Kennedy in Santa Fe he can explain everything."

"I got all out of Kennedy I needed when he said your ways were a little odd, then your display in the morgue. I also talked to Randall in Taos. She said you have visions, and she didn't like it. If it helps me catch this monster, I'll accept your visions."

For the first time since Landes found him on the floor, Connor relaxed just slightly. Ellis wasn't going to be a complete blockade to him finding Danny. He let out a sigh of relief. "Thank you. Can I go get my phone from my room? I need to get a little extra backup down here."

Chief Ellis let out a long breath. "More shifters no doubt. Look, bring in whoever you need to. Get this bastard off my streets. Then get out. Have you wondered why there aren't a lot of shifters in New Mexico other than that wolf pack up in Sheriff Callaway's district?"

Connor shook his head. "No." His gut tightened.

"We don't like your kind. We tolerate Cortez because he was here first, and the big treaty between shifters and humans that helped us win WWI makes us. But we do think it's for the best that most of your kind move on east or west. Some people, like Kennedy and Callaway, don't care. I do." Chief Ellis stood and started out of the room. "Oh, and make sure you clear everything with me before it happens. I won't have you endangering the good humans under my protection."

Connor sat there and stared at the chief's broad back as he turned down the hallway. He hadn't encountered that level of distrust of his kind in years. He had no control over where his visions were going to take him, but he hoped once they got Hernandez and left Albuquerque, he wouldn't have to come back for more than driving through on the highway. But right now, he had more important things to worry about. He had to find Danny and get him back.

Pacing didn't help him concentrate, but Connor didn't care. He hoped he wasn't wearing a hole in the carpet of the new motel room. Chief Ellis hadn't made him give an official statement. He'd told Landes Connor was working with the Albuquerque Police Department and was to get all the help Landes and the others could provide. To stay out of the way, Connor had moved his and Danny's stuff to the motel next door, which turned out to be run by the same chain, and was just slightly higher priced.

"Look, I'll be there in an hour," Lisa said. "What do you need me to bring?"

"Yourself and your sharp eyes. I can't find Danny. I need all the help I can get."

"No worries. I'm coming. Hey, have you tried contacting his pack leader?"

"Why?" Connor didn't think Ellis would like having more shifters underfoot.

"You two have a telepathic bond going on, right?"

"Right…ah how did you know about that?" Connor had thought he and Danny had done a pretty good job hiding the fact they were in a relationship.

"Connor, I'm a friend, I'm a shifter, and I'm a police woman. I'm a bit more observant than most. I could tell something was clicking with you two even if you were a little distant about things a month ago in the mountains. I could tell by the way you were treating him here in Santa Fe things had changed."

He sighed. "Yeah. But what does that have to do with his alpha, Cortez."

"It's my understanding that a pack bond, or a flock bond, works differently from a mate bond. The alpha, or even one of the pack, might be able to track Danny where you can't." There was the click of an ammo cartridge sliding into a pistol on the other side of the connection. "Now, I don't know this for sure. I'm a kestrel. Like mountain lions, we don't have pack or flock bonds. We just do mate bonds."

"I guess I can try." Connor wasn't sure how Cortez would handle a call from him. He looked over at the dresser where he'd plugged Danny's phone into the charger. He'd try anything to get Danny back.

"Now we also have to figure out why Hernandez changed his MO," Lisa said. "I'll think about that while I drive down. It's night, or I'd fly. Unfortunately, since the full moon's not out, I'm almost night blind."

"Drive safely." Connor hung up and set his phone down next to Danny's. He felt like he was invading Danny's life by using his phone without permission. But Danny wasn't there, and he wasn't getting anything useful in his visions.

Picking up the phone, he unplugged it and hit the button to turn it on.

The vision hit Connor hard and fast.

Ropes cut into his wrist.

His head pounded so hard he couldn't concentrate.

He opened his eyes. Everything was dark.

The pleasant aroma of rich soil filled his nose.

His spine ached.

Connor stumbled back and fell across the bed. He wasn't seeing where Danny was, he suddenly was Danny. Their bond was impacting his Sight. He held Danny's phone as tight as he could, but he couldn't find him again. There was something wrong, and he couldn't tell if it was with him or Danny. He couldn't lose Danny. He'd just found him.

With shaking fingers, Connor scrolled through Danny's few contacts to find Cortez. He tapped the name to connect the call.

"Daniel, tell me you have good news and have gotten that bear out of my territory," Cortez answered on the second ring.

"It's not Danny, it's Connor."

"His cat." He all but spat the words through the phone. "Why are you calling me and not Daniel?"

"Danny's missing. I think Hernandez took him." Connor blurted out. "I can't find him through our link. I'm hoping your pack bond can find him."

Cortez hummed for a moment. "He's a couple of hours away. I can feel him. He's still alive. Injured. Broken bones, maybe concussion." His voice grew distant like he was pulling the phone away and covered it with his hands. "Go find Jime!" Then he put the phone back to his head. "Where are you? I'll send Jime to you. He'll be able to find Daniel. He'll stay with you until the bear is dealt with."

Connor told him what motel and room he was in, then Cortez was gone, leaving Connor alone with Danny's phone and his fears. Try as he might, he couldn't get another vision from Danny's point of view. It was like Danny wasn't really there, but he was. He was still alive. Connor knew that. If Danny was dead, there would be a deep hole inside Connor that would never be filled.

Chapter Twenty-one

As consciousness returned, Danny coughed, trying to get some of the dirt and dust out of his nose. It was dark. His hands were bound behind his back. His tail bone hurt, feeling like something had been broken. He was face down in the dirt, but he was alive.

"Connor! Cat, can you hear me?" He pushed his thoughts out. His head recoiled against his efforts, sending waves of pain that slammed him back into oblivion.

"What do we have?" Lisa asked as she entered Connor's hotel room.

"Nothing new." Connor closed the door. Locking it gave him a sense of security he wasn't used to the action providing. "I've been trying everything I know to reach Danny. The one time I did, I was too deep in our bond to get anything useful. I know he's tied up. I know he's face down in dirt. He's hurt his lower spine. God, I just hope he can still walk. Something must be keeping him from shifting, or he'd shift and heal it."

"He's going to be fine." Lisa gave him a big hug. "Look, we've got a couple of hours until sunrise. We need to get some rest."

Connor shook his head. He'd not been able to sit down and relax since he got off the phone with Cortez. "I can't. I can't even sit still. I need to be doing something. I've already shifted and searched the parking lot of the hotel where Danny was taken from. I found the scent of the RV and followed it to the interstate. Lost it on the on ramp. Of course the semi that nearly hit me might've had something to do with that."

She frowned. "Okay. See, you're pushing too hard. You almost got hit by a truck. You're not going to do Danny any good if you get killed looking for him."

"You're right." He sat on the bed, placed his elbows on his knees and his head in his hands. "I never thought I'd feel this way about anyone, especially a wolf shifter. I remember something my grandmother told me when the first relationship I considered serious broke up. We were sitting on the porch drinking lemonade."

Lisa sat beside him and rubbed his shoulder. "What did she tell you?"

"I was lamenting the fact that I'd probably never find anyone who would accept both my shifter side and the Sight. The human I'd been with didn't want me to shift, and my visions made him uneasy." He looked up. "Can you imagine how you'd feel if Steve told you not to shift?"

"I'd probably kill myself." She chuckled. "Or him."

"I did have a short fling with a bobcat shifter, but I've never met another gay cougar. She held up her glass of lemonade and then pointed to my plastic tumbler. 'It doesn't matter what kind of vessel the lemonade's in, me Bairn, as long as it satisfies your thirst. Someday you'll find someone who satisfies the thirst inside you, and you won't care what he is. He may be shifter, or he may be human. You'll recognize the heart and soul inside the outer body.' She was right. I don't care that Danny's a wolf; I only care that he satisfies the thirst inside of me."

Lisa looked at him with a wan smile. "Grandmas usually know what they're talking about."

Someone knocked on the door. Connor sniffed. A canine smell that wasn't Danny hit him. He walked to the door and looked through the peephole before he opened it.

"Connor, Cortez says you got my Fuz Cuz kidnapped by a crazy bear shifter?" Jime stepped into the room. "Dude, that's some messed up shit."

"Thanks for coming, Jime. I think we're going to need all the help we can get." Connor closed the door behind him. "Lisa, this is Jime, Danny's cousin. I took your advice and called their alpha for help."

Lisa stared at the two of them. "Wow. You actually listened to someone other than yourself. Danny's having a great effect on you."

"Thanks. I think." Connor looked at Jime. "So can we use the pack bond to find Danny?"

"I tried on the way down here. It's all kinda fuzzy, but let's hit the road and see what we can find."

It was the first hope Connor had felt in hours. He grabbed his keys and his pistol. "Come on you two. I'm driving."

Things were warmer the next time he woke up. Danny lay there, keeping his breathing slow and regular. He wanted to try and move, but his head hurt so badly, he lay there, just enjoying each breath of dusty air that filled his lungs.

Then, something moved in the darkness.

"Your breathing has changed." Hernandez's voice was deep, but not gruff. It was the voice Danny remembered from the hallway that said they shouldn't kill cops.

"Why did you kidnap me?" Danny managed to get out between his dry cracked lips. His throat complained about the words and he coughed. That made his head hurt worse.

"He wanted to kill you. I don't know what to do. I don't like him bossing me around."

Danny remembered Connor saying something about Hernandez might be a multiple personality, or he might just be a turned shifter at odds with his animal half. "Who wanted you to kill me?"

"The bear. He still wants me to kill you. He says you're interfering with our hunts. I don't understand why I can still hear him. Killing the girls makes him be quiet. I kill them when he starts getting too loud."

The timing of the kills suddenly made sense. Even through Danny's pounding head, he could understand what Hernandez was doing. During the full moon, the bear that was now inside him, burst out then would still be trying to integrate with Hernandez for several days after the full moon, even after Hernandez returned to his human form. The killing of the hookers sated the bear for a time. Maybe the bear was getting stronger with each moon and pushing him to kill more frequently.

"Your bear will do that unless you find a way to work with him," Danny said. He'd had the talk with younger members of the pack, wolves in their teens, who were just starting to shift and were a little confused on how to communicate with the beast inside them.

"I don't want to work with him. Zack never said anything about having to work with the bear he put in me." In the darkness Hernandez moved. A wave of dust flowed up around Danny. "If I was working with him, you'd be dead now, instead of a problem I have to figure out how to deal with."

Light blazed in around Danny as Hernandez opened a door and walked out. The brightness hurt, hitting Danny hard. Tears ran down his face, and his head renewed its pounding. He pulled against the ropes, but they were too tight. The strain left him hurting and tired. He really wanted be untied and get something to drink. Connor was out looking for him. Danny held onto that thought. They had just found each other, there was no way Connor wouldn't do everything he could to locate him. He just hoped it would happen before Hernandez and his bear came to an understanding and the bear killed him.

Chapter Twenty-two

Although their search through the nighttime desert had been long and fruitless, Connor didn't want to head in and see Chief Ellis as the sun came up. Lisa had made a really good point and convinced him they should at least stop in and see if Chief Ellis had come up with any new info.

The Albuquerque police station was abuzz with activity as they walked in.

"You know, I can wait in the Jeep," Jime offered. "I'm cool with Danny being a cop, but so many overly-testosteroned humans with weapons make me nervous."

"Just be mellow and we'll all be fine," Lisa said. "Oh, and let Connor and me do all the talking."

Connor nodded. "Right." He spotted Chief Ellis standing talking to a couple other officers. "There's the chief." He headed through the squad room, nodded to a couple of the police officers he'd met the previous day. They looked at him like he was different from what he had been. The way they darted their eyes around showed their discomfort. Connor didn't like the idea they were nervous around them. That could end badly. He did his best to not let them know he sensed their nervousness.

"We were too late." Chief Ellis turned from the two men he was talking to as they approached. His smile was a little disturbing, considering they still hadn't found Danny.

"He turned the car in yesterday morning. He used the name Hubert King and paid with a credit card. He also had a driver's license in that name with an address in Tucumcari. The agent said he gave a cell phone number. She called the number while he was there, and it rang in his hand. I had it checked out and it's a burner cell. I checked the name Hubert King and the address. Mr. King had his ID stolen about a year ago when he was in Santa Fe. Said he thought he'd canceled all of his cards, but must have missed one.

"The car rental agent said something to Hernandez about the picture on the license not looking like him. He told her he'd cut and dyed his hair and got contacts since it was taken a couple of years ago. I asked the rental agency to hold off cleaning the car until you can get there. Kennedy told me you have your eccentricities about things like that."

Before heading to the car rental office, Connor looked at the map of New Mexico they had on the far wall of the squad room. "I bet he knows we're onto him."

"Other than him taking deputy Lupan instead of killing him outright when he killed the latest vic, what makes you think so? How would he know?" Ellis asked. His tone made it sound like Connor was some kind of simpleton. Connor wanted to say something and just storm out, but his vision of Danny in the desert stopped him cold.

"His mother probably contacted him," Connor explained in his most even, easy going voice. "She was overly protective when we questioned her. She doesn't realize he's killing her."

Chief Ellis frowned. "What do you mean, 'killing her'?"

"Look at all of the victims." Lisa cocked her head and put her hands on her hips, assuming her small-but-mighty pose. "Hispanic hookers just like his mother was. He hates her for how they lived when he was a kid."

"You could be right." Ellis nodded thoughtfully and tapped the map, hitting the spots where Hernandez had killed. "But this doesn't help us get your deputy Lupan back, or stop him from killing again."

"No it doesn't." Connor stared at the map, hoping something would come to him. "I think we need to run Hubert King's name through the New Mexico Property Database and see if he's purchased or rented anything recently. We might also have the credit card company get us records of all the purchases on the card that wasn't canceled. See if you can get King to leave the card active for now. If he keeps using it, we might be able to track his location by his purchases."

Chief Ellis frowned. "That's a lot of work for a couple of people. I've already got people going over the traffic cameras last night from the area around the motel trying to spot his RV."

It wasn't the first time Connor had thought about using the traffic cameras to try to find Hernandez, but it was the first time it was a decent option. They would've had to go back too far in Santa Fe, and not only were there no traffic cameras in Jemez Springs, the crime scenes were too far out of town. "Any luck so far?"

"We can see it got on I-25 and headed south." Chief Ellis walked over to the desk of a young woman who looked fresh out of the police academy. She was scanning through video. "We've been able to track him to I-40, but after that, we lost him. There are a number of truck stops on the western side of town, also a fair number of exits that head off into the desert."

"That matches what we've been trying to track," Connor said, looking over his shoulder at Lisa and Jime, who were back to staying fairly quiet and looked like they were trying to dissolve into the woodwork. They were all tired after spending the night trying to follow a fuzzy pack bond through the desert. They'd had a lot of stops and starts. He and Jime both hoped they could get a better fix on Danny if he was awake and able to return their telepathic calls.

"You get too far out there, and we're into county jurisdiction." Ellis leaned on the desk next to the woman looking a video. "I'm on good terms with Sheriff Ogden. If we need to get them involved, we can." He stared at Connor. "I'm not sure how warm his welcome to you will be."

"Then hopefully we won't have to involve him." Connor heaved a sigh. If there was one thing he wanted to avoid, it was more hostile human's running all over the place shooting silver bullets. Having Ellis' people involved was more than enough for him. "Now, we'll head over to the car rental agency and see if the Civic can give us any useful information. If possible, it would be good to have your forensics team go over it when I'm done."

"Then make sure you don't make a mess of the car," Chief Ellis said.

Connor nodded. "I'll do my best."

Connor sat in the Civic and opened himself up to the energies there. Conflict filled the car, but he couldn't get a good feeling for who it came from. There was also happiness, but he'd grown to expect that from the hookers Hernandez killed. The man knew how to work the women. He opened the trunk and looked around. There wasn't anything there that said it was anything other than a rental car. Everything was almost too clean, and Connor doubted Hernandez ever opened it, except at the rental agency.

"So, what is he doing?" Jime whispered to Lisa.

"It's his thing," Lisa replied.

"Oh, Fuz-Cuz said something about him having visions."

"And he probably won't with all the whispering going on," Connor grumbled as he knelt down and looked at the car's tires. They were standard tires, but there was a thick layer of red dust caught in the treads. "Lisa, do me a favor and get an evidence bag out of the glove box. I'd like to take some of this dust with me."

"It's just dust, Cat," Jime said, kneeling next to the back of the car.

Connor wasn't sure how he felt about Jime using Danny's nickname for him. "But it might help lead us to Danny if I can just relax enough to get a vision about the road it's from." Connor knew it was a long shot, but he was willing to take it. He had to get Danny back.

"Lead us to the road." Jime straightened, shaking his head. "Cortez is right, cats are crazy."

Ignoring him, Connor made a thorough search of the car, finding a few tumbleweed twigs stuck in the grill, and the bodies of a good number of grasshoppers. He doubted the insect remains would help much, but he pulled the tumbleweed sticks and had Lisa bag them. He still didn't have a good sense of direction beyond what Jime had been able to give him, but he was going to use that and the little bit Chief Ellis had said about the traffic cam footage showing Hernandez heading west. It was a start.

The cramp started in Danny's shoulders and worked its way down his arms and back. He was tired of lying there in the dirt, but every time he tried to move, his head hurt so badly he nearly passed out. The higher the temperature in the small shed — at least that's what he thought he was in — rose, the more his head pounded. He was beyond thinking he had a concussion, he was sure of it. He couldn't remember if a concussion was something shifting could help repair. Shifting could fix most non-life-ending injuries, but there were a few, mostly ones that caused mental damage, that it couldn't.

He really wanted something to drink, but it had been several hours since Hernandez had come to visit at sunrise, and Danny had almost given up hope when the door opened again. The mid-morning light rushed in, blinding him for a moment and making his head hurt worse.

"He's quiet now," Hernandez said, his voice little more than a whisper.

The absurdity of the statement, of Hernandez referring to his bear as a separate entity, made Danny want to laugh. Their animal sides weren't separate from them. Yes, he thought differently as a wolf, but his sensory input was far greater, and it made sense. But the instincts and urges of the animal weren't totally separate from the human. The only way shifters kept their sanity was by unifying their animal and human halves. Of course, he hadn't really known many 'turned' shifters. Almost every one he knew was a shifter by heredity…born that way.

"How do I get rid of him?" Leaving the door open, Hernandez crouched down next to Danny. "I agreed to this when Zack offered to turn me. He said it would make me powerful." He shook his head. "All it makes me do is kill to quiet the beast within me. I don't like having to kill. Getting the women to submit to me isn't as much fun when I don't leave them crying. The silence is wrong. They're supposed to be crying when I'm done with them."

The way his mind worked made Danny want to throw up, but there wasn't anything left in his stomach except bile which rose and made his parched throat burn.

"Tell me how to stop."

"You don't," Danny forced out through cracked lips. He did his best not to cough and let the bile rise farther. "You're a shifter now. The bear is part of you."

Hernandez stood. "No, there has to be a way," he shouted. "I'll find someone who can show me the way to be human again."

Danny almost asked him to stay, wanted to make up some kind of stupid ritual that he could make Hernandez do to stall him until Connor or the cops could find him, but he wasn't sure where to even begin to come up with something that would work. Not to mention, if Hernandez didn't bring him some water, he wouldn't be able to talk at all. Danny tried to roll over onto his side to alleviate some of the pain in his shoulders, but that just made it worse, so he lay face down in the dirt as the door closed and dusty darkness enveloped him again.

Connor put the evidence bags under his shirt, so they could be against his skin as he drove around. He didn't get impressions or visions from things like dust or plant matter very often, but he was desperate and willing to push his powers. Jime rode in the passenger seat, often with his head out of the window, or standing up, trying to get scents. Lisa flew in ever-widening circles, trying to spot the RV. There was something about being able to see what they were all doing, and having more happening, that gave Connor greater hope that they might actually find Danny or Hernandez.

Jime sat in his seat properly. "Cat, you might want to head southwest. I'm getting an impression of pack that way. Since most of the rest of the pack is up around Jemez Springs, there's a good chance it's Danny."

At the next intersection, Connor turned the Jeep to the right, heading west. "I'm not picking up anything yet."

"Don't worry. I'll keep you posted." He stood again, and the wind whipped his long black hair like a comet.

"*Jime says southwest,*" he reached out to Lisa.

"*Good. I'll head that way. So far, not seeing anything major. I'm also watching out for an eagle a mile north of here. She eyed me a few times, but I don't think she's hunting.*"

"*Just be careful.*" Connor would hate it if something happened to Lisa while they were searching for Danny.

"*Doing my best. Sometimes I really wish I was bigger. It would also make reaching things on tall shelves easier.*"

"*When we find Danny, I promise to get everything off tall shelves for you for a year.*" Connor knew how frustrated Lisa found things up high when she was in her human form. She was all of five foot nothing.

"*I'll hold you to that.*" Then she cut the connection. High above him she gave a sharp 'key-key' cry and banked to the south. She hadn't been able to fly at night, so she'd just been emotional support as he and Jime searched for Danny.

Jime dropped into his seat, running his hand through his hair as he did. "More south than west. He's out there somewhere. But all the dust from these dirt roads is hell on my nose."

"But you're following your pack bond more than your nose," Connor said as he made a left.

"Right, but dude, there's just something awesome about standing up in a moving Jeep while driving down dirt roads. We're working with the cops, so we don't have to worry about being pulled over."

Connor was about to say something when he caught something from the evidence bag of dust against his stomach. There was a slight pull toward the ground. He hit the brakes and brought the Jeep to a stop. He took his foot off the clutch before he had the Jeep in neutral. It jerked and died.

"What's up, Cat?" Jime asked as he let go of the bar in front of him that he'd grabbed hold of when the vehicle jerked.

"Got something." Connor didn't bother to pull the keys out as he jumped out of the Jeep. He knelt beside the Jeep and pulled out the evidence bags. He put the two on the road and put his left hand on them, one at a time. The bag with the dirt gave him a flash of the road they were on. There was nothing from the bag with the sticks. He put the bag with the sticks back under his shirt and kept the bag of dust in his hand. "This dust is from this road."

"So we're getting somewhere!" Jime grinned.

"We're getting somewhere." Connor swung back into the Jeep and started the engine.

"Connor, I've got the RV!" Lisa shouted through the link. *"It's about three miles from your current location. No sign of Danny, but the RV is pulling out of a short driveway near a small shed."*

"Which way is the RV heading?" Connor asked as he gunned the engine, accelerating as fast as he could. Dust billowed up around them as he shot down the road.

"Dude, warn a fella." Jime frantically grabbed the bar in front of him for stability.

"Sorry, Lisa's got the RV in her sights." Connor didn't even slow down as they topped a rise a little fast and the Jeep left the ground for several feet and came back down hard.

"He's heading right toward you."

"Check out the shed. We'll stop the RV." Connor scanned the road for a rooster tail coming their direction. He handed his phone to Jime. "Call Chief Ellis, his number's in my contacts. Tell him we've got Hernandez in our sights and tell him where we are. He's not getting away, but a bit of backup would be appreciated."

"You sure you want me to talk to him?" Jime asked as he started tapping the screen.

"I'm kinda busy right now," Connor bounced the Jeep over another rise. On the southern horizon, a plume of dust signaled a vehicle heading toward them.

"Hey," Jime said. "Is this Chief Ellis?…No, this isn't Connor., it's Jime. Connor's busy trying to keep the Jeep out of a bar ditch right now....Look. We've got the RV in our sights....Yes, that means we're pursuing it....I don't think he's going to listen to that...No. He wants some backup for when we bring this guy down." He paused for a moment, then relayed their location to the chief. "Thanks, dude." Then he hung up the phone. "That is one uptight human."

"He doesn't like our kind much," Connor said as he bounced over another rise.

"How are you going to stop that RV? It looks a little bigger than we are." Jime had a death grip on the dashboard bar.

"Yeah, it does. I just hope he doesn't want to crash and die." Connor waited as they drew closer together. He wished

Jime was a police sharpshooter who could take out the RV's tires or that they had some spike stripes they could drop or anything beyond what he was going to try, but saving Danny was worth losing his Jeep if the move didn't work. He could replace the Jeep. He could never replace Danny.

At the last second, he spun the steering wheel and hit the brakes. The Jeep slid sideways as it cut across the narrow dirt road, but it stopped and blocked enough of the road that Hernandez had to slam on his brakes and turn in an effort to not hit the Jeep. The RV had enough speed that it kept going, bouncing hard into the bar ditch and into the desert on the other side of the road.

Rocks, cactus, and dirt flew as the RV plowed through them.

Connor spun the wheel of the Jeep and went down, then up the bar ditch on the opposite side of the road. He hoped Hernandez wasn't going to be able to do much in the way of steering since the RV wasn't designed for off-roading. Crossing the road and heading out after the RV, Connor's hope of getting Danny back grew as he followed Hernandez's erratic trail across the rough terrain, heading toward a small house set a short distance from the road.

A heavy lump formed in Connor's throat. "Jime, we're going to have to stop him from getting to that house. We don't know if it's occupied or not. If he takes hostages, that would be really bad."

"And how are we supposed to do that?" Jime sounded a bit scared.

"We're shifters. We stop him. If the RV stops, we move out."

Jime shook his head. "Dude, I'm not Danny. My shifts aren't instant, and I can't shift clothed."

"Then start shifting now." Connor wasn't in the mood to coddle Jime. He'd hoped since Cortez sent him to help, that he'd be of some kind of use, and he had been, but he was going to need more.

Jime pulled off his shirt. "Fine."

Ahead of them, the RV turned sharply and Connor followed the move. He hoped the RV hit something, or broke something soon. If Hernandez was on foot, they had a hope of bringing him down.

As soon as he heard the RV start up and drive away, Danny worked at worrying the ropes binding his hands. He had to get free. Without knowing how far out from the city they were, he had no way of knowing how long it was going to take Hernandez to do whatever it was he was going to do and come back, if he was going to come back at all. He tried to shift just his hand into a paw. It was a trick he knew a few shifters could pull off. He'd tried it before, but he'd never managed it. Trying to shift hurt his head, but he tried to ride it out. Having his hands behind his back stressed out his shoulder as the shift progressed, but it was far enough for the ropes to slip off his paw, then he willed the paw back into a hand.

As soon as he stopped concentrating on shifting, the headache dropped from agonizing to just painful.

A sharp 'key-key' bird call startled him. He glanced around as a small raptor flew in through one of the holes in the wall. It landed in front of him, and seconds later, a naked Officer Collins stood there. "Danny. We found you."

Relief flooded through him. "Yes, you did. Where's Connor?" He forced the words out even as his throat complained.

"Coming down the road. I think he's cutting Hernandez off at the pass." She got a faraway look and frowned. "Yeah. They're now four-wheeling it across the desert." She knelt and untied the ropes around his ankles.

Danny worked on getting the knots off his other hand. "How far away?"

"About a mile and a half."

"Look. My head hurts too much to shift. I'm pretty sure I have a concussion. I can't help out at the moment. Leave me here. Go help Connor stop Hernandez."

She opened the door and stood there framed by the sunlight for a moment. "If you can make it out here, there's a hydrant next to where it looks like he's been parking the RV. I don't see any way to bring you water."

Danny forced himself to stand. The world swam around him, but he persisted. "A bit wobbly, but I'll get there. I'll stay there until you come back for me."

"Deal." She shimmered and shrank in on herself until a kestrel stood on the sand in the doorway, then she took off, flying hard.

The heat just outside the door was almost more than Danny could bear, but he forced himself to stumble forward. The hydrant was a classic lift handle model and there was even a short water hose attached to it. Danny got over to it and sat down before lifting the handle. It was tight, and his arm hurt enough he almost didn't get it going. Then it was up and water gurgled a couple of times before flowing out of the hose. It was cold and the best tasting water he'd ever had. He stuck his head under the hose and let the water soak his hair and run down over his body.

In the distance, something crashed.

"Thanks." Connor cut the mental link with Lisa off as he hit his brakes, sending Jime, who'd just completed his shift, into the floorboard. The RV had slammed into a narrow gully running across the property. It had been all but hidden by the sagebrush and rocks. From the loud crash when it hit, there were more large rocks on the other side of the dry ditch.

Jime jumped out of the Jeep as Connor cut the engine and followed. The dust was still billowing around them.

The mangled driver's door of the RV flew off as Connor and Jime approached the back. Connor pulled his pistol from his holster. It was loaded with silver bullets. He didn't want to take any chances with Hernandez. He wanted to bring him down like the rabid animal he was.

"Hernandez! Come out with your hands up." Connor stepped around the back of the RV.

Hernandez staggered out of the wreckage of the RV. He was nearly halfway through a shift. He stared at Connor, his dark eyes crazy. He roared and charged.

Connor fired. He felt like he was cheating. They were shifters. He was supposed to be facing the bear as a mountain lion with a wolf at his side. But he didn't care about the way things were supposed to happen. He'd heard from Lisa that Danny was safe. Hernandez needed to be stopped, and a silver bullet to the head would do that. He fired two more shots in rapid succession, just to be sure.

Hernandez jerked as each bullet hit. His momentum carried him forward and he crashed to the ground at Connor's feet. Blood oozed around Hernandez's head as Connor fired two more rounds into his back.

"Connor, he's down." Lisa grabbed his arm. "You can stop shooting."

"And Danny's okay?" Connor looked down at her, the pistol suddenly very heavy in his hand.

"Yeah. He says he's pretty sure he's got a concussion. I pointed him to water. He told me to come help." She let go of his hand. "But it looks like you've got this under control."

Connor nodded. Relief flooded through him as she took the gun from him. If Danny had a concussion, that would explain why telepathy wasn't working. "Can you stay here and handle Ellis when he shows up?"

"Let me grab my clothes out of the Jeep first." She turned to walk away. "Looks like the property owner is coming to see what's going on. Time to whip out my badge." She hurried to the Jeep and got dressed.

By the time she was done, Jime was back to human form and dressed too. "Okay. I'm going with you to get Danny."

Connor glanced at the two figures still several hundred feet away. "Can you stay with Lisa? The humans have guns. She's police, so they should listen to her. But just in case, I want her to have some backup." He could hear police sirens in the distance, but they were still several miles away. He'd probably meet them as he reached the road.

Jime frowned. "I guess."

"Thanks." Connor patted his shoulder, then got in the Jeep and headed back toward the road. He didn't want to waste any more time getting to Danny, and wasn't in the mood for police niceties.

Danny recognized the Jeep bouncing along the rough drive from the road toward him. There was a Jemez Springs Sheriff's Bronco following it. His head still pounded, but the water had made him feel better. When the gunshots rolled across the quiet desert, he wondered who had been shooting at whom. Seeing the Jeep made his heart jump. Connor was okay. There was no way he'd let anyone, not even Officer Collins, drive his Jeep.

Before the dust settled, Connor was jumping out of the Jeep and running to Danny. "Lisa said you were okay."

Danny managed to get to his feet. His throbbing head wanted him to stay on the ground and still, but he wanted to throw his arms around Connor and feel him. He really needed to know Connor was okay too. "Mostly."

Then Connor's strong arms were around him, holding him up. "I'm sorry I didn't see you getting attacked. I'm never getting in another tub or pool again."

"Don't be silly." Danny kissed him. "It's not your fault you have weaknesses like anyone else."

Connor kissed him back. "But I failed you when you needed me most. My weakness almost got you killed."

Despite the way his shoulder complained about the movement, Danny stroked Connor's hair. "But, it didn't. I'm okay."

Rusty cleared his throat, and they turned to look at him.

"You going to be all right?" Rusty asked.

"Need to have my head looked at," Danny said. "And my tail bone hurts."

Rusty shook his head. "I've been saying you need to have your head examined for years." Then he frowned. "I'll call for an ambulance to get you to the closest hospital."

"Sheriff Callaway," Connor stopped him from turning away. "How did you get here?"

"Well, I got a call this morning from Cortez. He said Danny had been kidnapped by the killer and you might need a hand in getting him back. It doesn't look like you needed any help. But I'm glad to see my deputy in one piece." He turned and walked back to the Bronco.

Danny chuckled and his head swam. "I guess the cat is out of the bag now." He clung a bit harder to Connor. "I think I should sit down."

Connor frowned. "Tell you what. I need to deal with the mess down the street. Instead of waiting for an ambulance, let's get Callaway to drive you in. He won't be needed here."

"Good idea." Danny wanted to shout, but was getting more lightheaded by the second. "Get me over there. I can lie down in the back of the Bronco."

"Okay."

It seemed to take forever to walk the short distance to the vehicle. Connor and Rusty helped him lie down.

Connor kissed his forehead. "I'll be at the hospital as soon as I can."

"Okay. I'll be there." As Connor closed the door, Danny closed his eyes and then did his best not to throw up as Rusty took off toward town.

Chapter Twenty-three

Connor nuzzled Danny's neck. "Time to get up, Dawg."

The gesture sent shivers across Danny's skin. "Um-m-m. Do we have to?" He asked sleepily. He'd had his first good night's sleep since getting out of the hospital in Albuquerque.

"Well, Rusty did give you time off. What do you want to do until the doctors release you back to work?"

"Can't I just sleep?" He'd been doing that a lot for the past week, and was getting tired of it. But he liked teasing Connor, who'd been so incredibly attentive since they'd wrapped up the case, Danny wasn't exactly sure if he was the same Cat or not. But he was still obnoxious, and growing more so every day. Danny didn't doubt he'd be back to normal about the same time Danny was.

"Nope. I need some exercise." Connor tickled his waist, something Connor had recently started doing. It went along with the increased obnoxiousness. "Come on. Rise and shine."

Danny rolled over and wrapped his arms around Connor. "I'll show you rise and exercise." He claimed Connor's lips with his. The doctor had cleared him for medium exercise as soon as his head stopped hurting enough he could shift. Until that moment, he'd held his need for Connor in check. He figured he'd waited long enough.

Visions of Rage

Connor drove Danny and himself over to the Star Café for breakfast. He'd been spending a lot of time taking care of Danny. It had been a long time since he'd put himself out in an effort to take care of someone. The feeling of being needed was nice. That morning was the first time Danny and he had been out together since bringing Hernandez down. It was great getting out, but somehow it felt like he wasn't going to have Danny to himself anymore, not that they'd been totally alone. There had been numerous reports to file with people in the various jurisdictions Hernandez had left bodies scattered through.

They'd also had to report in with Cortez and let the local alpha know that the rogue werebear had been dealt with. Cortez had been a lot more cordial to Connor after he'd rescued Danny. He'd even said Connor was welcome in his territory any time.

Overall it felt plesant to walk down the sidewalk side by side and into the restaurant like a normal couple.

Without waiting for the hostess, Connor led Danny back to the table they'd started feeling like was theirs before they went on their cross-county manhunt.

Angie walked up with a coffee pot. "You boys hungry? I heard about Albuquerque." She filled their cups. "Glad to know you got the guy."

"I'm just glad he didn't kill more people than he did," Connor said.

"I heard on the news his mother's suing the state for his death," Angie said.

"Good luck with that," Danny said. "They have enough evidence linking him to at least one of the deaths as well as kidnapping a police officer."

"Angie, bring me a short stack, two eggs medium, and a slice of ham," Connor said without looking at the menu. He'd eaten there enough that he had the thing memorized. "I'm hungry this morning."

"That sounds good to me, too," Danny said.

Jeri strolled into the café and over to their table. "What are you guys doing in town? I figured you'd be at home resting until the doctor said you could come back to work."

"Don't know about the dawg, but I didn't feel like cooking this morning," Connor said. He'd spent a lot of time over the past few days cooking, which was a vast improvement over the fast food he'd been eating while Danny had been in the hospital in Albuquerque.

Angie came over and poured coffee for Jeri.

"Same here," Danny said. "More like I didn't want to clean the kitchen afterwards."

Connor cocked an eyebrow at Danny. "You haven't cleaned a dish in two weeks." He knew because he'd cleaned everything Danny ate out of.

Jeri shook her head. "Doesn't that sound like a couple of men, Angie?"

"Hey, I don't mind," Angie replied. "They're both good tippers. You want anything to eat, Jeri?"

"Yeah, bring me one of those Danish pastries," she said. "Warm it up a bit, please."

"Will do." Angie turned and hurried off.

"Connor, Rusty said to tell you there's an empty desk in the office if you want to use it," Jeri said. "That is if you're going to stick around here."

"That sounds good," Connor said. "I've thought about leaving Santa Fe. I like the area here away from the city. More room to roam without people noticing me." He turned to Danny. "You up for a trip to Santa Fe tomorrow to get some things out of my place there?"

"Sure."

Jeri frowned at the two of them. "You guys do realize that the whole town knows you're a couple."

"Since when?" Connor asked, doing his best to act shocked but since Sheriff Callaway had talked to him in the hospital while the doctors had been examining Danny, he knew the department knew.

She got a faraway look. "Well, let's see. Since you've been in town, the number of mountain lion sightings has more than quadrupled. We figured it was you, but when Old Lady Flowers started reporting that, Penelope, her sheltie, had treed a mountain lion for several mornings running outside of Danny's house, Rusty and I figured out it was you, and you were sneaking into town so you guys could get together."

"I've been meaning to eat Penelope for years," Danny said under his breath. "So why didn't you two say anything?"

Jeri laughed. "We figured we'd let you take your time telling us."

"Sheriff Callaway told me they knew, when you were in the hospital," Connor said, then sipped his coffee.

"And you didn't tell me?" Danny stirred a little more sugar into his coffee.

"Slipped my mind," Connor said. "I've had a lot on my mind the past couple of weeks."

Danny blew him a kiss. "You're forgiven, Cat."

"Good." Connor hoped Danny would always be up for forgiving him the things he did.

Angie brought their breakfasts and they ate in silence. Connor hadn't realized exactly how hungry he was until the pancakes were there in front of him. Danny must've been hungry too, since he dove into his food with such gusto Connor was afraid he was going to chip a tooth on his fork.

Jeri finished her Danish. "You boys have fun. I need to go do some police work. Those speed traps aren't going to man themselves."

"Write lots of tickets," Danny said between bites.

"What did you have in mind for the day?" Danny asked as he wiped the last of his syrup up with a final bite of pancake.

Connor hummed a bit. For some reason his heart beat a little faster as he voiced what he'd been thinking. It almost felt like he was asking Danny on a date. "Thought a run in the mountains would be good, if you're up for it."

Danny pushed his plate toward the center of the table. "A run?"

"Yeah." He finished off his sausage. "You know, a four-legged run."

"Oh. That kind of run. Where are you thinking?"

"I thought about around the east fork of the Jemez River. We can take an easy pace." Connor needed to get out, but he didn't want to push Danny too hard until they were sure he was just fine.

"Sounds good." Danny grinned. "I could use a good run. I'm happy I can shift again without it hurting so much."

"Me too." Connor rose and paid their bill, making sure to leave Angie a big tip, then they left, walking side by side back to the Jeep.

Connor parked in a pullout on Route 4, jumped out, landed on four paws, and took off running.

Danny followed.

It was great that they could both shift so easily. After seeing how slow it was for Jime, Connor appreciated Danny's skill at assuming his wolf form even more. He knew some shifters had it easier than others, but he and Danny had it real easy and that made him feel like Danny was his equal in that way.

When they got to the river, Connor stepped into the clear stream and lapped at the water. Since he'd been unable to get a vision of Danny's kidnapping, he'd been doing his best to limit his time in water. He'd gotten to the point he could take a shower in under five minutes. He was worried he'd miss something important.

"Don't you know it isn't safe to drink out of the river?" Danny asked, rubbing up against him.

"Been doing it all my life," Connor said. *"Of course only in cat form."* Water in all its forms were a salvation for him; he wanted to get over his fear of missing things, so he could enjoy it again. He just didn't want to forget what had happened.

Danny lapped at the water. *"Tastes pretty good."*

Connor lay down and rolled in the cool current. He didn't totally submerge, hoping he could still pick up anything he needed to.

"Never knew a cat who liked water as much as you do."

Not being able to handle being wet anymore, and being reminded that it wasn't normal for a cat to like water, Connor stepped out of the stream. *"Come on."* He shook the water from his fur and ran into the brush.

Danny followed.

For half an hour, they chased each other around. First one in front and then the other. Connor kept looking back over his shoulder when he was leading, making sure Danny didn't look or sound too tired. He didn't want their run to undo any of the healing Danny had accomplished over the past weeks.

Finally growing tired, Connor flopped down on the grass with Danny beside him. He'd never found anyone who liked to run the way he did, or could keep up with him in the forest. If he'd had any doubts about how perfect Danny was for him, they'd vanished.

"This has been fun." Danny rubbed against Connor's side. *"We should do it more often."*

Connor licked Danny's nose. *"We could call this 'our place'."*

"Yeah." Danny put his paw over Connor's back, then laid his head on top of Connor's.

Connor purred in contentment and they dozed in the sun until it got too hot, then they rose and trotted back to the Jeep.

Chapter Twenty-four

Connor walked down the hallway of the Santa Fe Police Department. It felt like an ending of sorts. He wasn't sure if he'd ever be back there. There was no doubt in his mind that if Captain Kennedy called him, he'd come running to lend a hand, but he was leaving Santa Fe. He hadn't had a new vision, but he was moving to Jemez Springs. He was going to put his house up for rent…he liked it so much he couldn't bring himself to actually sell the little adobe bungalow. With Danny's help, the search was already underway for a cabin in the mountains near Jemez Springs that was big enough for the two of them.

The normally busy squad room was quiet, and Connor paused for a moment, wondering if there was something wrong.

"Cat, keep moving or signal, would ya?" Danny's strong hands pushed against his shoulders.

"Sorry." Connor resumed ambling toward the desk that had been his for a couple of years. Even though he wasn't a police officer, it still felt like his home. Officers looked up from their desks as he and Danny walked toward it. There was a bouquet of lilies laying on the center of the desk. He paused, then picked them up and smelled them. Even to his shifter's nose, they were nearly scentless. He frowned and put them back down.

"About time you got in here," Captain Kennedy said as he walked to the door of his office. "Come talk to me."

Connor glanced over his shoulder at Danny. "I've got Dawg with me."

"Lupan can be in on this." Kennedy turned and walked back to his desk.

"Come on, Dawg." Connor shrugged and walked into the office. Without a vision to warn him what was going on, strange butterflies filled Connor's stomach as he strolled across the office that wasn't nearly as empty as it sounded. He did note that Lisa's desk was empty, and she was sitting in front of Kennedy's.

They cleared the door, and Captain Kennedy gestured for the door to be closed. Danny did the honors, then grabbed a chair near the window and dragged it over to join the two in front of the desk.

"What's up?" Connor asked. He glanced at Lisa, but her face was still, revealing nothing of the situation they found themselves in.

"Officer Collins and I have been talking," Kennedy began as he picked his pen up off the desk and put it back down again. "You've been an invaluable help to not just this department, but this community. Without you, there'd still be several very dangerous criminals prowling the streets of Santa Fe. Between you and Collins, you've helped improve the relationship between the department and the shifter community. I don't know what I can do to repay that."

Connor waved his comments away. "Captain, you don't need to do anything. You know how I work. I go where the visions lead me."

Kennedy nodded. "I know. I have to admit, you've been a bit hard to deal with from time to time, but I'm very glad your visions sent you here."

"We've also been talking about something else," Lisa said, drawing attention away from Kennedy. "Shifter crimes are on the rise. Since we got back from Albuquerque I've done some digging, going outside the New Mexico area, and this week alone, I found several incidents where shifters were involved, either as the perpetrators or the victims, and sometimes both. Even found out Hernandez's cellmate, Zack, had a couple other cellmates over the years. They've all gotten out and gone on to commit other crimes. At this point one of them is off the radar." She shook her head. "We all know our criminal justice system doesn't really work, particularly on hardened criminals. The thing is, we're in need of more shifters on police forces, and possibly government task forces."

"Wait." Danny held up his hand.

Something started to form in Connor's mind. It wasn't a vision per se. There was no definite form of the feeling. But he felt a rightness at her words. There was a growing need since as the shifters spread out amongst the humans, not staying in the packs, prides and other groups they had for generations, there was more and more interaction, and not all of it positive.

"Are you suggesting that we form such a force?" Danny continued as Connor tried to understand what he was feeling.

Lisa shrugged. "Maybe, maybe not. I don't really know. I do know it was fun helping you two." She chuckled softly. "It's always interesting when Connor's around. I've gotten used to it. I don't want to be without it."

"But there aren't always going to be things we need to do," Connor interjected, not wanting the conversation to get away from him. "You know I can sometimes go months without a vision."

"I do." Lisa leaned back in her chair. "And during those times, I want to be based here in Santa Fe. This is where my family is, and my husband might appreciate having me home occasionally. Plus Kennedy wouldn't be able to run the department if I took off on him permanently."

"I don't know about that," Kenney huffed. "It ran pretty good before you guys got here."

Lisa laughed. "Right, and that was years ago. But anyway, we don't have to go out and declare ourselves a shifter force or anything right this minute."

Connor raised his eyebrows. "A shifter force?" There was an odd, proper feeling to the words. "You've been thinking about this."

"Maybe a little." Lisa gave him a soft, coy look that told him she wasn't above trying to manipulate him to get her way. "But you have to admit, we work well together, and Danny's a great addition."

Connor sighed and patted Danny's leg. "Yeah, he's great. What do you think, Dawg?"

"I think the Bird might have a good idea, but we'll have to think it over."

"Good." Kennedy grinned like he'd been in on the idea from the start. "I want you to know, if you need me to grease any wheels as you deal with other departments, don't hesitate to call me. Not all the cops out there are going to be so quick to accept your rubbing our human incompetence in their faces like we are here in Santa Fe."

"I know." If Connor had ever completely forgotten that, Danny was constantly reminding him and dealing with Ellis and Randall had been a major eye opener. It had been a long time since he'd dealt with the level of shifter bigotry and psychic distrust he had recently.

"Don't lose my number." Kennedy said and patted his desk. "You go enjoy life until the next vision takes you somewhere else. Collins is at your disposal, whenever you need her, but just remember to return her without a single feather out of place, she's my best shifter on the force."

"Only shifter on the force," Lisa corrected.

"Not for long." Kennedy smiled. "We've got an eagle coming through the academy right now. Should be ready for the street beat in a couple of months. If you're not out gallivanting across the country with these two, I expect you to show him the ropes."

"I'll love it." She grinned and stood.

Connor stood too. "Kennedy, it's been great working with you."

The Santa Fe chief offered him his hand. "You too, McGriffin. You always keep things interesting."

With brief handshakes, they parted, with Danny and Connor heading out into the squad room.

"Now what?" Danny asked.

Connor waved at his desk with the lilies laying there. "Now we pack up and head out."

"I'll give you a hand," Lisa said. "There're some boxes in the back room. I think a couple of paper boxes should be enough to carry everything. It's not like you had a ton of stuff."

"Sounds about right." Connor plopped down in his chair and started opening drawers. He glanced up at Danny and Lisa standing there staring at him. "What? You two get me a couple of boxes so we can get done here and on the road before rush hour hits."

They both grinned.

"Okay." Danny looked for a moment like he and Lisa had something else up their sleeves, but they didn't say anything more. They just turned and headed off to the storeroom, just down the hall toward the back door.

Connor tried not to think about the things he started pulling out of the drawers and setting them next to the lilies. It was several years worth of his life. Things were changing, but he was going to be with Danny, and that was the most important part of it, at least for him.

The glass pane in the Jemez Springs sheriff's office door rattled as Connor kicked it open. He carried a heavy box into the room.

Danny followed closely on his heels similarly laden. Connor was pissed off enough he'd been storming down the sidewalk from the Bronco. They were in the middle of their first fight, and Danny felt bad about it, but he wasn't ready to back down.

"If you'd watched where you were driving, you wouldn't have run over it," Connor bellowed as he stomped through the office.

"How was I to know you dropped it under the truck?" Danny returned. It had been a stupid move and they both knew it. Connor just wasn't ready to admit it was a dumb mistake and Danny wasn't going to back off until he did.

"Ah-h-h, Connor, I have Chief Kennedy on the phone for you," Jeri said cautiously, pointing to her headset.

"Put him on speaker, please. I kind of have my hands full," Connor said in a quieter voice.

"Sure." She hit a couple of buttons on the phone and the small light on top of the speaker on her desk came on.

"Hey, Kennedy, what's up?" Connor kept the box in his hand as he leaned against her desk.

Kennedy's voice came over the speaker. "Why aren't you answering your cell? I've been trying to reach you for an hour. It's going straight to voicemail."

"Some idiot ran over it with a truck," Connor said. He glared at Danny.

"It isn't a truck; it's an SUV," Danny exclaimed as he carried his box over to the desk Connor was going to be using in the office. Even though he often called the Bronco a truck, he wasn't going to let Connor get away with it, especially not until he realized they were being stupid and put an end to the argument.

"What-ev-er," Connor said. "It's still mangled beyond repair." He straightened and set the box on the empty desk beside Jeri's.

Jeri put her hand over her mouth to stifle her giggle.

"Okay, Connor," Kennedy said. "The police in Phoenix called right after you left here. They'd like your help finding a couple of missing boys."

Connor looked unseeingly at the wall behind Jeri's desk, then turned and looked at Danny.

Danny looked back, and for a few seconds they gazed at each other quietly.

"I'll still be here when you get back, Cat," Danny said softly.

"No." Connor shook his head. "I'm not going anywhere without you, Dawg. I told myself when you were missing, that if you were okay, I was never going to lose you again. You've been cleared for duty. You're coming with me."

Danny stood and silently looked into Connor's eyes for what seemed like a full minute. He lowered his eyes, removed his badge and gun, laid them on Jeri's desk, and stepped closer to Connor.

"Wither thou goest," he whispered. He'd been trying to figure out how things were going to work out. He knew beyond a shadow of a doubt that he didn't want to be parted from Connor, even for a little while, but he wasn't sure he could continue being a deputy if he was jaunting across the country, following Connor's visions.

Connor took Danny's face between his hands and kissed him.

Jeri looked on slack jawed and wide eyed. "Danny, you can't mean you're quitting."

Rusty stared. "She's right, Danny. You're not quitting on me." He walked from his office where he'd been standing in the door and picked up the pistol and badge. He handed them back to Danny. "You might need these. Connor's got nothing to back him up. This'll help, even if you're out of your jurisdiction."

Danny stared at the items in Rusty's weathered hand. "But you need me to quit so you can hire a new deputy." He wanted to take the badge and gun back, but the need to be with Connor was greater than his need to be a deputy.

Rusty pushed the two symbols of Danny's life against his chest. "I'm not about to *pay* you for running all over hell and back following his fool visions. I'll use that money to hire a new deputy. That cousin of yours was asking me about it last week, and Cortez wants one of his people on my force, he's even willing to pay half the salary to make it happen."

"Really?" Danny took the pistol and badge. He instantly felt better knowing he still had things that meant a lot to him.

"Really." Rusty patted Danny's shoulder. "Now get going and find those missing kids."

Danny placed his arms around Connor's waist and pulled him close. It felt so good and right to do it, even with

Rusty and Jeri watching. He kissed Connor again. Their life was changing, but it was changing in good ways.

Connor broke the kiss and said softly, "Let's roll, Dawg." He raised his voice a bit. "Kennedy, tell Phoenix I'm on my way. If you need me, call the dawg's cell. I'll stop and replace mine in Albuquerque on our way through. At least the SIM card is undamaged so I'll have all of my contacts."

"I can do that," Kennedy replied. "Also Lisa will be joining you in Phoenix. She's got to tell her husband, and book a flight. This is happening a bit faster than she'd been expecting. Looks like the Shifter Force has its first case."

Connor chuckled. "Tell her I'll text what motel we're at, and reserve her a room." He turned them around and walked out the door.

"Guess we need to go pack our bags," Danny said as they headed for the Bronco, then he stopped. "That's not my work truck anymore." His stomach knotted a bit. It might not have been the shiniest and prettiest police car on the planet, but it had been his. He hoped Jime would treat her nice.

Connor hugged him. "I know. But for now, we use the Jeep."

"Glad to hear Liza'll be with us. She did a good job finding me." Danny didn't like to think how long he would've been in that shed if she hadn't come along.

Connor nodded as they stopped at the Bronco. "She's great at surveillance. I think she'll be a good help to us. I almost wonder if she didn't set something up to get this shifter force thing going." Then he shook his head. "Nah, she wouldn't do that."

"Yeah, she wouldn't." Danny unlocked the truck and opened the door. "You think you can handle a few things without dropping them under the vehicle?"

"I promise I won't drop your flute CDs, or your phone." Connor held out his hands for things.

Without another word, Danny began emptying his old life into Connor's strong hands. He grinned as he worked.

"What are you smiling at, Dawg?" Connor asked.

Danny paused and kissed him. "I'm putting my life in your hands, Connor. I love you."

Connor chuckled softly. "And my life is in yours. I love you too."

After stopping in Albuquerque to get Connor a new phone, and driving halfway through the night, it was too late to stop in at the police department when they arrived in Phoenix. After midnight, Connor got them a hotel room near the police station and settled in, after leaving a message with the switchboard that they'd arrived and would be in first thing in the morning.

Danny spooned around Connor and rained kisses across his shoulders. "Goodnight, Cat. I love you." His heart swelled with a contented feeling.

Connor snuggled backwards into Danny. "Love you, too, Dawg. Sorry I got so upset about the phone. I know it was an accident."

"Apology accepted." Danny snuggled closer to Connor's back. He was glad to have the argument behind them. His mother always said couples shouldn't go to bed angry.

Connor closed his eyes and a soft purr started in his chest.

"Will you stop that infernal racket? We've only got a couple hours to sleep, and I'd like to get quiet shuteye."

The purr deepened.

"Tomorrow I'm buying a pair of earplugs." He stubbornly refused to say he was growing used to the sound. It was comforting and gave him a sense of belonging. It was like holding Connor as he fell asleep, it told him everything was okay. Their life was going to be chaotic, but as long as he held Connor every night and Connor purred them to sleep, life was going just fine.

"Go to sleep, Dawg." Connor kissed his hand and snuggled tighter into Danny's embrace.

Connor and Danny's adventures continues in "Visions of Shadows" available where ever you buy books.

If you'd like to stay on top of new releases and upcoming work by A.M. Burns, please join our mailing list.
And if you enjoyed this first adventure, please leave a review. It's easy and won't take you very long.

A child's cry shall lead them.

Connor McGriffin, psychic cougar shifter, can't resist when he's called to Phoenix to help find two missing boys. With his team at his side, he follows his visions and a hot trail through the desert and across the border. But there are more obstacles than ever before as he fights to interpret the images his psychic gift provides.

Danny Lupan is trying to adjust to his new role in life, Connor's partner and member of Shifter Force. When the system he's spent years in the middle of starts blocking them, he's got choices to make, some of them harder than he expected. Even as their team is on the cusp of earning their wings, tension from inside and out might pull them apart.

Emotions run high when the lives of children are on the line as Shifter Force races across the desert southwest, facing more danger than they could imagine, while they struggle to keep the cries Connor hears from becoming more graves.

Book 2 of the amazing new urban fantasy series, Shifter Force, is sure to keep you on the edge of your seat until the last incredible page.

Available everywhere books are sold

Stars are dying in the streets.

Falling stars, that's all his vision showed him, then his powers went on the fritz. For years Connor McGriffin, psychic cougar shifter has relied on his gift of prophecy to let him know where to go and who to save. But trapped in Los Angles, waiting for more information than just stars falling into the ocean, Connor is lost trying to help people, even himself and his team.

Danny Lupan, former deputy sheriff, and current wolf shifter agent, has gotten used to following his partner Connor, trusting in his visions to lead them where they were needed. When Connor's visions become unreliable, Danny and the rest of the Shifter Force must fall back on detective training to lead them where they need to go to stop the person blackmailing closeted shifters who have dreams of stardom.

Can Connor, Danny and the team find the clues and chase down the bad guys before more bodies show up? Things don't always go the way they thought, and when a rising star crashes back to Earth, they may be too late. Connor hates being late for anything.

The action never stops in book three of the exciting Shifter Force series. Run the streets and beaches with the team, as they try to catch falling stars.

Available at your favorite book store

A.M. Burns Bio

A.M. Burns lives in the Colorado Rockies with his partner, several dogs, cats, horses, and birds. When he's not writing, he's often fixing fences, splitting wood, hiking in the mountains, or flying his hawks. He's enjoyed writing since he was in high school, but it wasn't until the past few years that he's begun truly honing his craft. He is a previous president of the Colorado Springs Fiction Writers Group: www.csfwg.org. Having lived both in Colorado and Texas, rugged frontier types and independent attitudes often show up in his work.

Stay in touch with A.M. Burns through his website
www.amburns.com

and Facebook pages
www.facebook.com/authoramburns/

Feel free to drop me an email
andy@amburns.com

A.T. Weaver Bio

A.T. is a great-grandmother in her 70s who lives with her cat, Kiyah, in downtown Kansas City. She didn't start writing until she was 60. When a friend said he'd like to read a book where, 'the boy gets the boy and they ride off into the sunset', her response was, 'I can do that.' She's never liked to be told what she can or can't do. Even with her bad knees and age, she says, "Don't tell me what I can't do. Let me tell you what I can do."

Keep up with A.T at:
Blogsite: https://alixtheweaver.wordpress.com/
Email: alixtheweaver@yahoo.com
Facebook: https://www.facebook.com/alix.t.weaver
https://www.facebook.com/pages/A-T-Weaver-writer/149528070288

For several months,

Detective Greg Williams and his partner have been trying to catch the Black Fin gang. Their latest intelligence is good, so they go on their most risky raid yet. But things go horribly wrong. While recuperating from the wounds he received during the botched raid, Detective Williams and his captain realize there might be a leak in the Portland police department. When they begin digging, things get worse for Williams.

At the urging of his captain, Detective Williams heads into the mountains, hoping a little distance from the department will give the Black Fins and their police informants the opportunity to slip up. His working vacation soon takes turns he could never have imagined when he meets the reclusive writer, Ken Draiag, next door, who turns out to be more than Greg ever imagined. But the Black Fins aren't about to let Detective Williams rest, they soon track him down, but with Ken's help, Greg manages to stay alive and fight back as forces he never knew existed reveal themselves to be working against him. Will Greg survive the Black Fins' ultimate plot?

Available at your favorite bookseller

Catriona's Curse

A. T. Weaver

When Sunny Nelson walks into the house built by an ancestor, strange things start happening. First, he senses an attraction to April Davis. He hasn't been attracted to a woman since he discovered the difference between boys and girls. Of course as soon as he sees her brother, Jeff, he forgets April. Later, as he turns the old house into a B&B, he starts having dreams and visions about people who lived in the house. Together April, Jeff and Sunny discover the secret of Catriona's Curse.

Available on Amazon

O'Duirwood, druid dragon, enjoys his quiet life of solitude in the Colorado mountains. When the need arises, Tal is the one the Coalition of Magical Creatures calls on to handle problems no one else can. For years he's worked on his reputation as the thing of nightmares for those who step out of the shadows. He never realized what was missing from his life until his gets an assignment to travel to Yellow Sky,

Texas and help a witch and her students there stop a vampire invasion. Once there, he finds things were not as he was told. The witch is actually a werecoyote, and one of her students has eyes for Tal. Can Tal help stop the vampires in time to save his blossoming love? Will his heart, so long closed off from the world, be able to open to the touch of the handsome young mage?

Available where ever books are sold